The Humble Pawn

The Humble Pawn

Liz van Santen

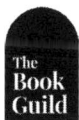

The Book Guild

First published in Great Britain in 2025 by
The Book Guild Ltd
Unit E2 Airfield Business Park,
Harrison Road, Market Harborough,
Leicestershire. LE16 7UL
Tel: 0116 2792299
www.bookguild.co.uk
Email: info@bookguild.co.uk
X: @bookguild

This work is entirely fictitious and bears no resemblance to any persons living or dead.

Typeset in 11pt Minion Pro

Printed and bound in Great Britain by 4edge Limited

ISBN 978 1835741 108

British Library Cataloguing in Publication Data.
A catalogue record for this book is available from the British Library.

To all those who pick up this book, thank you for giving my words a chance.

*'Even in the valley of the shadow of death,
two and two do not make six.'*

Leo Tolstoy

Part 1

One

'You look a bit gloomy today, Charlie. What's up?'

'I'm okay, just a bit shattered.'

'Oh, come on,' Sandy persisted, 'I know you better than that. Talk to me...'

The two friends dangled their legs over the steep, high wall that defined the boundary of the harbour. It had been a pleasant enough autumn day, but now a brisk north-easterly off-shore wind brought a sharp chill to the air. Charlie shivered as she watched the boats sway chaotically in the swirling spring tide, their halliards banging rhythmically against their masts.

Sandy had been a good friend to Charlie since she had fled Oxford two years before, to begin a new life with a new identity in Loss, a coastal town situated precariously close to the sharp edge of a steep cliff on the outskirts of Dartmoor. In Oxford, her name was Libby. She lived in a large Victorian house in a leafy area in North Oxford with her husband, a well-respected partner in a locally based firm of solicitors, and her springer spaniel, Dusty. She was a teacher and had taught in a large primary school for five years, but eventually she had to resign due to stress. Her husband earnt a healthy salary and, combined with their savings and investments, they had enough income to live a comfortable life. On the face of it, they had everything, but behind closed doors her life was increasingly catastrophic: a living nightmare. Finally, following a devastating incident, she had been forced to leave Oxford without a trace.

In Loss, she was Charlie. She had successfully applied to work as a live-in nanny for a family with two children: six-year-old Isabella and nine-year-old Daniel. The family lived in a huge and rather formidable house – a mansion called "High Cliff" – with commanding views of the hills of Dartmoor in the northeast and the Channel from a southerly aspect. Charlie lived in a spacious self-contained annex in the north wing, where she could find peace and escape the increasingly chaotic lifestyle of her host family.

Charlie sighed. 'The kids have been quite a challenge recently. They're really spoiled and don't seem to understand the word "no". James and Elsa have full-time demanding jobs in Bristol, and when they do see the kids they try to give them "quality time".' Brushing several strands of unruly hair roughly from her face, she muttered, '"Quality?" I'm not sure about that; the kids run rings around them; they rule the roost... and they get away with it!'

'God, it sounds like a nightmare. Poor you! I do wonder whether parents love their children too much these days, and are scared to upset them in any way, so they just let them do what they want? Perhaps they feel guilty about spending too much time at the office?' Sandy threw back her head and laughed. 'I don't think I'm going to try this parenting thing any time soon.'

Charlie creased her brow; she always valued the amazing pearls of wisdom her friend offered. 'I think you might be right; they definitely dote on Bella and Daniel. The trouble is, when I try to discipline them, they usually ignore me and do their own thing anyway. I want to be their friend, I actually want them to like me, but I nearly always end up getting cross with them.'

'But isn't teaching the kids the difference between right and wrong part and parcel of being a good role model and a good friend to them, Charlie? Bella and Daniel need you to be there for them, to give them clear and consistent boundaries, to praise them when they're being good, and to tell them off when they're being naughty. Surely it isn't just about being *nice*?'

'How on earth did you get to be so wise?' Charlie asked, affectionately nudging her friend's arm.

Sandy raised an eyebrow and smiled. 'Well, I was a child once, you know. It was a long time ago but...' She paused, pulling her flimsy raincoat across the vast expanse of bare chest, and noticed that Charlie's shoulders had slumped again. 'God, it's bloody freezing. Come on, let's grab a coffee.' She hauled her friend up, engulfed her in her arms, and propelled her towards a small coffee shop set back from the harbour. 'I've got a feeling there's more to this than just the challenging kids. What's really up, Charlie? I hate to see you looking so sad.'

The coffee shop was deserted except for an elderly

couple who leaned over their cups of tea, deep in conversation. It seemed to Sandy that they might be plotting their own suicides, they looked unbearably haunted. There was something depressing about this rather tired-looking cafe, definitely in need of some TLC after a busy summer season. The tables were simple – many levelled by strategically placed serviettes stuffed under a leg – and the metal-slatted chairs were very cold and uncomfortable. But it was a relief to hug steaming caffè lattes and feel the comforting warmth of the long milky drink. The night was drawing in and the fairy lights draped randomly above the filthy windows did little to light the gloomy cafe or lift Charlie's mood.

'Look outside, Sandy, it's just grim. Where did the summer go?' She sighed. 'I hate autumn and winter, the long dark evenings and the endless low grey skies and the rain.'

'But there is so much about autumn that is special,' Sandy said, as she gently stroked the side of Charlie's cheek. 'The heather is out on the moors at this time of the year. It looks like a massive purple carpet, draped luxuriously over every inch of the heathland in a deep rich layer of colour and life.'

Charlie looked at her friend in wonder. Sandy wrote poetry and was a talented musician, playing guitar and singing regularly in the local pub in the evenings; everyone loved her. 'You should write a song about the glory of autumn; it would be brilliant!'

Sandy's eyes twinkled. 'We need to walk the coastal path together, to feel the fresh sea air brush our faces, to hear the mighty waves crash against the blackened rocks that protect the coastline, and to study the gnarled trees, sculptured and battered by the enormous strength of the wind driving in from the Atlantic.'

'What about "Ode to Autumn" as a title for your song?'

Ignoring any ideas that she offered, Sandy threw her arms exuberantly into the air. 'Have you seen the gannets as they swoop into the sea from high in the sky to catch fish? How is that possible? They must have amazing eyesight to spot the tiny fish swimming in the ocean! I wonder how deep they dive? And the incredible birds of prey flying effortlessly in ever-increasing circles in the thermals; they don't seem to have a care in the world. Charlie, just look around you, nature is everywhere.'

Charlie observed Sandy as her friend became immersed in describing the wonder of nature. She was beautiful in every way. Her family originated from Cypress, and she had inherited a multitude of beautiful features: she had a dark olive complexion; thick black hair which she often tied back in a single rope-like plait and huge warm chestnut eyes, surrounded by long dark eyelashes that curled up at the ends. She wore colourful flamboyant clothing, stunning, but often ill-suited to the cold weather in Loss. She had a warm heart and the largest and most generous of smiles; she could light up a room in an instant.

'Hark at me, waxing lyrical about the autumn. But, Charlie, seriously, if I can ever be a listening ear, you know where I am. Sometimes I need to talk less and listen more.'

'Thanks, Sandy. I love your optimism.'

'I've got an idea,' she said, as she reached over and held Charlie's hand. 'You are still freezing; why don't you come back to my place tonight? We could have a large glass of Chardonnay and then…' She paused, grinning from ear to ear. 'I can think of lots of things we could do to warm ourselves up…'

Sandy loved everything about women, she loved to share and celebrate her body. She was a lesbian, she was proud and she was free. And she loved Charlie, always flirting outrageously, ever hopeful that one day she would tempt Charlie into her bed.

'You never give up, do you, Sandy!' she said, although she had to acknowledge to herself that she did sometimes feel tingles of excitement whenever she was close to this amazing woman. Memories came flooding back of a special time in a Parisian nightclub two years before. 'Never say never…'

'Don't you worry, hun, I will never give up!'

The dark clouds had gathered and were now scudding ominously across the steely grey sky, casting an eerie light across the harbour. 'It looks like a storm is brewing; I think we'd better dash before it pours with rain.' After a quick hug they rushed off in different directions. 'I'll text you tomorrow, Sandy.' She watched as her dear friend disappeared into the darkness.

Stumbling up the narrow uneven path that led to High Cliff, the rain started to fall, stinging her cheeks. Charlie quickened her pace as she felt the familiar and sickening terror bubbling up from deep within her.

Could she hear footsteps? She looked nervously over her shoulder.

Checking. Always checking.

'Is anyone there? Go away, leave me alone…'

Two

Dear Antonia Farouk,

Thank you for letting me consider your submission, *The Humble Pawn*, but I think I'll pass on this one. I wish you luck in finding representation elsewhere.

Kind regards,
Belinda Pollock

Submissions:
Painstork and Riley Agency
PO Box 356
London
E14 6PB

Antonia had endured the last two years translating the jumbled, often shocking, and always painful memories that dominated her headspace, into words on a page. She had risked everything. And someone, somewhere, had decided to pass. Belinda Pollock had decided to pass. She stared desolately at the screen. At least Belinda Pollock had given her the courtesy of a reply. She had submitted her manuscript to at least twenty agencies and publishers. Some had let her down gently by describing her work as "an interesting read" or "written with passion". Positive statements were usually followed by a *but…* "not suitable for our agency" or "not the genre we're looking for at the present time". But – Antonia fiercely hated the word "but" – she heard nothing back from the majority of agencies and publishers. Absolutely nothing.

She read the words on the screen again. "I think I'll pass on this one" left her feeling angry and fiercely driven. She would not give up. Her story must be told.

Her name was Antonia – within the confines of her annex in the North Wing, High Cliff – the proud and determined Antonia Farouk. Behind closed doors she lived and breathed Antonia.

Closing the lid of her computer, she padded across the wooden floor to the full-length mirror. Antonia always wrote at her best when she dressed in character; her outfit reflecting feelings and emotions that she attempted to translate into words on the page. She studied every minute detail of the image that stared back at her. Like the sheath of a sword, her crimson evening dress was figure-hugging at every point – from her bodice to her hips, to her hem. The thin shoulder straps accentuated the deep depressions formed by her collar bones, and the curve of her exquisitely toned shoulders. She turned sideways, her silhouette perfect, the extravagant satin trim running down the centre of her dress, gleaming in the flickering candlelight. The slit to one side exposed her shapely brown leg, allowing her to move freely. Her hair, one of her collection of wigs, tumbled down her back in loose light brown curls, shot through with gold. She finished off her elegant look, with a thick layer of matt red lipstick. She pursed her lips together and smiled with satisfaction. I will refine my story: I will tempt them with the sheer power of my words; of greed and jealousy; anger and betrayal; of love and loss.

They will not be able to resist...

***

After an unsettled night, Charlie lingered in the warm comfort of her bed for as long as she dared. Eventually she pulled back the duvet and padded over to the high Victorian window. She threw back the curtains to discover that the distant moorland hills had totally disappeared, shrouded by a thick layer of fog, and there was a distinct chill in the air. She shivered as she tried to ignore Bella's high-pitched screaming coming from the kitchen directly below her bedroom. *This could be a long day*, she thought wearily as she pulled on her faded jeans and a baggy grey jumper.

'Charlie, could you come down here for a second?' James shouted. 'We need to talk to you about something before we go to work.'

Her body stiffened and the tips of her fingers tingled. *Do they know?*

Charlie's hands started to shake as she hurriedly brushed her hair and glanced at herself in the mirror; she looked pale, gaunt and grey. She was apprehensive about what James and Elsa might have to say.

'Hello, Charlie. I trust you had a good night's sleep?' James asked in a rather formal manner. Without waiting for a reply, he turned to the children. 'Go and get yourselves dressed, my darlings, we won't be long.'

Bella stamped her foot, turned and flounced out of the room banging the door behind her shouting, 'I wanted toast not cereal. Ugh… I hate cereal and I hate you, Mum.'

James glanced at Elsa. 'She doesn't mean it, darling.' Turning to Daniel, who had remained quiet, hunched over a huge mound of cornflakes, he demanded, 'Go and play with Bella for a few minutes.'

Without looking up, Daniel left the soggy bowl of cereal on the table, muttering under his breath, 'If I have to…'

Charlie stood awkwardly to one side of the large kitchen, watching the embarrassing scene unfold. It didn't feel, at that moment, as if there was much love lost between the children and their parents.

'Come and sit down, Charlie. Now, we need to discuss…' James paused, drawing so close to her face that she could smell the coffee on his breath. 'Have you hurt yourself? You have a red scratch just under your nose.'

Charlie realised with horror that she had been stupidly, dangerously careless. She roughly rubbed a trace of red lipstick away with the back of her hand. 'No, I think it must be the lip salve I used this morning.'

'Okay, good. There's some coffee left in the cafetière, would you like a cup?'

Now feeling slightly queasy, she declined.

'We need to talk about the children.'

Charlie felt the tension drain away in an instant.

'We were called in by the school last week to discuss Daniel's progress. His teacher is very concerned about him. She said that he is sullen and uncooperative in class. He is often rude and belligerent, he doesn't have many friends, and, most importantly, he is falling behind in his schoolwork.' James paused, wringing his hands together. '"Falling behind with his schoolwork", you can imagine our dismay, Charlie.'

'I'm very sorry to hear this,' she said, although she felt that they should be far more concerned about Daniel's behaviour and well-being. It sounded as if his teacher was describing a very unhappy little boy.

'We expect Daniel to achieve academic success and, when he is eleven, to pass the entrance exams for Westbourne Manor. I attended Westbourne Manor myself, as did my father before me; it is a family tradition.' James shook his head. 'But, if he goes on like this, he will *fail* and have to go to Loss Secondary School instead. I'm sure you understand that this would be an utter disgrace for the family.' He hesitated. 'And, of course, a disaster for Daniel.'

Elsa, who had been quietly listening, now looked directly at Charlie with a cold hard stare. 'Daniel's behaviour started to deteriorate when *you* arrived at High Cliff.'

'Darling, perhaps we shouldn't be too quick to lay blame…'

The silence hung heavy in the air between them. Charlie now felt sick to the pit of her stomach. Were they really blaming her for the behaviour of their son? She shook her head, thinking about how much pressure Daniel must have on his young shoulders to achieve or to fail at the age of eleven. 'I have noticed that Daniel is showing signs of being very unhappy...'

'He's not unhappy,' Elsa interjected, 'he can't be, the boy has everything he could ever need or want...'

Charlie hesitated, calculating how confrontational she dared to be. 'But I don't think it's just about stuff, it's about giving children the time and space to be heard, to be listened to, and to be valued for who they are, as unique individuals. And to be loved.'

'Are you saying that we don't love our children, Charlotte?' Elsa spat out the words with venom.

James looked from Elsa to Charlie. 'I'm sure you don't believe that do you, Charlie?'

'No... and I'm sorry if I've upset you,' Charlie replied, folding her arms firmly across her chest. She turned her gaze to the branches of the silver birch tree bending in the wind just outside the kitchen window.

'We're worried about Bella too,' James said quietly, trying to diffuse the atmosphere. 'She is having tantrums that are more like those of a two-year-old. She actually scratched Elsa on the face yesterday,' he said, pointing to the angry red mark just above Elsa's left eye. 'She's usually such a kind and happy little girl. It's like she's been touched by the Devil.'

Charlie looked at James in disbelief. To associate a six-year-old child with the Devil was more than she could take. She weighed up the situation and decided it was not worth voicing an opinion so, instead, she turned to Elsa, looked her in the eye, and asked, 'So, what do you want me to do? Hand in my notice?'

Three

Saturday night at the Ferry Boat Inn was always a lively affair. A sandwich board placed by the entrance to the pub advertised the live music event in large letters: "Sandrine – Our very own jewel in the crown!". This particular evening the locals swarmed into the pub in their droves to hear their favourite local musician. Not only was Sandrine a great singer and guitarist, but she was also beautiful. Many of the punters, both men and women, enjoyed feasting their eyes on her striking olive complexion, dark brown eyes and curvy body, as they supped their ale. The bar staff, already run off their feet, were serving the crowd that had gathered round the bar. The pub offered a selection of local craft beers, ranging from a light fragrant summer ale to the rich chocolatey stronger ale. There were large jars of pickled eggs on the counter, a platter of sow ears for the dogs, and a large blue donation box supporting the Royal National Lifeboat Institution. Luckily cash was used more than credit cards in this pub, so loose change often ended up in the box supporting a very worthy cause.

Old Jimmy sat in his usual rocking chair set back from the bar in a small alcove by the window. He was as old as the hills: his face rugged and brown, weathered by years of working in the wind, the rain and the sun. His long white hair was pulled back loosely into a ponytail, and he wore a faded checked shirt and jeans that were fastened up with an old leather belt, tied well below his rotund beer belly. He held his pewter tankard, engraved with his name, "James Legg", with pride, and slowly sipped his favourite syrupy dark brown ale.

Jimmy had lived in Loss all his life – seventy-nine years – and he was well-respected in the town for his fishing adventures and his riveting stories, colourful tales of the sea. He owned a small working boat called *Maverick* and every day he headed out to sea at dawn to haul in the lobster pots and to make his daily catch: mackerel, bass, pollock and other fish that took the bait, and then sell to the local fish market for cash. He understood the sea, he had an inner sense of where to go each day for the best catch. Jimmy loved nothing better than to fish on the Skerries, just east of Start Point; bobbing about on the waves, line in hand, and chatting to the throngs of black-headed and herring gulls that surrounded his boat, ever-hopeful of a tasty morsel.

'Hey, Joe, how does that old sea shanty go? You know, the one about her topsails all-a-quiver. Can you give it a go for us?' he asked, his lined face breaking into a wide smile.

'Of course, Jimmy, I know the one you mean, "The Wild Goose".' Joe stood up straight, filled his lungs and started to sing with gusto. Everyone around him joined in enthusiastically with "Ranzo, Ranzo. Away-hey!" as they swayed in time to the words they sang. The rich powerful voices filled the pub and Jimmy beamed. When the shanty had finished, his eyes twinkled. 'That were grand, lads! The ditty always makes me think of our beautiful Sandrine... Nuff said!' He smirked, pretending to look abashed. Everyone laughed.

'Come on now, Jimmy, we all know she bats for the other side!'

'I know, me old mate, she's just beautiful!' Jimmy said, smiling kindly.

The locals were fully aware of Sandrine's sexuality: she talked and sang openly and earnestly about her love of, and for, women. This intrigued them, they loved her even more for her honesty and self-respect, but it didn't stop them lusting after her.

Charlie smiled to herself as she waited patiently at the bar. Sandy, the proud all-woman woman, will flirt outrageously with the adoring punters, enjoying all the attention; she'll give them a good evening's entertainment, and then she will leave. Charlie bought herself a pint of golden ale, calculating that it would last her for the whole evening. It was a session beer – only 3.8% – so she would be able to keep her wits about her. Clutching her glass, she pushed past groups of friends talking and laughing together, spilling some of the golden liquid as she did so. Finding one empty chair near an area of the pub set up with speakers, a stool and a single microphone, she sat down heavily on the sticky wooden chair, relieved to have found an empty space.

Feeling fed up and, frankly rather angry about her conversation with James and Elsa the previous morning, she had decided to go out for the evening to cheer herself up, but she couldn't get the incident out of her mind. The children were clearly very unhappy and out of control at home and at school, and the parents, or at least Elsa, seemed to blame her for everything. They refused her offer of resignation, and suggested, instead, that she adopted a "firmer hand" and controlled the kids with "a rod of iron", especially Daniel. James would enquire about some extra tuition for Daniel. The family, including Charlie, would go sailing one weekend. And then, "everything will be fine". As if it were that simple. Charlie felt that the parents were abdicating responsibility; they were happy to brush everything under the carpet and were not prepared to lift a finger themselves to improve anything. She wondered why parents have children at all, if they were not prepared to invest sufficient time, attention, and love. She exhaled, her calm features belying the agony she felt; James and Elsa had no idea how lucky they were to have been able to conceive two children.

Her thoughts were interrupted by the huge round of applause that had erupted as Sandrine entered the stage area, carrying her guitar held by its decorated strap over her shoulder. She sat down on the stool resting her guitar across her knee, and beamed at the audience, grasping the microphone with her left hand. 'One two, five, six, nine, ten.' The sound check was a brief affair. She tuned her guitar in a thrice and now she was ready to play. The audience hushed in eager anticipation.

Tonight she wore bright stripy voluminous harem pants, drawn into a wide cuff at each ankle, showing off her gold anklet, immaculately pedicured toes and sparkly high-wedge flip-flops. Her purple satin shirt complimented her outfit beautifully and hugged her shapely figure, exposing a tantalising glimpse of cleavage. Her thick black curly hair was secured in a multitude of beaded and braided plaits, a few strands of hair falling seductively across her face. When she panned the audience with her huge dark chocolatey eyes, she made every individual person feel special. When she smiled, she lit up the room.

But Sandrine was not perfect. The middle finger on her left hand was missing. She never tried to disguise this; instead, she embraced and celebrated her disability with a bold and striking fern-shaped tattoo that traced the inside of her ring finger and her index finger, finally curling artistically up her left arm. The way she played her guitar was quite extraordinary. Sometimes she laid the guitar on its back across her knees – slide guitar style – and this enabled her to use her remaining fingers and her thumb to shape the chords and individual notes. Sometimes she held her guitar in the traditional way and stretched her thumb behind the narrow-fretted neck to capture the lower notes. She overcame her physical challenge with skill, verve and style. Her guitar playing was sublime.

Spellbound, Charlie listened to the rise and fall of Sandy's powerful velvety voice. She had a wide repertoire of songs, some dating back to the sixties – she loved the music of Joni Mitchell, Carole King, Carly Simon, Joan Baez… But equally she adored singing songs of more recent artists – Christina Aguilera, Madonna and Lady Gaga. All her idols were women; strong women singing songs with a powerful message. She also liked to sing her own compositions, voicing her feelings about love, war, struggle and hardship. This evening, she had chosen to sing "Beautiful" by Christina Aguilera. Charlie listened intently to the lyrics as Sandy sang but she struggled with the sentiments expressed. The darkness and horror of her past returned to her in an instant. Tears started to flow unchecked down her cheeks. Thoughtless words had hurt her. Spiteful words had damaged her. Damning words had destroyed her.

Sandrine glanced across at her friend and sensed her sadness. Turning herself to face Charlie, she continued to sing. As the song came to an end, Sandrine added her own thoughts, 'Just remember, y'all, no matter who you are, or what you look like, we are all *beautiful* in our own way.'

A hush descended, before rapturous applause and cheers filled the pub and well beyond.

Charlie suddenly felt completely drained and decided to leave the session early. She felt guilty about not waiting to congratulate Sandy on her amazing performance, but she was glad to leave the hot stuffy atmosphere of the pub behind and to gulp the fresh air of the cold evening. As she wearily climbed the steep and winding path to High Cliff, the overwhelming nightmare of her past coursed through her head.

Perhaps one day she would be forgiven for her huge and deadly mistake.

Four

Saturday morning dawned bright and clear. The weather looked promising, and James decided to go ahead with his plans to take the family and Charlie sailing in an attempt to restore family peace and harmony. He had checked the Inshore Waters forecast the day before. It predicted a south-easterly 3 to 4, veering southerly 2 to 3 later, sea state slight or moderate with good visibility. Over the following twenty-four hours the red warning line had spread to the whole of the British Isles, including the coastal area, Lyme Regis to Lands' End. Strong winds were predicted, south-westerly 5 to 7, sea state moderate or rough, with heavy rain, perhaps thunder, and poor visibility. It wasn't a good forecast, but he decided to take a risk, thinking that, if he waited for perfect conditions for sailing in Britain, he might have to wait a long time.

After a chaotic breakfast, the family bundled into their litter-filled Espace and headed off towards Dartmouth where *Snow Goose* – a forty-two-foot Swan – was kept. The yacht was moored up on "trots" – in a line of boats, with a buoy at the bow and the stern. By the time they reached Dartmouth, the river was a lively hubbub of activity. The Dart Express cut its normal route across the water, ferrying the locals from Dartmouth to Kingswear. The pontoons were all fully occupied with boats rafted up, some three-abreast. A colourful array of small dinghies, out for Saturday morning racing, weaved in and out, perilously close to the yachts swinging on their buoys in the middle of the channel. The gig boats were out for their weekly training; two enthusiastic teams of muscle-bound women, following instructions from very small men with extremely loud voices. The constant cry of the gulls could just be heard in the distance over the frenzy of human activity.

Charlie loved everything about Dartmouth: the imposing and impressive castle at the harbour entrance; the colourful busyness of a thriving coastal town; the comforting sound of the old steam train chugging and whistling its way from Kingswear to Paignton, and further upriver, the peaceful tranquillity of Dittisham, a picturesque village set in the glorious green countryside of Devon.

After taking the yacht club launch out to *Snow Goose*, they set off down river towards the harbour mouth, narrowly missing many of the obstacles that Dartmouth harbour presented. James stood behind the large steering wheel, barking incomprehensible instructions to his unwilling crew, and blaming everyone but himself for the poor handling of the boat. He liked to think of himself as an experienced yachtsman but, as Charlie thought wryly, *he is more like the guy that "has all the gear and no idea!"*.

At last they left the stress of Dartmouth harbour well behind and were now sailing towards Start Point. Progress was slow because James had mistimed the tide times, and they were plugging the tide.

'Darling, can you take the wheel, I want to see how many knots Daniel can remember. Dan, use that blue line over there and tie a bowline.'

Elsa reluctantly took the wheel. She looked ill at ease and clutched the wheel with a vice-like grip. 'I'm not feeling too good,' she said grumpily, 'so don't be long.'

'What the hell are you playing at, Daniel? I've shown you how to tie a bowline hundreds of times. You ought to know by now, for God's sake.'

Daniel's hands shook as he twisted the thick unforgiving warp between his fingers.

'No, that's a bloody granny knot,' James shouted, now totally exasperated by the ineptitude of his son.

'James, give me two minutes with Daniel and we'll show you the perfect bowline. Come on, Dan,' Charlie said encouragingly, looping the line over her forearm. 'Let's go down below and work it out.' Charlie didn't know very much about sailing, but she did know how to tie a bowline. She sat beside Daniel with the line spread across her knee. 'Right... the rabbit comes out of the hole... round the tree... and back down the hole again... and there you have it, a bowline.'

Daniel looked up at her in disdain. 'You sound really silly...'

'I might sound silly, Dan, but the rabbit story helps me to remember how to do it. Try for yourself. I promise you; it works.'

Daniel took the line in both hands and quietly recited

the story as he twisted the line. On the second attempt it worked. 'I don't need a baby story to do a bowline,' he said scathingly.

'Okay, Dan, let's go up and show your dad.'

The young boy sat beside his father and successfully tied the required knot, his head was bowed, his face creased in concentration, but Charlie could detect a slight movement of his lips as he silently mouthed, 'The rabbit comes out of the hole…'

'Not bad,' James said, clearly surprised.

Daniel threw a quick glance of gratitude towards Charlie. 'Of course I can do a bowline, Dad!' he said, puffing his chest out proudly. 'I'm not totally stupid.'

'Next time I'll test you on a round turn and two half hitches,' James said darkly.

Looking out towards the Skerries, Charlie spotted a small red fishing boat, *Maverick*, surrounded by gulls; an elderly man leaning over the side with his arms outstretched, obviously struggling with the weight of his catch. It was old Jimmy. A week had passed since Charlie had gone to the Ferry Boat Inn to hear Sandrine – Sandy – perform. She hadn't seen her friend since that evening, and wondered if Sandy was annoyed that she had left early. She had tried to text her several times, but the signal was always hopeless at High Cliff. Charlie missed Sandy and resolved to make more of an effort to contact her after the weekend.

'I'm bored, Mum, are we nearly there yet?' Bella asked sulkily. 'I want to go home.'

Elsa looked at her crossly. 'We've got hours to go yet. Go and read a book…'

Bella stamped her foot. 'I don't want to read a book…
I've got nothing to do. *Nothing.*'

'Shut up, Bella, you're driving me up the wall,' Daniel
said grumpily.

Bella suddenly lashed out and hit Daniel, square across
the cheek with full force, making him fall back against the
wooden hatch with a loud crack.

'That is enough,' shouted Elsa, 'go to your cabins
now. I don't want to see either of you until you decide to
behave. Most kids would give their eye teeth to go sailing,
but not you. Spoilt brats, both of you. Now get out of my
sight!' she hissed.

Bella flounced down the steps and Daniel meekly
followed, looking downwards and nursing his wounds.
Charlie slipped down below unnoticed, where she stayed
until they arrived in Salcombe. The kids played on their
iPads at opposite ends of the cabin.

'Why the hell did we ever have bloody children?'
James bemoaned.

Then the arguments started: James and Elsa argued
about the children; about work; about money; about life,
until their words faded away in the wind.

The next morning the family awoke to a raging storm.
Torrential rain hammered against the semi-open hatch,
drenching part of the front cabin. Dark clouds scudded
across the charcoal sky; a fearsome gale ripped through
the harbour.

'I've got an important meeting tomorrow. I have to go
back to Loss today,' James said, staring bleakly out of the
porthole. He hesitated. 'Perhaps I should catch the train

back and leave you here until the weather improves?' he asked hopefully.

'Don't you dare leave us here on this godforsaken boat,' Elsa muttered.

'But I really don't think it's safe to go out in this weather…' James persisted.

Elsa glared and said nothing.

He sighed deeply, he realised he had no choice. 'On your head be it.'

Five

'We need to pick up more supplies before we leave,' James said firmly. 'Charlie, please come with me and Elsa can you get the kids up and ready for a long and bumpy passage.'

Charlie looked nervously from James to Elsa and nodded reluctantly. 'I'll just get my jacket and waterproofs.' This weekend was turning into her worst nightmare, and all she really wanted to do was hide under the covers and stay there until they arrived back in Dartmouth.

'I'll check the lines are secure before we go ashore,' James said as he brushed past Elsa and up through the hatch. He watched helplessly as the boat lurched against the unrelenting side of the pontoon, only a few semi-inflated fenders were saving the hull from serious damage. 'The harbour taxi has arrived,' he shouted.

As Charlie climbed unsteadily from the cockpit onto the pontoon, she was shocked by the sheer force of wind and driving rain that beat against her face as she battled to stay upright. The cheery taxi skipper held her securely by one arm and levered her firmly into his small motorboat. 'Good weather for ducks, I say!' He wore yellow oilskins and a wide brimmed sou'wester that partially covered his weather-beaten face, but Charlie could see his wide grin. 'Hold on tight, you two, we'll be there in a jiffy.'

After hurriedly thrusting some coins into the taxi driver's outstretched hand, they half-walked and half-ran up the causeway, now completely drenched from head to foot. James peered down at his new designer knee-high sailing boots and sighed heavily. 'They cost me an absolute bloody fortune, and my feet are soaking wet.'

'Come on,' Charlie shouted impatiently. She pointed to the illuminated sign above the local supermarket. 'Let's go inside before we catch pneumonia!'

It didn't take long to select a few provisions: bread, baked beans, soup, pork pie and pastries; and then they waited in a small queue at the checkout. All of a sudden, Charlie felt a sharp prod on her shoulder. She looked round to see a middle-aged couple staring intently at her.

'Excuse me but don't I know you from somewhere?'

Charlie froze.

'Yes, I'm sure I've seen you before… or seen your photo somewhere? Do you recognise her, Ems?' Peering over his metal framed glasses, he added, 'Are you from London… or around Oxfordshire somewhere?'

'No,' Charlie stammered, shaking her head.

The man looked at his wife, totally mystified. 'She looks different, I think it's something about her hair, but I'd recognise that face anywhere.' He paused, looking puzzled. 'Or at least I think I would…'

Charlie averted her gaze, her mind racing. 'I'm sure I have a double somewhere, I often get mistaken for someone else,' she said, in a falsely bright tone of voice.

James, keen to join in with the conversation, commented, 'Charlie, it's a small world, perhaps these good people *have* seen you before.'

'It isn't very likely…' Charlie muttered feebly.

'Darling, I don't remember anyone called Charlie, and I usually have a good memory for names,' his wife volunteered.

Andy studied Charlie's face in silence. 'It will come back to me… how I know you, I mean. It will…'

'Well, if you do solve the mystery, feel free to come and visit us.' James suggested generously. 'We live at High Cliff, in Loss. We have the biggest and highest house in the town, you really can't miss us.'

Charlie glanced at James in disbelief, before quickly turning back towards the checkout. The colour drained from her face.

They hurriedly threw the shopping into the "bag for life" and braced themselves for the storm that was still raging outside. 'Hope to see you again,' James shouted, as they fought to open the door. Charlie did not look back.

The harbour taxi was waiting to take them back to the boat. 'I hope you're not crazy enough to venture out in these conditions.' He laughed, but then he glanced at James, who was staring steadfastly into the distance. 'If you think it's bumpy in here, mate, you should see the harbour entrance. I've never seen such enormous waves,' he said, throwing his free hand into the air. 'It's force 6 to 7 out there today. Which way are you heading?'

'We have to go back to Dartmouth today.'

'Is anything that urgent?' he asked incredulously. 'It would be much safer to stay put today. But if you really have to go, make sure you study the tide tables carefully, check that you sail over the sandbar and around Start Point at exactly the right time so that the wind and tide are in your favour.' He paused before giving a stark warning. 'Or, mark my words, you *will* run into serious trouble. It's dangerous out there.'

James muttered something inaudible, before paying the well-meaning taxi skipper and clambering back on board. The mood was sombre as James poured over the tide tables spread across the chart table. Daniel and Bella, now dressed, stared at their iPads in silence. Elsa set the oven on its gimbals and battled to light a flickering flame under the kettle, just as the cups toppled and slid halfway across the work surface. 'Shit!'

'For God's sake, shut up, Elsa,' James spluttered, 'I've got to think…'

Charlie had stored the provisions in the bilges and now sat dejectedly in her cabin. Her mind was reeling from the unfortunate meeting in the shop. Did they recognise her? Would they remember her? The horror of her past was threatening to catch up with her; more rapidly than she had planned.

'The tide is ebbing, so if we leave now, we should be okay,' James said, feeling less confident than he sounded. 'Dan and Bella, I think you should stay below deck. Elsa, you take the wheel, and Charlie and I will cast off the lines. Let's go.'

As the lines were released, the mast was abruptly taken

by the wind and the boat was blown off the pontoon, leaving Charlie and James to leap perilously aboard.

'I'll take her from here,' James said as he pushed Elsa roughly aside to take over the steering of the lurching yacht. 'Go below and check the kids.' Elsa glanced back at the Bag – the area of the harbour where they had moored overnight. An eerie silhouette of tall masts rose proudly beneath a fast-moving blanket of low cloud, as they duelled with each other for survival. She began to feel nervous and very sick.

The unwilling crew stayed below, leaving James to manoeuvre the boat out of Salcombe Harbour, across the sandbar and out into the open channel, before heading east towards Start Point. Charlie sat between Daniel and Bella, thinking it would be a good plan to form a barrier to stop any fights that might erupt. But the kids were fully immersed in the games they were playing on their screens, and they sat in silence. Elsa had retreated into the front cabin, appearing periodically in her life jacket, to clamber up the steps of the companionway, clip on, and empty her stomach contents into the sea, cursing as she did so.

'Are we all going to drown?' Daniel whispered, his head bowed, as he snuggled close to Charlie. 'I'm scared.'

'No, Dan, we'll be fine. I know it feels bumpy in here, but it feels worse than it is. *Snow Goose* is a very seaworthy boat. She is perfectly capable of handling these conditions,' she said, giving him a reassuring hug, although she was quietly very concerned about the clueless skipper and the weak crew.

James had successfully negotiated the sandbar and now turned towards Start Point. The waves to the stern were the biggest he had ever seen, but the tide was flowing underneath them, enabling the yacht to cut efficiently through the water, and the small scrap of gip which he had unrolled, gave even more speed. Running his gloved hands lovingly around the large wheel, he felt glad that he had wisely invested in a well-constructed vessel, specially designed for long voyages and rough seas, although it was very expensive.

Daniel nestled into Charlie's armpit, clutching his knees up to his chest. This was unusual for Dan; he was normally very independent and detached. 'Please don't tell Dad how scared I am, he already thinks I'm a wimp and…' His words trailed away as he buried his face in his hands.

'What's the matter, Dan?' she asked softly. She ran her hands gently over his rounded back.

'It's just stuff at school,' he said, his eyes filling with tears.

'What's going on?'

'The kids hate me… I don't fit in.' He paused. 'I'm different.'

'Why do you think you're different?'

'I just am,' he said resignedly. 'They can't stand me.'

'I wonder why? I can't imagine anyone hating you.'

'They do though, and I can't make it right.' He shook his head in despair. 'I don't know what to do.'

Charlie knew only too well how cruel children could be to each other. 'But it's good to be different. Just imagine how dull the world would be if we were all the same.'

'I try to be like them,' he said, lifting his head to glance sideways at Charlie. 'If I'm naughty in class, maybe they will like me?'

'Your dad did mention to me that you have become increasingly disruptive in school,' Charlie acknowledged. 'I think you know this isn't the answer, is it, Dan?'

'But you don't understand,' he said, jutting his jaw out defiantly. 'If I misbehave at school, I am safe.'

'How does misbehaving make you safe?' Charlie asked, finding his revelation rather puzzling.

He looked directly at her. 'Because when the teachers get angry with me, the kids are too scared to bully me or hit me; they know the teachers are watching…'

Bella looked up from her iPad. 'Wimpy Dan, Wimpy Dan…'

Charlie gave Bella a withering stare. 'That is enough!' Returning her gaze to the unhappy boy beside her, she said quietly, 'We need to talk more about this, Dan. It will get easier though, I promise you.'

The storm continued to rage as James single-handedly navigated the boat through the choppy restless sea around Start Point; it felt to him more like a dangerous voyage around Cape Horn. He breathed a sigh of relief as he left the lighthouse safely behind them and began the sail across the considerably calmer waters of Start Bay.

'Dad, is it safe to come up?'

'Yes, I think we are through the worst now, thank goodness.'

Charlie, Daniel and Bella crowded into the cockpit, but Elsa stayed down below, still feeling nauseous and exhausted from the bumpy passage. The dark grey clouds had disappeared as quickly as they had arrived, devoured by a deep blue sky and a low watery sun, which cast shimmering sparkles across the blue water.

James pointed to the large structure on the cliff that marked the entrance to the mouth of the River Dart. 'If it wasn't for the day mark it would be very easy to miss Dartmouth altogether,' he said.

'Why isn't there a big signpost in the sea to show everyone the way?' asked Bella brightly.

Everyone laughed and the tension drained away. James hauled in the gip and started up the motor. 'We'll be in our berth soon,' he said encouragingly as he carefully steered a course upriver – Dartmouth on one side and Kingswear on the other – leaving the Town Jetty to port, and manoeuvring round the familiar red-hulled boat, *Salt Winds of Dart*, before edging nervously into their allotted mooring on the trots.

As Elsa stepped onto the yacht club motor launch that would take them to shore, she turned back and glared at James. She spoke her words slowly and ominously. 'If you *ever* expect me to come on this godforsaken tub again…' She paused. 'I *will* leave you.'

Six

Dear Antonia Farouk,

The Humble Pawn

Thank you for your submission. We aim to read submissions within twelve weeks of receipt.

If you have not heard from us twelve weeks after your submission was sent, please assume it has not been successful in this instance.

We wish you all the best of luck,
Submissions at Four Hedgehogs Publishing

Having submitted her manuscript thirteen weeks ago, she had heard nothing, again. Absolutely nothing. She had spent two and a half years vomiting her life story into words on a page and she had heard nothing. They had not even given her the courtesy of a rejection. At least a rejection was *something*. But this… this was *nothing*. And nothingness felt to Antonia like a black hole, a voluminous chasm. Hell on Earth.

And Antonia knew that time was running out.

'What are the chances?' she muttered under her breath. 'Two random people in the middle of nowhere recognising me.' Wringing her hands nervously, she whispered, 'I must take more care…'

She strode over to the mirror. This evening she wore her "little black dress", the symbol of a dangerous woman, to reflect the words on the page. Coco Chanel once said, "A woman can be overdressed but never over elegant." Yes, Antonia looked elegant and chic in a simple black number. She would have to go back to the drawing board, she would entice and seduce with her sentiments. She would not dress up her story with fancy or insignificant words, she would keep it simple. Her unique story. Nothing more, nothing less.

***

'Who the hell invented the institution of marriage?' Charlie bemoaned as she and Sandy sat in the Ferry Boat Inn early on Saturday evening enjoying a frothy pint of Jail Ale. A week had passed since the ill-fated sailing weekend and the two friends had not had a chance to meet up until this evening. 'It's totally ridiculous. How can anyone be expected to stay with the *same* partner forever and ever, Amen?'

'Where on earth has this come from?' asked Sandy in surprise. She had grown very fond of her new-found friend, but she was beginning to realise how little she knew about her or her life.

'I don't believe in wedded bliss and happy-ever-after stories, it's a load of rubbish,' said Charlie dismissively.

Sandy creased her brow. 'I suppose marriage can work, I know one or two couples that have been happily—'

Charlie tossed her hair back. 'Don't be so naïve, Sandy, it's a terrible idea. People change.'

'Do you think that we should just live together and forget about the whole marriage thing?'

'Ooh yes.' Charlie smirked. 'Let's all live in sin, sounds a lot more fun to me! But seriously, young couples these days seem to focus all their energy on *The Big Day*, with all the trimmings – the giggly hen do at a posh health spa, the drunken stag weekend, doing heaven knows what, in Berlin.' She took a deep breath. 'The silk dress, a fairytale vision of loveliness, the Italian handmade shoes, rock oysters and champagne – but they seem to forget about the life-long promises and commitments they make to one another. It can start well – candle-lit dinners, romantic holidays in faraway places, electrifying sex...' She hesitated. 'Actually, the electrifying sex probably comes before the marriage!' She sighed deeply. 'But then the harsh reality of life descends like a thick black cloud – boring jobs, snotty-nosed kids, pyjamas in bed, arguments, affairs...'

'Oh dear, there isn't much hope is there?' said Sandy with a frown.

'I think there should be a ten-year renewal written into the contract, so that partners would have to work harder to make their marriage work, if it is worth saving, or, if not, they could simply walk away. People should read the small print before they commit themselves to a life sentence.'

'"Read the small print", "a life sentence", you're such a cynic, my friend,' said Sandy, raising her eyes to heaven. She glanced around, a steady stream of locals had flocked into the pub for their customary session of drinking, chatting with their mates, listening to music and generally having a good time. She turned to Jimmy who sat close to them and had listened intently to their conversation. 'What do you make of all this, Jimmy?'

He clutched his trusty tankard of ale and looked at Charlie and Sandy in turn with a twinkle in his eye. 'Well, I did have a few adventures before I tied the knot.' He threw his head back and chuckled. 'Me and my mates, we used to pile all our surfing gear into the old yellow Volkswagen camper van and head to Newquay as often as we were allowed. The surfing was pretty good, but you wouldn't believe what we got up to in the back of the van with the local gals! Oh my, I could tell a few stories… My ol' mum wondered why we had so many cushions and sheets in the van… little did she know!' He suddenly became serious. 'I have often wondered if I fathered any children I didn't know about back in the day…'

Keen to avoid the embarrassment of hearing the gory details of his sexual encounters, Sandy asked, 'When did you get married?'

'I met my Mrs when I was nineteen. She was a real beauty, and I knew right away that my Maisie was the only one for me. We wed in a tiny church just a stone's throw from here. It was a small family affair, lots of flowers. I remember the day like it was yesterday... She was a rare one all right.'

'How long were you married?'

'We were wed for fifty-nine years and three months.' He stared blankly into space. 'I lost her to cancer four years ago... but I know she wanted me to be happy after she'd gone, so, here I am.' He raised his tankard, 'Cheers to you all!' Turning his gaze upward, he added, 'And here's to you, my lovely Maisie.'

'What is your secret for a happy marriage, Jimmy?' Charlie asked, intrigued.

Jimmy sat silently for a few minutes, deep in thought. 'We were always the best of friends, through the good times and the bad, we laughed together, and we cried together. Love *is* important,' he acknowledged, 'but it ebbs and flows like the tide. Our friendship was forever. She was, and is, my best mate.' He pondered for a moment, taking a noisy slurp of his ale. 'But of course we went through rough patches. We used to fight like cat and dog – she sometimes drove me up the wall – but we never let the sun go down on an argument. When things got really tough, I went out on *Maverick* for a day's fishing. I've always loved the big wide-open space of the ocean, and the solitude that it gave me.' He chuckled. '"Peace, perfect peace, with loved ones far, far, far away." But I never once strayed – I'd be lying if I didn't admit I was tempted once or twice – but Maisie was my rock, my everything. I wouldn't have swapped her for the world... And she was such a sexy beast!' A ripple of laughter followed by a spontaneous burst of applause broke out from the dozen or so locals that had gathered around him to listen to his pearls of wisdom. The wise old man of the sea grinned from ear to ear. 'And I wouldn't change a thing.'

Seven

The double-decker bus hurtled along the narrow coastal road from Dartmouth towards Start Point at breakneck speed, brushing perilously close to overhanging hedgerow and houses lining the route. Charlie and Sandy chose to sit on the top deck so they could enjoy the stunning panoramic view of the Devon landscape. Blankets of purple heather covered the rolling hillside, creating a dreamy haze of colour. Farmers in green and red combine harvesters cut the corn and gathered in the harvest for the winter months ahead. Straw bales were positioned randomly in burnt ochre fields, reminding them of the oncoming of autumn. The bus passed through tiny hamlets with dwellings like dolls houses, immaculate well-tended gardens and trees heavily laden with fruit, all surrounded by weathered stone walls, beset with remarkably resilient clumps of daisies.

At last the bus came to rest at a bus stop alarmingly near the edge of a steep cliff. 'This is where we get off,' Sandy said cheerily.

'Where on earth are we going? It looks like you've brought me to the middle of nowhere.' Charlie laughed.

'Phew, it feels so hot after sitting in the bus with the air conditioning on.'

'You'll see…' Sandy grinned as she took Charlie's arm and steered her towards a well-worn track that led down towards the beach. She had planned a surprise day trip for her friend, and the weather was perfect. The path in front of them was narrow and steep, and partially blocked by thistles and stinging nettles. Pink and white wild orchids rose proudly above the lush green vegetation.

'Look at this, Charlie,' Sandy said, pointing to the branches of a tree heavily coated with lichens and moss. 'You don't get this in town.'

'Really, I've never noticed it before.'

'It just shows you don't come to the coast often enough!' Sandy smiled. 'Lichens and moss won't grow if the air is polluted or if everything has been sprayed with horrible chemicals by the farmers.'

As they made their way to the beach below, they paused occasionally to admire the buzzards and other majestic birds of prey, as they glided effortlessly, wings outstretched, catching the uplift of air as they rose above the cliffs. They listened to the clear song of the skylark, hovering high above them. At last they negotiated the last rocky part of the path and arrived on a largely deserted sandy beach. It was hot and they were looking forward to plunging into the sea. They threw off their shoes and enjoyed the hot sand trickling between their toes.

'Let's relax for a moment, Charlie, I need to tell you something about this particular beach. It is very special.'

'I can see that, it's stunning.' Charlie sighed happily. 'It almost feels like we're on a desert island.'

'This is Pilchard Cove and…' She hesitated. 'It's a naturist beach.'

'Does that mean that we're likely to see a lot of birds?'

'Yes, we may well see some birdlife!' Sandy giggled. 'But I think you are confusing "naturalist" with "naturist". A naturalist is someone who studies the natural world. A naturist is someone who believes it is good and healthy to be naked.'

'You mean we go naked on this beach?' she asked, raising her eyebrows in mock horror.

'Yep… I promise you, it's the best feeling in the world,' Sandy said as she began to undress.

'I'm not sure I'm ready for this,' Charlie said, shaking her head nervously. 'Anyway, I've brought my new snazzy bikini to wear today.' Glancing at her friend who, by this time, was naked, she was struck by Sandy's natural unassuming beauty; there was no embarrassment, no awkwardness; she made no attempt to hide any part of her body, there was no posturing; she looked supremely happy and content in her body and totally in tune with the environment.

'Give it a go, Charlie. Once you've done it once, I'm willing to bet that you'll never look back.'

'Okay, I'll try, but I'm still not really sure…'

It was not Charlie's first experience of naturism, but this was in her past life. She must not tell. She reluctantly peeled off her clothes until she was bare. She looked down at her body and bit her lip.

'Come on, let's go,' Sandy suggested brightly. She held her friend's hand, and together they ran towards the sea. Charlie gasped as she plunged into the deliciously cool water and the gentle waves caressed her body. 'Do you fancy swimming out to that buoy over there?' she asked, pointing to the large yellow float about fifty metres away.

'Yeah, why not?' said Charlie. She started to enjoy the luxurious sensation of the waves massaging her body as she moved through the water. The low sun cast a glittery pathway on the sea before them.

'Isn't this heaven on earth?' Sandy said happily.

'It's totally magical.'

As they swam further from the shore, the bottom fell away under their feet and the deeper water became darker blue and colder. After a few minutes, they had successfully rounded the buoy and headed back towards the beach, rising and falling, as they were carried by the waves. Stepping onto the warm damp sand, her whole body tingled with pleasure.

'Hang on a minute,' Sandy said, running over to their solitary pile of belongings a little further up the beach. She rummaged in her rucksack and pulled out a floppy wide-brimmed hat. 'I have to be careful in the sun, Charlie, I don't want to spoil my dazzling beauty with any wrinkles or unsightly blemishes, do I now?' She raised her eyes to heaven and giggled and tossed one or two damp strands of hair away from her face. Together they walked hand in hand by the water's edge until all the water had evaporated from their bodies and they were completely dry. 'Isn't it great, you don't have to worry about soggy sandy towels or wet bikinis.' She paused. 'Anyway, whoever invented the idea of *putting on clothes* to go swimming? It's just crazy if you ask me.'

Charlie shrugged her shoulders. She had to agree with Sandy, and she had loved the freedom of swimming with nothing on, but now that they were back on land, she was beginning to feel self-conscious again, rather exposed.

'Do you see the house on the top of the cliff over there?' Sandy said, pointing to a huge glass-fronted dwelling with a luxurious balcony overlooking Pilchard Cove. 'One day, I'm going to live there,' she said, nodding her head confidently. 'I'm going to win the lottery and buy that house.'

As they stretched out on their striped beach towels, Charlie began to feel curious. 'How did you get into naturism, Sandy?'

'I stumbled on this beach, quite by chance, a few years ago. It was one of the hottest days of the summer, and the beach was much busier than it is today. Kids were building sandcastles and paddling in the sea, supervised by their attentive mums and dads. Groups of teenagers laughed and joked with each other, and older folk basked in the sun. And everyone was naked.'

'Were you shocked?'

'I was surprised, but not shocked. I realised that what I was seeing was unique and very special, and now I visit this beach as often as I can. It is usually very peaceful here, especially during the week.'

'Tell me more.'

'Naturism gives me the freedom to enjoy the forces of nature on my body – the sun, the wind, the rain – there is nothing like it. I feel connected to the earth when I'm naked. Grounded.'

Charlie listened intently.

'We are all equal when we are naked. It doesn't matter if you're the richest person in the world, or the poorest student, naturism is a true leveller. No one wears designer clothes, Rolex watches or huge rocks on their fingers. It doesn't matter if you are an eminent judge or a humble shopkeeper, material wealth and status are irrelevant. When you're naked, there is nothing to hide behind.' Sandy paused, looking at her friend, who had now carefully positioned a towel to cover the lower half of her body.

'The thing that struck me the most on the beach that day, was that there is no such thing as the "perfect body". We come in all shapes and sizes; it doesn't matter if you are fat or thin, unless of course your weight is affecting your health. It doesn't matter if you have a disability – I will never forget a woman that proudly walked along the beach. She had a double mastectomy, and she made no attempt to hide her scars. She was truly natural and beautiful. She was free. It doesn't matter if you are young or old...' She paused, drawing breath. 'Am I going on about this too much?'

'No, carry on, I'm really fascinated by what you're saying...'

'I worry about kids these days, obsessing about their appearance, taking endless selfies, using filters to make their faces appear perfect, or paying lots of money for fillers and lip plumping and other unnecessary cosmetic surgery. They have tummy tucks, boob jobs, bottom fillers, and going on stupid diets, sometimes seriously damaging their health. And all for what? It seems so horribly fake to me.'

'And what is your point?' Charlie asked, looking more serious now.

'I think that if anyone has poor body image or low self-esteem, they should try naturism. They would soon realise that there really is no such thing as a perfect body. They might decide to focus on being good, being kind and being happy, instead of wasting their time on things that really don't matter.'

'Well, I do believe I'm one of those *horribly fake* people,' muttered Charlie angrily.

Sandy looked at her friend. 'What are you saying?'

Charlie hesitated, staring blankly at the cloudless sky above her.

Sandy placed her hand gently on Charlie's arm. 'Tell me...'

'It all started when I was eleven years old. Puberty arrived, and with it came horrendous periods, spots and mood swings. My friends told me I was fat. I hated myself. I remember thinking that, if this is what it is like to be an adult, I didn't want any of it.' Her eyes welled with tears. 'I was bullied mercilessly by my so-called friends. I was trolled online, I had to read evil and malicious messages, and see grotesque images. I wanted to die.'

Sandy rolled onto her side, supporting her head on her hand, listening to the disturbing story that was unfolding.

'Did you tell anyone about how you were feeling, Charlie?' she asked quietly.

'No, I didn't, my mum and dad were too busy arguing, and I felt too intimidated at school to say anything. I thought seriously about taking my own life. But instead, I went on a diet. I strived to make myself look better in the eyes of the world. It started well. I was in control.' The fingers of her left hand formed a tight fist, her knuckles turning white. 'But then it took over my head. All I could think about was losing more and more weight. I was convinced that the more weight I lost, the better life would be. But I was starving myself to death. I spent hours of each day in my bedroom, searching online. I read unhealthy websites promoting anorexia nervosa, and other eating disorders, as a healthy and positive way of life. I read online forums where sufferers bragged about how much weight they had lost, posting horrific emaciated images, describing themselves as beautiful and powerful... And the worst thing is that I believed every word.' She took a deep breath and sobbed. 'I nearly died, Sandy.'

'I'm so sorry this happened to you.'

Charlie sat up and hugged her knees to her chest. 'I can't talk about this anymore, it's just too painful.'

'That's okay, I just want you to know that I'm always here for you, Charlie. I can't promise to have all the answers, but I am a very good listener.' Sandy put her arm around her friend, and they sat together, the silence only broken by the distant cry of the gulls. After a while, Sandy jumped up and ran towards the water's edge, inviting Charlie to follow her. Together they stared out towards the horizon. 'I don't know if I should say this,' said Sandy, 'but I think you're bloody gorgeous.'

They laughed, as they watched the blood-red sun slowly disappear into the sea.

Eight

'Darling, I don't know what more we can do. I just don't understand why Dan is behaving so badly.'

'James, you're pathetic. Why the hell can't you control your son?' Elsa hissed. 'You're so weak. How did I end up marrying you?'

'I do my best,' James stammered, 'but it obviously isn't good enough.'

'*You* are his father, the person he is supposed to look up to, his role model, God help me!'

'Perhaps I should visit the school again?' he asked quietly.

'Don't blame the bloody school, James, you need to look closer to home.' She stared at him dispassionately. 'It is all your fault.' With that, she banged her half-drunk cup of coffee hard down on the worktop and left the kitchen, slamming the door behind her. 'I give up!'

Daniel stood dejectedly by the window. 'Dad, it's not your fault, it's mine,' he said, tears streaming down his cheeks. 'I'm sorry... Are you and Mum going to split up because of me?'

James turned to face Daniel, and spat out his words. 'Do you love your mother?'

'Yes, I do,' Daniel mumbled.

'Speak up, boy. I'll ask you again. Do you love your mother?'

'Yes, I do, Dad,' Daniel said in a flat tone of voice.

'And do you love me?' James asked, as he walked slowly towards Daniel.

'Yes,' he stammered.

He leant over so close that Daniel could feel droplets of saliva on his face. 'Then for God's sake, stop snivelling and act your age. I expect more of you than this, Daniel. Mind your step, I will be watching you like a hawk.'

He turned away, leaving Daniel alone in the kitchen.

Charlie had listened to every word from the next room. She wondered how James and Elsa could have such little understanding of their son. It seemed to her that Daniel was being attacked and manipulated on all sides: from his family, his friends and his teachers at school.

'Hey, Dan, are you okay?'

'Not really,' he said tearfully. 'I'm really worried that Mum and Dad will split up and all because of me.' He looked unbearably sad.

'Right,' Charlie said brightly, 'go and put your shoes on, we're going into Loss for a coffee and a chat. I'll let your dad know that we'll be out for a couple of hours.'

'What about Bella?' he asked quietly.

'I'm sure your parents can look after her. She's busy on her iPad, so she probably won't notice that we've gone out anyway.'

The coffee shop was quiet when they arrived. Dan stared forlornly out of the window. 'There's nothing like a comforting cuppa to cheer you up.' Charlie smiled as she pressed a steaming mug of weak milky tea into his outstretched hands. She studied the young boy in front of her: he had an unruly mop of ginger hair that flopped heavily over his forehead, partially covering his pale freckled face. His mellow brown eyes were set too far apart, making him appear as if he had a squint. Over the past few months he had grown very tall and gangly, his elbows and knees too big for his limbs, but his voice had not yet broken. He didn't look comfortable in his skin.

'It's not been a good day has it, Dan?'

'No, it hasn't,' he said, putting his head in his hands. 'I just feel thick and useless.'

'I don't agree,' Charlie said, 'you're extremely bright. Haven't you just finished reading the entire *Harry Potter* series?'

'Yeah, they were brilliant stories!' Daniel answered, breaking into a smile. 'I felt really sad when I finished the last book. I've borrowed the Philip Pullman trilogy, *His Dark Materials*, from the school library to read next. And after that, I want to read *The Hobbit* and *Lord of the Rings*. I can't wait!' He sighed heavily. 'I guess I escape into my own world when I'm reading. I get absorbed in the story and forget about all the horribleness in my life.'

'It's fab that you can enjoy reading, I envy you; I find it really hard to get totally engrossed in a book... but tell me about the *horribleness* you talk about.'

Daniel became sullen. 'It doesn't matter.'

'It does matter, Dan, *you* matter a lot.'

He shrugged his shoulders.

'I want to tell you something about myself. I was bullied at school.'

Daniel looked up, surprised by her revelation.

'The kids at school teased me for being fat.' She paused. 'Actually, teasing is too nice a word... I was bullied for being overweight.'

'How did you deal with it?' asked Daniel, becoming interested in what Charlie had to say.

'My so-called friends posted evil messages and horrendous images online. Even at home, I could never escape their bullying. I lived with it every waking moment – a living hell. I've rarely felt more alone than I did then. Large groups of kids used to wait outside the school gates to taunt me; they called me all the names under the sun. I began to believe the words they were saying – that they were right.'

Daniel listened intently. 'How did you get through it?'

'I had a very tough time,' Charlie answered, gauging that it wouldn't be helpful, or wise, to go into detail about her illness. 'I didn't confide in anyone, but now, with hindsight, I wish I had. I kept it all to myself. I should have told my parents, or one of the teachers at school, or anyone that I trusted. I realise now that to talk to someone about what is worrying you, even if it is very painful, will make you stronger, and give you the armour you need to resolve what is happening, with help and support. But it can be daunting to take the first step.'

'They call me names like ginger whinger, carrot top, ginger nut, matchstick, and other even more disgusting names. They must be pretty stupid though. Don't they know that carrot tops are green, not orange?'

Charlie had wondered whether the colour of his hair might be something to do with the problems Daniel was facing. She had heard in the news a couple of weeks before, that there was a move afoot to put "gingerism" on a par with racism and sexism, as a hate crime, since people have been badly wounded in anti-ginger attacks. Some people had even taken their own lives because of the bullying. She knew that what Dan was describing to her was serious and disturbing. 'Do you know, Dan, you're very special. Only two per cent of the population on the entire planet have red hair?'

'Really? Only two per cent? That's awesome,' Dan said, looking a little brighter now. 'But the kids won't know that.'

'And what about all the famous people that are very popular and have red hair? Ed Sheeran is pretty cool, isn't he?' Charlie asked.

'Yep, he's cool. I wish I could sing and play the guitar like he does.'

'He's got ginger hair. I think he's really good-looking, along with half the adult population!' Charlie smiled. 'And what about Prince Harry?' she asked, raising her eyebrows quizzically. Dan frowned. 'Okay… You've seen the *Harry Potter* film series haven't you?'

'Yes, it was totally brilliant,' said Daniel, smiling.

'Isn't Ron Weasley a redhead?'

'He does have red hair,' Daniel acknowledged. 'Ron is Harry Potter's best friend, he never got teased about his hair in the books. In fact, no one mentions the colour of his hair, except Draco Malfoy of course, and Harry

Potter soon puts an end to that!' He paused. 'Ron is very good at chess, perhaps it is more important to be good at something, than about hair colour?'

'You're right, Dan.' She inwardly winced at his reference to a game of chess. It brought back horrific memories that she would have to live with every day of her life.

'And I suppose, who wants to be Draco, running to tell the teacher every time he wants to get Harry in trouble, and buying himself into the Quidditch team, when he could be ginger and win the house cup?'

'Aren't the kids that are bullying you just a bunch of mini Dracos?' Charlie volunteered.

'Haha, a bunch of mini Dracos, I like that. But when I think about it, all the Weasleys have ginger hair… And Harry Potter ends up with Ginny Weasley, because his soulmate had to be a redhead.' He paused. 'It doesn't help me though, because none of the kids read Harry Potter.'

'I feel sorry for them, Dan, they're missing out, not reading these brilliant stories.' She took a long sip of coffee. 'What else do they taunt you about?' Charlie asked, inviting Daniel to tell her more about his troubles.

'They tease me because I live in a big house and go sailing. They think I'm nothing but a posh rich kid. They taunt me about my accent. The other day they pulled me into the bushes and bullied me into saying, "utterly butterly". They all jeered and told me it was "uttly buttly", but they're wrong aren't they, Charlie?' Dan said, his words tumbling out in one long stream of emotion. 'I might talk posh but there's absolutely nothing fancy about me.' He paused. 'I looked up, "posh" on Google, and do you know, it might be short for "Port Out, Starboard Home". On the ships travelling between Britain and India years ago, the most desirable cabins – the ones that didn't get the afternoon heat – were on the port side out and the starboard side home. These tickets were stamped "POSH". No one knows if this is true, but it's a great story isn't it, Charlie?'

'How interesting; you're a mine of information, you could certainly teach me a thing or two!' Charlie commented, impressed by the sensitivity, intellect and insightfulness of the nine-year-old boy sitting opposite her. 'Dan, it's good that you are opening up about what is happening to you at the moment. It can't be easy...'

'There's so much more, Charlie,' he said sadly.

'Come and talk with me whenever you feel like it, Dan. I'm not going anywhere... Can I share with you some of the things that I learnt when I was being bullied?'

'Of course, Charlie,' he said softly.

'Children that bully others have often been bullied themselves. They are weak and cowardly. It is these kids that have the problem, not you.'

Dan stared sadly into the depths of his tea.

'It's wise to try and ignore them if you can; don't give them the satisfaction of showing them that you are upset or angry. Just walk away.'

'I find it hard to ignore them, their words hurt me too much.'

'There is a saying, "sticks and stones may break my bones, but words will never hurt me",' Charlie recited. 'It's not true, is it, Dan?'

'Words can damage you just as much as being punched in the gut.'

Charlie took a sharp intake of breath. 'I agree, Dan.' She was taken aback by the way he could express himself so clearly. 'You are strong enough and brave enough to walk away, to ignore them, not to retaliate…' Charlie gave a deep sigh. 'I bitterly regret…' Her words trailed away.

'What do you regret, Charlie?' he asked, now looking puzzled.

'Never mind, it's just something I did in my past that I wish I hadn't done.' She hesitated. 'Dan, don't change your behaviour, or anything about you, to try and be like them. You are one in many millions!'

Just at that moment Sandy bounced into the coffee shop. 'Hi, you two, I hope I'm not interrupting anything. I'll just get a coffee, and then can I join you?'

Charlie glanced at Dan who was smiling at Sandy. 'Of course!'

'How's it going?' Sandy asked, glancing at her friend, aware of tension in the air. 'Have you been talking about serious things? Trust me to butt in, like a bull in a china shop… or Sandy in a coffee shop!' She threw her head back and laughed.

'No, you're not interrupting us,' Charlie said. 'I think we've finished our conversation for the moment, haven't we, Dan?'

Daniel nodded, relieved that Sandy had arrived to lighten the atmosphere. 'It's great to see you.'

'What have you been up to, Dan?' asked Sandy cheerfully

'Not a lot really...' Daniel said, shrugging his shoulders.

'Charlie told me that you went sailing to Salcombe.'

'Yeah, it rained all the time. It was an awful weekend.'

'Oh dear, at least the sun's shining today,' Sandy said, exchanging glances with Charlie. 'Hey, last time we met, you mentioned that you like dancing. How's it going?'

'The kids at school think I'm a sissy for liking dancing,' he said sadly.

'That's nonsense!' Sandy retorted. 'Do you know that the male dancers from the Royal School of Ballet train with an American football team to keep themselves fit? A dancer has to be as strong as an ox!'

'They think dancing is only for girls. They call me Nancy Boy.'

'Don't listen to them, they're talking a load of rubbish.' She paused, and then her face broke into a wide smile. 'Have you seen the musical, *Billy Elliot*, it's a fabulous show?'

'No, never heard of it,' said Dan, shaking his head.

'We must go and see the show together; it's brilliant. It is about a young lad growing up in an extremely masculine working-class society in Durham. He begins to learn ballet and, although it is a struggle to begin with, he discovers that, through dance, he can express himself creatively, and he can embrace his individuality. *Billy Elliot* positively challenges gender roles and expectations that ballet is only for girls – it challenges homophobic prejudice – that all male dancers are gay.' She paused. 'People can make ignorant assumptions and, I might add, that there is absolutely nothing wrong with being gay. The show is all about being open-minded and accepting who you are, as a unique individual.'

'It sounds amazing, I would love to see it!' Daniel smiled from ear to ear. Charlie listened quietly; this is exactly what Daniel needed to hear.

'What kind of dance are you into at the moment, Dan?'

'I love street dancing,' he answered. 'I've been watching kids on YouTube; they're unbelievable acrobats, so cool! I've started practising. I can already do a few moves but I'm not very good yet.'

'That sounds great, Dan. I've got an idea,' Sandy said, her dark eyes shining with pleasure. 'My great friend, François, is an amazing dancer. Can you believe he used to perform regularly with The Ballet Rambert in the West End? He has retired now, but he's determined to share his passion for dance with interested students of all ages. François owns and runs The South Hams School of Expressive Movement and Dance, not far from here. He teaches a wide range of dance, including ballet, tap, modern, freestyle and creative dance. I loved watching some of his students, mainly lads of about your age, perform breathtaking street dancing in the square at Dartmouth just the other day. Wow did those kids draw in the crowds! Would you like to go to his classes? I could have a word with François if you would like me to?'

Daniel wriggled with excitement. 'I would love that, Sandy, yes please.' His face suddenly crumpled. 'But what would my dad think?'

Nine

Dear Antonia Farouk,

The Humble Pawn

I trust this email finds you well.

I wanted to email you today with regard to your manuscript that you sent us recently. I think you have something really raw, compelling and distinctive here. The subjects you have tackled are by no means easy and it's so brave of you to have drawn on your own experiences so deftly. I commend you. I am very interested in working with you on it. I enclose a draft contract for you to sign.

Thank you and I look forward to hearing from you.

Regards,
Ms Prudence Beecham

Castle View Publishers
PO Box 526
London
SE4

Antonia stared at the screen. Nice words. Kind words. Can I dare to dream? She eagerly opened the attachment. It looked professional and expensive, and horribly glossy. It had twenty-three numbered clauses, complex legal gobbledygook, and signed by Ms Prudence Beecham herself, in perfect italic lettering.

So easy to sign, so easy... So far so good. Yes, I should sign. I will sign.

But wait.

10. AUTHOR CONTRIBUTION

10.1 It is mutually agreed that The Author shall pay a contribution consisting of £5,000 GBP in accordance with the terms of this Agreement contained herein, before the work is released to the trade.

Antonia turned away from the screen and slowly rose to her feet. She heaved her body up to full height and gazed at her reflection in the mirror. This evening she wore a grey silk wraparound dressing gown, tied in at the waist. She longed for her story to be told: it wasn't much to ask was it? But Ms Prudence Beecham had filled her head with anger. Emotion flooded her face in wet saltiness. Her legs gave way, her body folded in despair. She drew her knees into her chest and buried herself deep in the slippery folds of her dressing gown.

I have to pay £5,000 for the privilege of getting MY book published? I have to pay for the pain I suffered, translating the Devil into words on a page?

Who has £5,000? The rich? The privileged? The entitled? But wait, there is more.

16. TERMINATION AND REVERSION OF RIGHTS

16.1 If at any time after the expiration of two years from the date of first publication The Publisher shall determine that there are not sufficient sales of the work to enable it to continue its publication and sale profitably, it shall be privileged to dispose of the copies remaining on hand as it deems best, subject to the provisions with regard to royalty set forth in Clause 10 of this agreement.

The Publisher is privileged to dispose of the copies remaining on hand as it deems best. Privileged?

Chuck them on the scrap heap. Reduce them to pulp in a matter of minutes.

And there you have it. The sadness and pain of life, reduced to waste for recycling or landfill.

***

Dartmouth quayside was alive with a hubbub of activity. Young children dangled their crabbing lines over the edge of the high wall, into the water below, one or two dangerously close to toppling in. Elderly couples sat in amiable silence, clutching a cup of tea in both hands and gazing at the colourful array of boats bobbing about in the harbour. A group of hardy open-water swimmers had just returned, shaking the water off their ruddy blotchy skin, like dogs, before donning enormous waterproof coats and plastic clogs. A young couple sat on a nearby bench, deep in conversation, heartily digging into a mouth-watering carton of fish and chips.

Sandy and Charlie sat side by side, idly passing the time away, people-watching and sipping cool pints of Tribute served in plastic containers. 'This won't do,' said Charlie, shaking her head. 'I think we need some exercise. Do you fancy walking part of the coastal path around the castle?'

'Yeah, I suppose so, although I'm feeling pretty lethargic today,' Sandy said, smiling lazily at her friend. 'Okay, let's go while there's still some heat in the sun.'

They quickly drained their beers and began the long climb through dense woodland, towards the mouth of the Dart, breathing in the musky aroma of damp brackens and ferns, mingled with steam from the train journeying from Kingswear to Paignton on the other side of the river.

'Have you ever studied these incredible stone walls, Charlie?'

'No, I haven't. It must have taken years to build them, and now they are almost completely covered over in ferns and undergrowth. It makes me wonder why they bothered in the first place.'

Sandy laughed. 'Oh, Charlie, you're such a heathen!' She ripped some greenery aside to reveal a wall with an unusual vertical course of stone. 'It's amazing how they constructed these walls back in the day. Look, they split the stone into narrow pieces and stacked them vertically, instead of horizontally; they didn't use any mortar, that's why they are called drystone walls. Don't you think it's incredible that they have stood the test of time? These beautiful stone walls must be literally hundreds of years old. And they are holding back tons of earth from collapsing onto this narrow path.'

As they walked further, Sandy began to describe some of the history of the area: that Kingswear is first mentioned in history back in the twelfth century when it became a popular landing site for overseas pilgrims who were on their way to Kent to pay homage to the murdered Archbishop of Canterbury; Thomas Becket. 'There have been a few epic historical voyages that started right here. Can you imagine a host of ships sailing out of Dartmouth and helping to defeat the Spanish Armada?' she said, her eyes shining with excitement. 'When World War Two came, literally hundreds of vessels sailed from here for the invasion of Europe... Elizabethan adventurers left Dartmouth to explore the New World, and the Pilgrim Fathers sailed off from here to settle it.' She took a deep breath. 'This area is steeped in history. I find it really fascinating; I often wonder about how our modern world is shaped by significant events of the past.'

Charlie listened with interest, realising how little she knew about history. She had opted to study geography instead of history at school, and now she was beginning to regret it.

'Our history teacher was so stuffy and boring; I gave it up,' Charlie said sadly.

'I didn't particularly like history at school, but when you live in a town like Dartmouth, history comes alive for me. I live it and breathe it; it is real, I didn't read it in dusty textbooks.'

Suddenly the path widened into a grassy clifftop area,

enjoying breathtaking views across Start Bay. The sky was cloudless, and the sea was azure blue and as calm as a millpond. 'Let's take a breather for a few minutes,' Charlie suggested. They found a small rocky outcrop on which to sit, threw off their rucksacks, and took a few deep breaths of the fresh coastal air.

'Sandy, can I ask you something?'

'Of course, Charlie, anything, anything at all.'

'It is quite personal,' she warned. She looked down at Sandy's left hand with one finger missing, and the striking fern-shaped tattoo that traced the inside of her ring finger and her index finger, curling up her left arm.

Sandy smiled sadly, lifting her left hand into the air in front of her. 'You want to know how this happened, don't you?'

'I'm sorry. If you don't want to tell me, I would totally understand.'

Sandy's face darkened. 'My parents came from Cypress. My mother was forty-two when she gave birth to me. My father was a carpenter, a talented craftsman, but he wanted more for me. My parents didn't want me to become a housewife or a mother, a shopkeeper, or a secretary; they were fiercely determined that I should become an eminent lawyer or a consultant surgeon. Nothing else would be good enough for their daughter.'

'It sounds to me like they wanted you to aim high, and for you to enjoy some of the advantages and opportunities that they didn't have.'

Sandy turned to face Charlie. 'No, they weren't thinking about me or my welfare at all. It was all about status and pride. All they worried about was what other people thought of our family, and I had to live up to their expectations. I had no choice.'

Charlie listened quietly.

'But the trouble is, from the time I took my first steps and uttered my first words, I loved to dance, I loved to sing and I loved to draw and paint.' She paused. 'But none of it was good enough for my parents.'

'What happened, Sandy?' asked Charlie, edging closer to her friend.

'I badly wanted them to love me,' she said, creasing her brow. 'But nothing I tried was ever good enough. They even sent me to an expensive all-girls private school when I was eleven, in the hope that I would excel in all my exams. God knows how they afforded it! But what they didn't realise was that the school prided itself on achieving every pupils' potential, whether it be in academic, creative or technical subjects. The teachers were brilliant; they recognised and fostered my love of music, art and dance. One of the teachers even lent me her guitar to play…'

'That explains why you're such a great musician.'

'But then this happened,' she said sadly, looking down at her hand.

'What happened?'

'I was in my dad's workshop, using a jigsaw to cut shapes into a lump of plywood. My dad was busy varnishing a rocking chair he had just made; he wasn't watching me. I simply forgot that my other hand was underneath, holding the wood in place. It all happened in a flash. I didn't feel a thing.' Her dark eyes glistened with tears. 'There was so much blood...'

Charlie slipped her arm around Sandy's shoulder. 'How old were you?'

'I was fourteen. I thought my world had fallen apart. I had grown to love my guitar, but how was I going to play it now?'

'It's incredible how people can adapt and learn new techniques to compensate...'

Interrupting her friend, Sandy continued, 'But after this, something really unexpected happened. My mum and dad started to show more interest in me, we were more like a family. I could have a laugh with them, they seemed to believe in me, I truly believed they loved me.' Sandy put her head in her hands. 'But I was wrong. I was lulled into a false sense of security. I thought I could confide in them, tell them anything...'

'And...'

Sandy took a deep breath. 'We had enjoyed a lovely day on the beach, swimming, laughing, and eating fish and chips. I felt so happy; I had faith that my parents loved me unconditionally. We started to chat about school and friends, and I gauged that the time was right to share with them that I liked girls, that I might be a lesbian. I thought they would be pleased that I was growing up and beginning to understand my own mind and body, but instead, all hell broke loose. They abandoned me on the beach. Charlie, I was only fifteen and they threw me out of the house. They disowned me, and I have not seen or heard from them since that day.'

'Oh, Sandy, I'm so sorry.'

'I am a lesbian, it is the very essence of me,' Sandy said passionately. 'And I'm proud of who I am. Isn't life all about friendship and love? It doesn't matter about the sex, gender, or race of the people you get close to, as long as you love and respect them for who they are.'

'You are so right, Sandy, and I love you for it,' Charlie said, as she gently stroked the side of her face. 'And I think you are beautiful, through and through.'

Ten

The path became grassy as they closed the metal latch of the old wooden gate and began the undulating walk inland, heading back towards Dartmouth. Rolling hillsides, dotted with large farmhouses and orange and pink-tinged fields stretched before them. Sandy and Charlie walked in silence, both reflecting on the significance of the conversation.

'How could your parents disown you for being honest, for being you?'

'I have no idea. I'm still Sandy, whatever my sexual preferences, I'm still their daughter.'

'It's ridiculous. Their loss,' Charlie said, hoping that she wasn't dismissing the importance of her friends' words too quickly. 'How did you survive, Sandy, you must have been very scared?'

'I was petrified, I had no idea what to do. I drifted for a while, I slept on park benches, begged for food and smoked discarded fags. I met the wrong people. I took drugs and began to drink heavily. One morning, after a particularly rough night, I woke up determined to take back control of my life.'

'So what did you do?' Charlie asked, squeezing Sandy's hand gently, 'I can't imagine how you must have felt.'

'I hitchhiked into Plymouth and made my way straight to the council offices, where I was directed to Children's Services. The staff in the department were kind and caring. They listened to what I had to say; they knew that emotionally I was pretty broken. They placed me in a temporary foster home that they had assessed as being appropriate for my needs.'

'My goodness, Sandy, what was the foster home like?'

'It was here that I met Betty, a true earth mother, my saviour! She was as short as she was wide, with a doughy dimpled face, tiny glittery eyes and grey hair swept back in a bun. And she had the biggest and heartiest of smiles!' Sandy said, her face radiating pleasure. 'She welcomed literally hundreds of troubled children into her home over many years. She was, and is, one in a million. Although Betty ran a tight ship, always expecting great things, we were happy and sensitively looked after. She valued each and every one of us.' Sandy raised an eyebrow. 'And she had the biggest cosiest bosoms... when I felt sad, or happy, I buried my face deep into her ample flesh. I breathed in her soothing voice and absorbed her wise words. I felt safe.'

'Did you tell Betty the reason why your parents disowned you?' Charlie asked quietly.

Sandy shook her head. 'I wanted to, but I was terrified about what she might say. I was only fifteen, and my fear was that if my parents threw me out of my house, would Betty do the same?'

'Weren't you tempted to confide in her?' Charlie persisted.

'Of course I was, but I was very confused and frightened. I became withdrawn and spent most of my time in my room. I wasn't ready to share my secret with anyone,' Sandy said sadly.

'Perhaps you should have done?' Charlie suddenly realised the irony of what she had just suggested. She had also not shared the dark years of her life with anyone.

As they walked over the brow of a sun-burnished hill in silence, dramatic views of the Dart Estuary opened out before them. Kingswear basked in the early evening sun, as the first lights twinkled in the tiny cottages on the other side of the river.

'But some good came out of it all, Charlie,' Sandy said, 'it was during this time that Betty said that I could borrow her son's guitar, while he was at university. During many months of solitude, I spent hour upon hour exploring ways of playing the six strings of the guitar with my four remaining digits. I discovered the power of my thumb! I realised I *could* play the guitar and sing. I could overcome my disability.'

'And you are a brilliant musician,' Charlie acknowledged.

Sandy spread out the fingers of her left hand. 'I realised that, instead of trying to hide my disability, I should highlight it, be proud of it. I decided to have a tattoo. After all, losing my finger was the reason I was so determined to become a musician... and it is rather wackily wonderful,' she added with a grin.

'You're amazing, Sandy, not only to overcome adversity, but to positively celebrate your "disability" with a beautiful tattoo for all the world to see, is awesome!' She glanced at her friend. 'Did you ever tell Betty that you're gay?' Charlie asked, keen to return to the earlier conversation.

'I did, but it took three years of agonising before I finally found the nerve to confide in her. By this time, I was at college taking an arts degree, but I used to visit my foster home regularly. Betty had been so kind to me over the years, I had come to love her, I owed it to her to be honest.'

'So you spilled the beans?'

'Yes, I did, as simple as that. I just blurted it out.'

'And what did she say?'

'Well, it was the biggest non-event really,' said Sandy, smiling. 'She didn't think it was a big deal at all, just a personal and loving part of me. She had known all along, because of some of the things I had said.' Sandy put her hand over her mouth to suppress a giggle. 'And because I shooed away all the good-looking boys that ever came to visit!'

'I bet loads of boys fancied you, Sandy!' Charlie laughed.

'Yeah, there were quite a few. Betty was shocked to hear why my parents had thrown me out of my home, thinking they were misguided, uneducated, old-fashioned and heartless.' Sandy paused. 'She did warn me about the ignorance, prejudice and discrimination that I might have to face. She told me just to ignore them. "They're only words, after all".'

'But words can wound you, harm you, damage you...' Charlie muttered, looking away.

Sandy paused, absorbing what Charlie had said before continuing. 'She told me to enjoy life to the full. Be happy.'

'And are you, Sandy? Are you happy?'

'I think I am, most of the time. But I'm not really sure what happiness is, I guess it's just a state of mind, kind of ethereal...' She started to sing, her body swaying in time to the words she sang. 'We've all got to stop worrying about silly stuff!' She threw her head back and laughed. 'I find dope helps!'

Charlie put her arm firmly round Sandy's shoulders. 'I wish I had a fraction of your courage, then I would be happy.'

'Well, I think we need to grab happiness when we can, otherwise it might pass us by!' With that, she pulled Charlie deftly towards her, swiftly cupping her breasts. 'Bloody hell, now this is what I call happiness!'

'I can't...' Charlie stammered, pulling away. 'I'm not ready...'

'What is it, Charlie? I know there is something troubling you, please tell me. You know what they say, a problem shared...' Charlie's behaviour was puzzling, and Sandy was beginning to wonder if she was hiding something from her.

Charlie gazed towards the horizon and said nothing. She suddenly slumped down on the grassy bank and put her head in her hands. 'It's just a part of my life that I can't talk about.'

Sandy hesitated. 'Is it during the years when you had anorexia?'

She looked directly at Sandy. 'I will always have anorexia,' she answered angrily, 'the demons are always there in my head. Always. They will never leave me, they haunt me.' She hit her head hard with the flat of her hand. 'Every day, they haunt me.' She drew breath and her words cut through the air like a knife. 'But no... this is *not* my darkest nightmare...' Her words trailed away.

'It must have been horrendous, Charlie, I can't imagine what has happened to affect you in this way.'

Charlie's voice softened. 'Be patient with me, Sandy. When it comes to sex, I don't seem to be able to accept any pleasure, I feel too guilty about what has happened. I feel the need to punish myself; the workings of my brain are complicated, it's not you.' She locked eyes with Sandy. 'I will get there, I promise.' She bowed her head and hugged her knees tightly to her chest.

The late-September night crept over the dark hills of Dartmoor, black, illuminated only by the distant lights of Dartmouth. Autumn was stealing in, sending with it a sharp chill to the air. Sandy listened intently. What could possibly have happened?

'I will tell my story, but all in good time, when I am ready.'

Sandy considered their conversation and was reminded of the strange case of Dr Jekyll and Mr Hyde – the fight of good over evil – and it worried her. There was so much about Charlie that she knew nothing about, but, at that moment, she felt strangely close to her friend. 'There's more to life than sex; you're safe with me,' she said in a soothing voice. 'No need to talk any more, but I am always here for you.'

'Sandy, I'm sorry,' Charlie said, with deep sadness in her voice.

'Come on, let's grab a quick pint in the Ferryboat before closing time.' With that she grabbed the crook of Charlie's arm, and they walked together in silence.

***

Hello,

Thank you for the opportunity to consider your manuscript. Unfortunately, I did not feel passionate enough about your work to be able to offer representation at this time.

As an author in a fiercely competitive market, you need an agent who can be an absolute champion of you and your writing.

Best of luck finding the right agent for your work.

Regards,
Elara Presley

Magenta Agency
London E7

'Elara did not feel passionate enough – *passionate enough* – about my work,' Antonia muttered. 'But I feel – *passionately* – that my story must be told. What must I do?'

She stood erect and studied her reflection in the full-length mirror. She wore a simple cream dress, made with delicate folds of soft taffeta. The luxurious material caressed her body, a perfect fit. The robe revealed just a subtle suggestion of her shapely figure underneath; modest and understated, and yet sensual and glamorous. As she swayed, a multitude of silver sequins glittered in the candlelight. 'Perhaps I should offer my body to Elara Presley, in return for her goods and services,' she said alluringly. 'I could show her the true meaning of the word *passion*.'

Suddenly she froze, her face taut, her eyes expressionless. The terror of her past flashed before her.

I am nothing but a sacrificial pawn. My story is not worthy. I am not worthy.

Suddenly everything became clear.

Antonia turned her back on her image, strode to her desk and opened the lid of her laptop. She highlighted the last eight chapters of her manuscript, her hands hovering above the keyboard: shaky, clammy, and then she pressed delete. Delete. The words, the lies, the deceit, disappeared from the screen in an instant. Her fingers alighted on the keys, and she typed, furiously, the words spilling out onto the page. The truth must be told. And Antonia knew that then, and only then, would publishers and agents fight to publish her story: the shocking truth of an unexplained death.

Part 2

Eleven

Oxford: Two years earlier.

Libby glanced down in horror at the enormous "all-day breakfast" that she had just ordered; it was enough to feed a family of five. Two fried eggs, glistening with oil, carefully balanced on top of a tangled mound of streaky bacon, and surrounded by several rounds of blood-and-fat impregnated black pudding. Two chunks of tomato added a subtle touch of health to the otherwise unhealthy calorie-laden feast. And, just in case she was still hungry, a mountain of butter-soaked toast was included in the price. She sipped her black coffee and watched as people passed by the window of the small cafe. It was mid-July and the covered market was strangely quiet for this time of the year, but the popular coffee shop opposite was packed with people, young and old, ordering espressos and lattes, pastries and a wide range of treats, all at highly exorbitant prices. Young people perched precariously on low rustic wooden crates in the tiled passage outside the entrance to the shop, enjoying their chosen beverage, steam rising from their recyclable mugs, all deep in conversation.

'You're miles away!' Amelia said in her rather piercing voice. 'What do you think, Libs?'

Realising that she had not heard a word her friend had said, Libby shrugged her shoulders. 'What about?'

'Well, hun, I was asking you about the merits of us leaving the European Union. Did you vote to stay or leave?' After a brief pause she added, 'And what do you think about Scotland becoming independent?' Amelia giggled and took a large swig of coffee. 'Only joking, Libs!' She knew only too well that Libby was not politically minded at all. It wasn't that she didn't care, she was simply not interested in anything to do with current affairs, and she made no attempt to hide this fact. 'Actually, I was asking you something much more important. Would you and Alex like to come for dinner on Saturday evening?'

Libby glanced at her friend. She had long thick auburn hair that curled in all the right places, and piercingly blue eyes that she often used to her advantage – she could beguile or chastise in an instant. She had a bright smile and perfect teeth; she oozed affluence. Today she wore an ankle-length yellow and cream tie-dye jersey dress that hugged her body and accentuated her rounded belly. As she talked, she gently stroked her unborn child with intimate pleasure and affection.

'I'm seven months gone so we haven't got many Saturdays left, please say you'll come, hun. And now that you've finally thrown in the towel with your wretched job, you've got all the time in the world.'

Libby reflected sadly how she had been forced to resign from her position as reception teacher at the local primary school. Her stress levels had gone through the roof with all the planning, target setting, assessments and the prospect of an inspection looming on the horizon. She had enjoyed, and was committed to, working with the children, but she had no choice but to leave for the sake of her health and well-being.

She pressed her palms together in a prayer position. 'Come on, Lib. Tom has already sorted out the menu, and I will organise the aperitif... and entertain our guests of course.'

Amelia seemed to have it all: a beautiful house, a gorgeous-looking husband, a great job in finance; all that, and she was expecting a baby. Libby thought about her own circumstances. She had been married to Alex for a year when they decided to try for a baby. That was four years ago and, after a lot of carefully timed mechanical sex, two unsuccessful IVF treatments and all the painful emotional turmoil that goes with it, they still had no baby. The reason they were given was "unexplained infertility". The medical staff really had no idea why they hadn't conceived. She wondered whether she was envious or jealous of Amelia, perhaps she was both; she wasn't sure of the difference between the two, but jealousy seemed a stronger emotion; yes, she was jealous of her friend.

'What say you, Libs?'

'It sounds great, Amelia, I'm sure we can but I will need to check with Alex before I can say for definite. Is that okay?'

'Yeah, sure, text me as soon as you can.' Amelia had become aware that Libby didn't seem as happy or carefree as she used to be. She gasped. 'Oh my goodness, Libs, feel this little sproglet kicking.' She guided Libby's hand towards one side of her swollen belly, and just as she made contact, the unborn baby catapulted her hand away with a swift kick. They giggled, but then Libby quickly turned away to conceal her aching sadness. Although the fertility clinic was efficiently run with knowledgeable and caring staff, it was very expensive, and the ongoing stress was taking its toll on their marriage. Alex was often disgruntled these days, blaming her for many things, especially their fertility issues. Over the past few months he had called her "the womanless woman", "barren" and "useless". But then he would hold her close and reassure her that he loved her, and that everything would be fine. Libby was always left feeling confused about his true feelings. She had chosen not to share the fertility problems they were facing with any of her friends, but it made some conversations with Amelia unbearably painful. She braced herself for what she knew her friend would ask next.

'Isn't it about time you and Alex had a baby? Why don't you take the plunge, Lib, then our kids can be best mates as they grow up? Just imagine the mischief they would get up to!'

'We will,' Libby muttered quietly, 'when the time is right.'

'For God's sake, Libs, if you wait until the time is right you'll wait forever – until you have a bigger house, a better job, more money, a garden with a climbing frame and a tree house, blah blah blah...' She sighed extravagantly and shook her head. 'Don't wait until your womb has shrivelled and your eggs have rotted and Alex has no more swimmers; do it while the going's good.'

Libby averted her gaze, her eyes welling up with tears. If only Amelia knew what agony they had gone through for years. How could something this natural be so easy for some and the hardest thing in the world for others? 'We will have a baby when we're good and ready. But I have to say that we have a lot going for us at the moment. Our bank account is healthy – we have more than enough money to lead a comfortable life – and the freedom to do what we want when we want. We may yet decide not to have a baby at all. Who knows?'

'Come on, Lib, I know how much you love kids. Do you expect me to believe that you don't want to have one of your own one day?' Amelia persisted.

'What is to be will be,' Libby retorted, keen to bring the conversation to a close. She played with her congealed plate of food in front of her. 'I thought I was hungry enough for this, but I've lost my appetite. How about we go for a cheeky cocktail at Cafe Calypso? The sun is just about passed over the yardarm.'

'Sounds great, although I'll have to stick to a non-alcoholic delight,' Amelia said resignedly. 'Have we got time to pop into the baby boutique just round the corner? I can never resist…'

'No, I think we'd better get a wiggle on, I've got stuff to do this afternoon,' said Libby. She was keen to avoid the inevitable baby shopping binge that would follow. Leaving the cafe, they ambled up the dimly lit passage passing by many empty closed shops 'Goodness, isn't it sad to see the covered market with so many failed businesses? It feels like a lot of the market is empty and boarded up now. It used to be thriving fish mongers, butchers, fruit stalls, an incredible delicatessen, and now it feels as if Oxford is losing one of its finest assets.'

'Do you know why this is, Libs?' Without waiting for an answer, Amelia continued, 'It's the hugely high rents, so I've heard. And then when you add the business rates on top, it's unaffordable for many small businesses. All that will be left in the end will be trinket shops, Oxford souvenirs and cafes, the high street is dying. And as for the famous Oxford Covered Market, they've killed the goose that lays the golden egg.'

'Maybe that's a bit harsh, Amelia, these small businesses may yet recover…'

'Yeah, I hope you're right, hun, but I sometimes think the *powers that be* don't live in the real world. They're even plonking flowerpots in the middle of roads in parts of Oxford to thwart local traffic, how do the emergency services—'

Their conversation was interrupted as they dodged past the bustling throng of Chinese tourists taking photos of an impressive selection of cheeses temptingly displayed in the French cheese shop near the entrance of the market, before heading towards Cornmarket Street. As they turned down the tiny passage that led towards Cafe Calypso, they paused to listen to the sound of a homeless man singing haunting words of despair; strumming gently on his old, battered guitar, a cap with a few coins placed in front of him, ever hopeful of a few pennies to see him through another day. One or two passers-by had stopped to listen. If he had been born into another world, he might have been famous; he might have been rich; but the reality was that his life was a struggle, every day, a struggle. Libby, mesmerised by the musician, began to think about her own life. She used to be happy; to be curious; to be excited about the future. When she was a child she was often commended for her natural curiosity, asking endless questions to satisfy her thirst for knowledge. But now things had changed. She had started to question her own existence: what if she had decided to have an early night instead of going out to the pub with her friends that fateful night, when she first met Alex. What if? Her life would have gone in a totally different direction.

'Come on, Libs, you're such a dreamer!' Amelia laughed, propelling her friend towards the eye-catching blue and yellow frontage of Cafe Calypso. 'Right, my shout; what do you fancy?'

They sat down at the bar and poured over the extensive cocktail menu: there were almost too many choices, but in the end Libby chose a *Sex on the Beach*. She loved the subtle flavours of peach, orange and cranberry mixed with vodka, a seductive combination. 'I've always enjoyed sex on the beach,' she said wryly.

'Okay, if you're having a *Sex on the Beach*, I'm going for a *Safe Sex on the Beach*.' She laughed. 'The mocktail has everything except the main ingredient, vodka!' Amelia winked extravagantly. 'Sensible, but not nearly as much fun!'

Libby watched as the dark-haired barman expertly shook each cocktail, his impressive, bronzed biceps bulging as he skilfully blended the precious ingredients; his slim hips gyrating as he poured the thick frothy liquid into the glass before finally adding the perfect finishing touch with a flourish – a large twist of lemon and a Morello cherry. 'Wow! Did you watch the guy behind the bar mixing our cocktails? Combining his sexy moves – seductively, gorgeously – with his obvious skills and knowledge. Now that's what I call a pure art form!'

'And that is what I call pure eye candy!' Amelia exclaimed. 'He is drop-dead gorgeous isn't he?'

As Libby sucked the delicious liquid through a straw, she glanced around the crowded cafe, now a lively hubbub of conversation with the cheerful sound of Calypso guitar playing in the background. 'I wish we were lying on a deserted beach somewhere in the Caribbean, soaking up the sun, feeling the sand between our toes and listening to the gentle waves as they lap against the shoreline,' Libby said wistfully.

Amelia looked at her friend with concern. 'What is it, Libs? You haven't been yourself for a while now. Why don't you tell me what's going on?'

Libby wondered whether it was because she hadn't had a lot to eat, but she was rapidly beginning to feel tipsy. She found that when she drank alcohol, it would often accentuate the mood she was already in: if she was happy, a drink would make her feel happier; if she was sad or depressed – as she was today – alcohol would make her worse. And the vodka had gone straight to her head. She gazed into the distance, her chin shaking with emotion.

'Is this about Alex, Libs?' Amelia asked quietly. 'Are you two going through another rough patch?'

'No,' Libby stammered, dismissing her friend's suggestion, almost too quickly. 'Alex does his best…' She bit her lip. 'He sometimes gets frustrated with his work… and with me.' She looked up and a single tear ran down her cheek. 'But he is really sweet, he loves me, and that's all that matters.'

Amelia sat quietly, absorbing what Libby had just said. She remembered the last time her friend had gone through a rough patch with Alex; she never knew what actually happened, but it had almost broken Libby. Over the last couple of years, things seemed to be looking up. It was hard to know how to support her friend because Libby was always guarded about her troubles, and Amelia knew that, without second guessing, it was impossible to know what happened behind closed doors.

'But love isn't always enough; you need friendship and respect for each other.' She reached over the bar to hold Libby's hand. 'Are you two okay?'

Libby roughly wiped her cheek with the back of her hand. 'Come on, let's enjoy our cocktail,' she urged. 'We are devoted to each other; I know we'll get through this. We did before, and we will again.'

Amelia suddenly turned her head. 'God, Libs, I think I just saw Alex with his arm around a rather elegant woman with long blonde hair; they just left through the side door. It couldn't have been him could it?'

Libby watched as the door closed. 'No it couldn't have been Alex, he's in London today.'

'I'm sure it was him, Libs. I'd recognise his curly brown hair anywhere.'

Libby put her hand to her mouth. 'No, it can't be…'

Twelve

'Why didn't you ask me first, Libs? You know I don't like Tom and Amelia; they think they're so bloody posh.' Alex stooped in the middle of the spacious bedroom peering at himself in the mirror. His body, once muscular and toned, was now showing signs of middle age – frequent nights out drinking with his mates was taking its toll – his previously flat tummy now protruded over the strained elastic of his boxer shorts. Fine wrinkles were beginning to appear under his eyes, but Libby reflected, he still had the roguish good looks that had caught her eye when they first met.

'I just thought we might enjoy an evening out,' Libby said forlornly. 'We haven't been anywhere for months.'

'I've got pressing things I need to do for work, Libs,' he argued. 'I haven't got the time to drop everything and go out for dinner. When did you arrange this anyway?'

'Amelia and I were having a pre-lunch cocktail on Wednesday at Cafe Calypso...' She paused. 'Actually, Amelia thought she saw you leaving the cafe with a woman. Were you there, Alex? You told me you were in...'

Alex turned and smiled, almost too brightly. 'Darling, it was just a work meeting.'

'Yes, but I thought you were…' Libby stammered.

'You know how plans change so quickly in the office. I was supposed to be in London on Wednesday, but instead I had to meet a client. It was an emergency.' He suddenly turned to face Libby. 'You do believe me, don't you, darling?' he asked, holding her hands tightly in his.

'Yes, of course I do,' Libby said, although doubts were creeping in as to whether he was being totally honest with her. Why had he not mentioned this before?

As they parked the car in the long tree-lined avenue that led to Amelia and Tom's house, Libby dreaded the evening ahead. Her friend greeted her with a warm hug; the bump of Amelia's unborn child fitting neatly into Libby's concave stomach like intricate pieces of a jigsaw; the juxtaposition of new life and hope with emptiness and hopelessness.

The initial awkwardness between the two couples evaporated as the wine flowed freely, lubricating the increasingly animated conversation. The smoked salmon and prawn starter, followed by a generous helping of beef Wellington slipped down easily, and Libby began to feel her tension drain away, almost as quickly as her wine glass. Perhaps the evening would be a success after all. Libby glanced across at Alex and Amelia who were now deeply engrossed in conversation, their faces almost touching. She couldn't help but wonder what they were talking about, but she had the horrible feeling that it was about her; they kept looking in her direction and whispering conspiratorially.

'Surely you're not as bad as Alex suggests, Libs?'

Libby could feel beads of perspiration appear above her top lip. She shrugged her shoulders. 'About what?' she asked warily.

'Alex says that he has confiscated your car keys because you're a nightmare behind the wheel,' Amelia said.

Alex threw his head back and laughed. 'She can't even get the car out of our driveway without some sort of drama! The other day she even backed into the wall at the front of our house; it's not as if walls move is it? It's been there for bloody years.' He turned to Libby. 'I just want you to be safe, darling,' he added with a smile.

'Well, I suppose it is a big deal to damage your shiny Maserati,' Amelia conceded, glancing across at Libby who now looked embarrassed and rather crestfallen. 'Maybe you just had a bad day, Libs?' she added sympathetically.

'I wonder if I could have a drop more wine?' Libby asked, keen to divert attention from the embarrassing exchange. She added quietly, almost inaudibly, 'I used to be a very good driver, but now…' She shook her head sadly, her words fading away as her glass was replenished. She took a large sip of wine and her mind started to race. Alex had taken the car keys from her handbag two weeks before, and, by doing so, he had made her more dependent on him. He had more control over where she went and with whom, she was beginning to feel trapped. But was he right? Perhaps she was a danger to herself and to others on the road.

'God, Libs, if I so much as threatened to take Amelia's car keys away from her, she would eat me alive,' Tom said, 'She's always gallivanting about in her beloved Mini

Cooper, going heaven alone knows where. I don't mind, as long as she comes back in a good mood, and perhaps a treat for supper.' He took a deep breath, waiting for Amelia to complain – she usually objected to his rather sexist comments – but she remained quiet, so he continued. 'But these days, she's usually bought something expensive and totally unnecessary for the sproglet.' He paused, raising his eyes to heaven. 'The other day she came home with a cradle that we are supposed to attach to our bed. Can you imagine having a snuffly, screaming baby in your bedroom, every single night? Crazy if you ask me!'

'You've got a lot to learn about being a parent, Tom,' Amelia said firmly. 'And by the way, you're right, I would be furious if you stopped me from driving. Libby, if you ever need a lift anywhere, you know where I am. It may be more difficult after the baby is born, but do ask, I always will if I can.' She turned to face Alex. 'And, for the record, I don't think you should have the right to take Libby's car keys without her permission.'

A heavy and uncomfortable silence descended around the table. Amelia swilled her wine, self-consciously studying the arch windows left on the deep sides of her glass. 'Yep, this is a good vintage, it shouldn't give us too much of a hangover tomorrow. It must have cost you an arm and a leg, Libs?'

'I don't know,' Libby said quietly, 'Alex chose it from his wine collection in the cellar. I don't really know much about wine, except that I usually enjoy it.'

Alex shot her a frosty stare. 'Good wine is wasted on you, Libs, I might as well buy cheap plonk from the

Co-op.' His voice softened. 'I prefer the Bordeaux wines myself, rather than the New-World wines – New Zealand, Australian or Californian. Bordeaux wines are medium to full-bodied, with aromas of black current and plums with earthy notes of wet soil or pencil lead. The final taste is prickly, savoury with mouth-drying tannins...'

'Alex you sound like you've lifted that straight out of a posh guide to fine wines!' Amelia said, lifting her glass to her nose. 'I'm blowed if I can smell black currants, and thank God I can't taste, or smell, wet soil or pencil lead! Who makes up this stuff anyway?'

'You heathen,' Alex said with a forced smile. 'I have tasted many fine wines in my time, some costing up to £800 a bottle. A Châteaux Lafite Rothschild can cost thousands. These vintage wines are lovingly grown on the vine – it's all to do with the terroir – and aged in oak barrels. They are rare, exquisite and truly delicious.'

'The trouble is that if I was offered a glass of wine from a bottle as expensive as that, I think I'd find it hard to swallow!' Amelia laughed. 'I might well be a heathen, but a £6 bottle is fine by me, don't you agree, Libs? I don't need, or want, hints of wet soil or pencil lead. To be honest, I'd rather have a wine box, you get more in it! But the trouble is, drinking too much alcohol is a bad idea, especially when you're pregnant.'

Alex sighed heavily. 'I'm wasting my breath on you, Amelia, please can you top up my glass, but only a third full, otherwise I can't appreciate the bouquet.'

Amelia sloshed the wine carelessly into his glass, muttering under her breath. 'What a bloody wine snob!'

She paused, looking round the table with a tight smile. 'Anyone for pavlova?'

The desert arrived, huge, creamy and generously covered with "fruits of the forest" berries; deliciously mouth-watering for those with a sweet tooth, but Libby didn't want any more food. 'Amelia, please could I have a small portion? I'm rather full from the delicious beef Wellington.'

'Libby watches her weight; she works hard to keep her figure,' Alex commented.

'Of course, Libs, said Amelia, cutting a small slice. 'I'm rather full too but, surprisingly, I always find I have a little room left for something sweet!' She laughed. 'Although with this bump in the way, it will be a bit of a struggle!'

Libby glanced across at her friend. She was envious of Amelia and Tom, they were always open and honest with each other; they bickered, but they also laughed together. Occasionally Alex couldn't resist putting her down in public, like this evening, undermining her for her perceived ineptitude behind the wheel of a car. Sometimes he just couldn't help himself. But normally he kept his grumpiness hidden behind a friendly facade. It was a different story in the privacy of their own home.

'Alex, I visited James Fox on Brompton Road the other day – he really does have the best collection of cigars in the whole of London – and I selected some Monti Christos, amongst others. Shall we retire to the patio for a whisky and a smoke and leave these good ladies in peace?'

'Perhaps Libs would like a cigar as well, Tom? It's not only men that enjoy a good cigar I'll have you know,'

Amelia suggested, turning to Libby. 'It's so outdated for the men to "retire to the drawing room" isn't it? Well, Libs? Do you fancy one?'

Libby declined and the two friends were left alone around the table.

'Libs, are you all right? You seem really sad,' Amelia said, moving her chair closer.

'I'm okay, as I told you before, we are going through a bit of a bumpy patch. We've been here before and I know that we will get through this. We love each other and that's all that matters.'

'But, Libs, I've heard you say this before. Love means nothing if there is no friendship, or empathy. Love is just an empty promise, it means nothing.'

'Amelia, you don't understand. I am devoted to him. I want my marriage to work.'

'You're right, Libs, I don't understand, but it doesn't stop me from being worried about you. This isn't the first time I've heard Alex put you down in this way. Men have an awful lot to answer for… God, now I'm being sexist,' she said, covering her mouth with her hand in mock horror.

'Alex has been under a lot of pressure at work recently, working long hours and dealing with difficult staff.'

'You mean like the attractive woman he left the cafe with last Wednesday?' Amelia asked quietly.

'He told me that it was a work meeting, and I believe him,' Libby answered firmly. 'He has a lot on his plate at the moment, and I must be there to support him.'

Amelia looked at her friend; once bubbly and outgoing, now introverted; once feisty and refreshingly rebellious, now a shrinking violet. 'But, Libs, do remember that you have needs too.'

Libby's shoulders began to shake uncontrollably as tears flowed freely down her cheeks, leaving black smudges of mascara in their wake. 'Oh dear, I think I've had too much wine…'

'Libs, you are beautiful, intelligent and funny – yes, inclined to be a bit batty at times,' Amelia said, putting her arm affectionately around Libby's shoulders. 'But you are unique.'

Thirteen

The cream-and-black-trimmed Mini Cooper sped ably through narrow South Oxfordshire lanes, finally turning into the long drive of Blackmore Rest Home – a residence for gentlefolk – a residence for families with shedloads of money. The formidable "home" appeared in the distance; an impressive turreted stone-built structure, striking against the steely grey sky. It was a residence not unlike a French château: full of history, full of antique furniture, full of the elderly.

Amelia parked the car in the last available space in the modest car park between a shiny red Range Rover, parked carelessly across two marked bays, and an egg-yolk-coloured Lamborghini. 'The car park is very full today, I think they must have a managers meeting,' Amelia said with a wry smile. 'Anyway, Libs, this place is surrounded by glorious vineyards, I'm going to explore the possibility of buying some English sparkling wine. I'll see you later. Shall I collect you in a couple of hours? About six o'clock?'

'That would be great,' said Libs reluctantly. She dreaded her regular visits to see Alex's elderly mother. Alex always found excuses not to go to see "the old bat". Since his mother had begun to exhibit the symptoms of senile dementia, he believed any visits were a waste of time; his mother would not remember him or his visit, he would spare himself the inconvenience.

As she approached the pillared entrance, generously surrounded by climbing roses and jasmine, she breathed in a mixture of sweet jasmine, congealed beef stew, disinfectant and urine. She glanced to the left of the high-ceilinged entrance hall to a shelf dedicated to residents who had recently passed away, with kind messages from the families expressing their gratitude to the staff at Blackmore, and surrounded by colourful – some may say tasteless – arrangements of plastic flowers. Behind the shelf was a seating area with a coffee machine and a collection of daily newspapers. Libby had never seen anyone sitting enjoying a coffee in this area, but it did look inviting. She idly flicked through the visitors book to see who had last visited Florence – or Flo as she was usually called – noting that none of Alex's family had visited for months. Flo, through no fault of her own, had been the cause of Alex and his two brothers becoming estranged from one another. It all began when they took on the joint role of powers of attorney, working on behalf of their mother. She reflected sadly how the family, and distant relatives, had initially circled around Flo like vultures, before they realised that Blackmore would probably eat up most of their inheritance, the will was already set in stone, and that no amount of visits, or reminders of how poor they were, would make any difference. She feared that Alex had plans to use his knowledge and expertise to his advantage regarding the will and inheritance, but he had not shared any plans with her. She hoped she was wrong.

Flo had effectively been placed in Blackmore Rest Home – a beautiful place, an ivory tower, and been forgotten.

'Hello, can I help you?' asked Doreen, a member of staff, looking dubiously at Libby leafing through the visitors' book. 'Are you looking for something?'

'No thanks, I'm just here to see Flo. How is she doing?'

'Ah, I'm not sure, I'll just ask in the staffroom,' she said, turning away.

After a few minutes, waiting for Doreen to return, Libby decided to make her way to Flo's room in the east wing of the property. She wearily climbed the stairs, luxuriously covered in a thick pile green carpet, decorated with pink rose buds, that led to room number thirty-one. The carpet smelt brand new, and Libby couldn't help but wonder why they had replaced what seemed like a perfectly presentable carpet with another; where did the money come from? What about the world's resources?

She knocked on the door and shyly walked in. The room was empty, the bed left unmade, and magazines were strewn on the floor in disarray. Libby feared that something might be wrong. Flo always sat in her chair, hardly ever leaving the room except at lunchtime. She jumped as a male member of staff popped his head round the door. 'It's your lucky day,' he said brightly, 'it's pre-dinner cocktail hour. All the residents are in the Morning Room, and, if you get down there pretty swiftly, you'll be offered a drink too!'

Libby sighed. 'Okay, thank you.' As she entered the Morning Room all the elderly folk were clutching one of a variety of cocktails: vibrant blue concoctions, glasses containing more greenery than liquid, cherry-topped frothy drinks; all hunched in Edwardian uncomfortable but extremely elegant chairs. Flo was sitting in the bay window, apart from the others, staring desolately into her chosen cocktail. The room was silent apart from a well-meaning member of staff rushing around rather aimlessly, reminding them what fun they were having. 'We could almost be in Barbados, couldn't we, my ducks? Isn't this wonderful?'

Flo raised her eyes to heaven. 'What is she on?' she muttered. As Libby walked towards her, she saw the tiny hint of a smile. 'At last, someone has had the decency to visit me.'

Libby drew up a chair and sat beside her. 'How are you, Flo?'

'How the hell do you think I am? Bloody awful.' Suddenly something caught her eye and she looked horrified. Staring at the care worker, she screeched in a piercing voice, 'Just look at that fat bottom! That didn't just happen did it? How did she get that fat?'

Libby's eyes darted apologetically from the conscientious care worker to Flo, who was now pointing directly at the accused member of staff.

'Have you noticed the trees outside? The leaves are just turning red and brown, such beautiful colours,' said Libby.

'You're not listening to me, why is everyone so fat in here?'

Libby had noticed that Flo had put on a few pounds during her time here, and wondered, rather cynically, if it was a deliberate strategy to overindulge the residents, in the hope that they would live longer, resulting in increased funds going in to the, already healthy, Blackmore bank account.

'Well, I think cocktail hour is a great idea,' said one of the more lively residents. Her dark eyes twinkled with pleasure. 'I'd like another *Blue Lagoon*, please.' She rallied the other residents as she beckoned to the care worker, swinging her empty glass high above her head. 'Come on, you lot, live a little, that's what I say! We're a long time dead!'

Libby smiled; it was good to hear one of the residents with a spirit of adventure. She had often thought that the elderly clientele should rise up, have a revolution and dig their escape through the solid walls of Blackmore – like the valiant soldiers dug tunnels during the first and second world wars – to escape. But, as she reflected, even if they were successful, there was nowhere to go; the home was in the middle of the countryside, miles from anywhere.

But perhaps she was being rather unfair. As she scanned the room, some of the residents looked calm, almost content, as they stared into the depths of their cocktails. The staff were generally well meaning, needs were met – on the surface anyway – perhaps it wasn't too bad. For some anyway.

'Where's my son? Where is my Alex?' Flo asked angrily, her words cutting through the air like a knife. 'Why doesn't he visit me? Why does he always send you?' Her face creased; her lips pursed tightly. 'I'm not interested in seeing you, how he ever ended up with the likes of you beggars belief. He is worth so much more…' She took a sharp intake of breath. 'He's clever and wise, my Alex. You…' She spat out the words with venom. 'You are worth nothing.'

Flo had never believed Libby to be good enough for her son, but, as she had got older, her dementia taking hold, she had become increasingly vocal about her utter disdain of her daughter-in-law. Her words were bitter and cruel.

'Tell me about Alex when he was a boy, Flo.' She tried to brush aside the familiar script; the hurtful words that Flo regularly directed at her.

Flo's face softened as she started to recount memories from many years ago. 'Alex was my firstborn, he was bright, articulate and fiercely driven. He wanted to learn, he needed to know everything. He was exhausting, always asking endless questions: Who? Why? How? It was enough to drive me mad, I can tell you.' She smiled. 'His teachers were often out of their depth, Alex seemed to know a lot more about Latin, ancient history and the English language than they did. He flew through his school years, passing every academic exam he ever took with flying colours. He strived for perfection, one hundred per cent perfection, anything less than perfect was simply not good enough.'

'Was he a happy child, Flo?'

'Alex has always been ambitious and focused. He didn't need friends; he didn't need anyone. He was self-reliant and self-contained. He couldn't relate to anyone he considered less able than himself, he preferred his own company. But was he happy? Does it matter? He has made a success out of his life; he is a partner in a well-respected firm of solicitors… Although I have to say that I'm disappointed he didn't aim higher; he could have been a barrister. Now that would have been a huge achievement.' She stared vacantly into space.

'I'm proud of him, he won a scholarship to the University of Oxford, and graduated with a high second-class degree. That is a real achievement,' Libby said. She was beginning to feel annoyed that Alex's mother, although recognising some of his academic success, seemed ultimately disappointed.

'But he should have got a first,' Flo hissed, 'but his head was turned, stupid boy.'

'What do you mean?'

'Heaven alone knows what happened during his three years in Oxford, studying law. He once told me that during the years he spent attending his prestigious private school, most of the boys focussed on the three R's – rugby, rowing and rogering…' She paused, looking slightly puzzled. 'I thought that the three R's meant something entirely different, but never mind. Alex resisted all three R's at school, preferring to focus all his efforts on studying. By the time he got to Oxford, things were different; he still wasn't tempted by rugby or rowing – he was hopeless at sport – but he was certainly interested in the final R. Rumour has it that he was a leading light in one of the most prestigious libertine clubs.' Her eyes widened. 'My Alex, a libertine, fancy that!'

Libby listened intently, always impressed and a little

surprised that Flo could remember minute detail from many years before, and yet she often couldn't remember what happened yesterday or the day before. A care worker had once explained to her that dementia can be likened to an overflowing glass of water. The water that splashes over the side of the glass represents the short-term memory, it overflows and is forgotten, but the water at the bottom of the glass remains constant; the long-term memory. Libby found the analogy helpful, giving her some understanding of the way Flo's mind worked. But was Alex really a libertine?

'And Alex had a fiery temper, especially if he couldn't do something. When he was a baby he screamed because he wanted to crawl. When he was a toddler he had almighty tantrums because he wanted to talk. As he got older, he realised that he was not good at art, in fact he was terrible, but he insisted on trying, but it always ended in disaster. He used to vent his frustration by hurling his paints against the wall. He simply could not accept failure. But…' Flo hunched her shoulders, the pain of the years etched on her face. 'He had to be in control. In the end, he took control of me and his father. He got his way. Ted and I constantly argued about how to discipline him, and in the end, Ted left us.' She flinched. 'Was I such a bad mother? I tried everything…' Suddenly she looked guiltily at Libby and bit her lip. 'Alex thought he knew best, and no one else's opinion mattered to him. But he is my son, my firstborn, and nobody is perfect.'

Libby leant over and held Flo's hand. 'Why have you never told me this before?'

'Because it hurts to remember…' she said, holding her head in her hands.

'Tell me about your other sons, Flo – Matt and Andrew,' Libby said compassionately. She changed the subject to spare her more pain.

'They weren't clever like my Alex. Matt, my youngest, has always been more interested in art and music than any sensible subjects. He even likes to dance; a son of mine, a man, who likes dancing. All he wanted to do as a child was bang on his stupid drum and prance around like an idiot.' She put her head in her hands and sighed. 'There is officially no hope…'

'But it sounds like Matt was incredibly creative and fun-loving, how wonderful. And don't forget that some of the best dancers are male. What does he do now?' Libby knew the answer, but she was keen to see whether Flo remembered, or recognised any of Matt's considerable achievements.

'I think he plays guitar and is the lead singer in a pop group,' she said dismissively. 'He could have done so much better. Why did we waste all that money on private education?'

'I believe Matt is making a huge name for himself in the music world and is currently on tour in America. This week he is performing in Philadelphia, and I'm told that ticket sales are going through the roof! You should be very proud of Matt.'

'I suppose so,' acknowledged Flo, 'but he'll never make any money.'

Libby had so much more that she wanted to say about

the power of the arts, and how successful her youngest son is, as a solo singer, a multi-instrumentalist and a founder member of one of the most popular up-and-coming bands of the decade. She would return to this subject with Flo another day, but it was almost time for Amelia to pick her up.

'And what about Andrew?'

Flo turned away. 'I have absolutely no idea.'

Fourteen

Libertine:

A person, especially a man, who freely indulges in sensual pleasures without regard to moral principles.

Someone who forms their own opinions and beliefs about religion. A freethinker.

Libby clutched her phone, reading and digesting the definition of a libertine. Could Alex have been an unbridled libertine at university? Is he still a libertine?

'Wow, Libs, perhaps Alex made up his own rules when it came to sex at Oxford. Perhaps he slept with hundreds of women, and men, perhaps he had a whole lot of fun...' Amelia exclaimed, as they pulled away from Blackmore and headed back towards Oxford.

Libby looked sideways at her friend. 'I despair of you sometimes...' Amelia was a good friend, but they often had completely opposing views over many things in life. She was always refreshingly open and honest and, as close friends, they could generally agree to disagree, without adversely affecting their friendship. Libby had noticed recently that, in society, people had become more judgemental and divided than ever before about many issues; often politically driven; often quick to adopt, what she saw, as the biased view of the mainstream media. The art of healthy debate had been lost in favour of fixed unerring judgements with a lack of compassion, understanding, or respect for an alternative viewpoint. She must listen to Amelia; she might change her view. She might learn.

'The trouble is, Flo has dementia; it's hard to know what to believe. How do I separate fact from fiction?'

'Libs, never let the truth get in the way of a good story!' Amelia laughed. 'But, if it is true that Alex was a libertine when he was a student, then perhaps we should say, all power to him! Life is short, if he had some amazing sexual encounters and experiences, then who are we to judge?'

'So you don't think that it is immoral to sleep around, Amelia?'

'By suggesting that being a libertine is simply about, "sleeping around" you are immediately imposing your own moral judgement, Libs. Perhaps we don't know enough about the philosophy to judge.'

'You might be right, Amelia, although I'm not convinced.'

'If all sexual encounters are consensual – agreed by everyone involved – and you practise safe sex, then one could argue, what is the harm in that? I'm being Devil's advocate, Libs, but I can really understand arguments in favour of being a hedonist, seeking out pleasure in life, in the unsettled society we live in. Shouldn't we seek out what brings us joy? I don't think we should automatically dismiss it as something wicked or immoral. After all, is it more honourable to be a libertine, than a partner in a marriage having an illicit affair?'

Libby was brought back to reality with a jolt. Was Alex with a woman, a lover, in Cafe Calypso? Was Alex involved with another woman? Was he having a secret affair? He had been less than convincing when she had questioned him about his movements that day.

But this was not Libby's main concern. The words that Flo had said coursed round and round in her head:

He had to be in control. In the end, he took control of me and his father. He got his way.

Libby started to go cold as she thought about her own marriage: Alex had recently taken her car keys, effectively preventing her from driving the car. "I'm only thinking of you, and your safety, Libs." Only last week he had removed her name from their joint bank account, telling her that he could no longer trust her to make sound financial decisions. "Don't worry, darling, I will make sure that you have everything you need; and I will invest my money wisely." *My* money wisely… And she had meekly agreed, believing that Alex knew best.

Was I such a bad mother? I tried everything…

Libby shuddered. Is history repeating itself? Is Alex intimidating? Is Alex a bully?

But he is my son, my first born, and nobody is perfect.

Libby sighed with relief. Of course Flo was right. *Alex is my husband and I love him. And nobody is perfect.*

But the words that she couldn't erase from her mind, was Flo's answer when she questioned her as to why she had never told her about this significant part of her life before; about the control and the break-up of her marriage: *Because it hurts to remember...*

Storm clouds were gathering, the light was fading fast as the car drew up outside her house. Libby glanced at her watch, it was nearly eight o'clock, and she was surprised to find the house shrouded in darkness. As she unlocked the front door, she wondered why Alex wasn't home; he hadn't said he was going to be late. Without hesitating, she threw her raincoat on the kitchen sideboard, selected a large wine glass from the cupboard, grabbed a chilled bottle of Sauvignon Blanc from the door of the fridge-freezer and poured herself a generous slug of wine. Although it was the height of summer there was a distinct chill in the air, and the sitting room felt uncomfortably cold. She put her wine on the coffee table and sat down heavily on the leather settee, drawing up her legs towards her chest. Dusty – a liver and white springer spaniel – who had waited eagerly for her to arrive home, bounded up cheerfully and drew his rough tongue over her face affectionately, leaving behind a thin trail of saliva. 'Oh, you soppy old thing... At least somebody loves me,' she said, wiping her cheeks and gently pushing him away. All at once, Dusty sprawled heavily across her knee, his sides rising and falling, as he buried his nose deep into her crotch. Libby absentmindedly stroked one of his sleek velvety ears, her mind full of questions. Is Alex lying? Is he having an affair? Is he with her now? Who is she?

A deep shiver ran through her body as she scanned the room. The sitting room was immaculately tidy with a matching cream three-piece leather suite; a walnut coffee table strewn with a selection of newspapers, including *The Guardian*, *The Telegraph* and *The Times* – Alex liked to read papers that reflected a range of political perspectives. A book, *The Anatomy of a Scandal*, lay to one side, a fringed University of Oxford bookmark positioned between two pages towards the end of the book. She turned her attention to the artwork displayed around the room. The common feature of all the prints displayed was the portrayal of nudity, usually of a nude woman. Alex particularly admired the work of Botticelli and was impressed by how this great artist could capture the very essence of beauty, sensuality, erotism and the forbidden in a single painting. A framed reproduction of *The Birth of Venus* – his favourite piece – hung in pride of place, on the chimney stack above the wood burner. The painting represented Venus: a curvy female nude, her genitalia hidden by her long hair and a hand carefully positioned to hide one breast; a study of the hidden and the exposed; sensual, erotic, tantalising. The other pieces of artwork displayed included a portrait of Adam and Eve, and a Picasso drawing of nude female – eloquent in its simplicity; formed with just a few strokes of the lead. As she studied the artwork displayed around the room, she noticed that something was missing – a framed David Hockney print that she had bought – and it had been replaced with an extraordinary painting of a mass of naked bodies intertwined, interconnected. She wasn't sure who the artist was, but she knew she disliked the painting. A few weeks ago she had found framed photos of her dear departed parents, once displayed proudly on the windowsill, now stored in a cardboard box under the bed. A few months earlier, unbeknown to her, Alex had sold the grandfather clock that Libby had inherited from a great aunt; a piece of furniture that she had looked after lovingly for many years, and had sentimental, and probably monetary, value.

She sat in the semi darkness, tears streaming down her cheeks. She realised with horror that Alex had removed any trace of her, or her life, from the sitting room, in fact from every room in the house. Alex had control. She shuddered.

She glanced at her watch; it was ten thirty. Where was Alex? Dusty grunted, scratching his ear with one of his hind legs vigorously, and then stretched out languorously on his back. Libby smiled sadly. 'You haven't got a care in the world have you, Dusty?' she said as she tickled the soft down of his underbelly. Carefully sliding herself out from under him, she drained the rest of her wine and carefully placed the glass between the pile of newspapers and the book on the coffee table. Anxious now, she drew back one of the curtains in the bay window and peered out into the darkness. The dim streetlight by the front gate illuminated a group of youths laughing and joking, all clutching beer cans, obviously inebriated after a night out. But there was no sign of Alex. Perhaps he had been in an accident? Perhaps he was with his lover? She checked her phone again: no message. She rang his number twice, but it went straight to answerphone. Deciding not to leave a message – he would probably think she was harassing him if she did – she decided that there was nothing she could do. She closed the curtains, turned on the porch light for Alex and let Dusty out for his late-night outing in the back garden.

She pulled back the sheet and wearily climbed into bed. Turning off the lamp, she closed her eyes, her whole body alert, listening and waiting for Alex to return. The sound of the key turning in the lock disturbed the silence of dawn. Alex cursed loudly as he tripped on one of the stairs, before going to the bathroom to relieve himself of an extraordinarily long stream of urine, and then stumbling into bed. As he turned towards her; she breathed in the stench of his alcohol and garlic-fuelled breath. He threw one arm aggressively across her chest, pinning her to the bed. 'Where did you go?' he asked angrily. 'I waited for hours, but when you didn't turn up, what else could I do?' With that, he roughly pushed her away. 'It's all your fault.' He turned to her, his face contorted in anger. 'I'm sleeping in the spare room.'

As Libby drew her hand over the crumpled sheet where he had lain, her heart beat fast in her chest; she thought she could detect the merest hint of floral perfume subtly combined with her husband's sweat.

Fifteen

'You'd better start packing, Libs, we're going to Paris on Friday for a long weekend.'

Libby stared at Alex in disbelief. 'You're not being serious? We can't just drop everything and go. What about Dusty?'

'Darling, I thought you'd jump at the chance. Where is your spirit of adventure? Don't you want to go to the most romantic city in the world?' Alex asked. 'Most women would give their eye teeth to be whisked off to gay Paris by the love of their life.'

Libby stared forlornly out of the window. It had been pouring with rain for days, and the thought of escaping the bleak weather, her dark thoughts and doing something totally different should have been appealing, but she didn't seem to be able to summon up the energy or enthusiasm to do much at all these days.

A week had passed since Alex mysteriously disappeared for the evening, arriving home at dawn. There had been no explanation, no discussion whatsoever. Questions spun round and round in Libby's head. Was it all her fault? What had she done? Or not done? If she had returned earlier from seeing his mother, perhaps he wouldn't have gone out? But she believed that the problems were more deeply embedded than this. If she paid him more attention – pandering to his every whim – would he love her more? If she was more alluring – more attractive, more exciting in bed – would he need a lover? Self-doubt was creeping in, slowly, insidiously. Were the ever-widening flaws in their marriage her fault?

'Darling, an old friend of mine, Roland, and his wife, Eloise, have invited us to go to Paris with them to visit one of the most prestigious nightclubs in Europe.' He paused. 'I forget the name of the club, but it sounds incredible: al fresco, fine dining, more champagne than you could ever drink, a magnificent French burlesque show, dancing the night away... Roly's description of the nightclub was eloquent, breathtaking.'

'It does sound interesting, Alex,' said Libby flatly.

'*Interesting*? Is that really all you have to say?' he said, throwing his arms up in despair. 'It's one of life's experiences we should grab with both hands.'

'If you say so, Alex...'

'I'll give you some money to go shopping, Libs. You will definitely need some sexy lingerie for the club, and a smart dress or two. We are leaving on Friday, early morning, so you have a few days to sort out your wardrobe.'

'What is the dress code for men?'

'I have to wear a pair of chinos, a smart shirt and a pair of loafers.'

'So, men only have to wear smart clothes that they could go to work in, not even a tie, but women have to dress like sex goddesses?'

'Yeah, I suppose so… but women enjoy dressing up and feeling sexy don't they? You could give it a go couldn't you, Libs? I know it will be a struggle for you but…'

Libby was used to Alex's put-downs, but they always hurt. She certainly didn't feel sexy or alluring; she felt downtrodden and useless. 'Okay, I'll go into town tomorrow and see what I can find.'

'A little boutique on the high street called MeMe's has a fabulous range of lingerie.' He averted his eyes. 'Or so I'm told…'

***

The three women strolled up the high street towards MeMe's.

'Libs, I just couldn't resist coming to help you choose some silky lingerie. I might be tempted to buy some myself, I'm sure Rick would love it if I did!'

'Oh come on, Ali, you don't wear sexy underwear just for Rick do you? After all, if you want to tempt a man into bed, wouldn't he whip it off in a flash anyway? What a waste of money!'

'I have to admit that all my pants and bras are comfortable, rather grey from too many coloured washes, and as for the elastic, but does it really matter? Nobody sees my knickers away, apart from Rick of course,' Ali said with a grin.

Rachel pursed her lips. 'Well, I wear silky underwear for me, and only me, because it makes me feel confident and sexy. I always wear exotic lingerie – underneath a dynamic outfit, of course – when I'm delivering presentations. My slinky underwear is my intimate secret, it makes me feel all-powerful, and,' she crowed, 'my presentations are usually bloody brilliant!'

Libs reflected how different her two friends were. Ali – a talented fiddle player in a local folk and blues band – was expressive and creative; inspirational; and refreshingly understated. She wore jeans and an old baggy jumper most of the time, and her hair was usually seriously in need of a tidy-up. Her appearance was well down her priority list. Rachel, by contrast, was a fiercely driven freelance consultant, advising businesses on leadership and management, and delivering enterprising, well-produced training packages. Always immaculately dressed, preferring bright colours and figure-hugging outfits, and highly made up, Libby often wondered how Rachel ever managed to walk in her high heels. Rachel was single but she always had a string of lovers – to satisfy her needs, and to make her feel good. On the face of it, they all had very little in common, but they were the best of friends.

The boutique was small but attractively laid out with a tempting selection of silky lingerie, uncomfortable-looking whalebone basques, stockings and suspenders, and an extraordinary selection of sex toys for adult play. And the boutique was extremely purple: MeMe's looked like a high-class brothel. Libby's eyes widened. 'I've seen enough, I'm off.'

'Come on, Libs,' Ali cajoled, 'now that we're here we might as well have a browse.'

'Can I help you?' asked an assistant, her face caked in many layers of beige makeup. 'We have all sizes, and everything is "three for two" today!' Her face broke into a wide smile, showing a set of perfectly white veneers that seemed too large for her small features, although her top lip was suspiciously plump.

Libby muttered her thanks and turned away to study the array of lacy, frilly and flouncy underwear on display. She could not imagine herself wearing what she considered to be ridiculous garb, although when she drew her hand over a pair of shiny French knickers, she was pleasantly surprised to find how soft and silky they felt.

'Here you are, Libs,' said Rachel, thrusting a pile of items into Libby's hands. 'These are the ones for you: sexy, lacy, pretty and alluring. I didn't think you would go for bright crimson strings or thongs without gussets…' She laughed. 'I certainly would though! See what you think. I can't wait to try these on.' Rachel had selected a red satin basque with multiple hooks and eyes, a striking red dress and a pair of sheer black stockings. 'It could take me a while to do all these fastenings!' She giggled. 'Ali, I think I might need your help.'

Libby gratefully accepted Rachel's selection, entered the changing rooms and undid the curtain tie to release the heavy velvet curtain that would give her some privacy. She peered at her reflection in the gilt-edged full-length mirror in front of her; she looked haggard, like an old woman. She sighed as she peeled off her jeans and T-shirt and stepped into a cream satin basque, beset with small stones that sparkled in the artificial light. She pulled the ties that zig-zagged underneath her chest and looked again in the mirror. She was surprised; the overall effect was incredible. The garment accentuated the natural curves of her body in a way that she never thought possible. She reached into her handbag for her brush and slowly pulled it through her curly light brown hair. She could hardly believe it, she looked exotic, shapely… and sexy. Reluctantly, she climbed out of the basque and put it to one side. She then selected a cream bra with an intricate lace trim – but this was a bra with a difference. The minimal garment simply consisted of a thin supportive strip that she wrapped around her upper torso and fastened at the back; her breasts – supported on the underside by two shallow satin pockets – were proudly displayed, like two spectacular pink blancmanges perching on plates. She teamed the bra with a classy pair of French knickers; the two matching garments accentuated her well-toned legs and her shapely breasts. Finally, she slipped on a cream "light as a feather" cross-over dress, made of many metres of soft taffeta. Libby sighed with pleasure as she felt the luxurious material caress her body, fitting her like a glove, glamorous and stylish, showing the merest suggestion of her shapely figure underneath. As she swayed gently, the delicate folds of the dress echoed her movement, like an exquisite dance. The silver sequins sewn into the fabric glittered, like the brightest stars in the night sky. It was extraordinary; she felt as if she was looking at the reflection of another woman; a sensual woman; an elegant woman

Ali's jaw dropped as she gazed at Libby. 'You look simply beautiful. It is as if that dress was made especially for you.'

Libby smiled coyly. 'I don't look too bad do I?' She hesitated. 'But can I really wear this to a stylish nightclub in Paris? Is it formal enough?'

'Relax, darling, you look simply gorgeous,' Rachel commented in her smooth velvety voice. 'And just remember, Libs, this nightclub is in gay Paris, the city of high fashion. You will look classy and fabulous. I'm pretty sure you'll turn a few heads.' Rachel sighed luxuriously as she fluttered her eyelashes. 'You lucky bugger.'

Libby stole a last glance at her reflection in the mirror. She felt more confident about her body than she had done for years. The dress and lingerie were classy and elegant, and not, as she had feared, cheap and tasteless. As she handed over the thick wodge of cash that Alex had given her, she smiled, feeling surprisingly delighted with her purchases. The beige makeup-caked shop assistant wrapped each garment lovingly in white tissue paper and placed the items carefully in a golden bag with "MeMe" artistically inscribed diagonally in deep purple lettering. Thanking her for her trouble, Libby smiled again. Alex might be pleasantly surprised. Or shocked.

The clouds had dispersed, and the sun shone brightly as they left the boutique, carrying their wares, and made their way towards a newly opened restaurant further up the high street towards St Clement's.

The restaurant was spacious and heavily ornate, each wall sporting an extraordinary and diverse – some might say random – collection of framed artwork; everything from the post-impressionist characteristic artwork of Van Gogh, to the modern pop art of David Hockney. Huge chandeliers hung – rather audaciously, in Libby's view – from intricately decorated ceiling rosettes, mounted at regular intervals on the high domed ceiling. Luscious green plants curled around the numerous Roman-style pillars, reaching upwards towards the light. A smartly dressed waiter led them to a small wooden table, hidden in a dimly lit alcove, semi-obscured by a flourishing rubber plant, decorated with a prolific array of warm-white fairy lights. The chairs scraped noisily on the tiled floor as they sat down and studied the menu.

'This place is a bit posh isn't it, Rachel?' said Ali as she glanced around. 'I bet the drinks are going to cost a small fortune!'

'My round,' Rachel said, as she spread her crimson lingerie across the table. 'I'm really pleased with my shopping, and I've even got a new toy to play with!' She thrust an oblong unopened box onto the table with a flourish. 'I can't wait to try this out. I'm sure it will give me the most awesome orgasmic experience.'

'Put it away, for goodness sake.' Libby looked around anxiously. 'Thank God no one heard you,' she added crossly.

The waiter appeared, carefully balancing a tray of drinks on his shoulder. Rachel hurriedly thrust her wares back in the bag. A knowing smile flickered across his face as he placed three large glasses of Chardonnay on the table in front of them. 'Let me know if you would like anything from our extensive lunch menu. *Côte de boeuf* is the chef's recommendation today.'

Ali turned to Libby. 'Are you pleased with what you've bought, Libs? I think your outfit is dreamy.'

'I don't know. Sometimes I feel as old as the hills. I wonder now whether I look a bit like mutton dressed as lamb.'

'Oh come on, Libs,' Rachel interjected, 'mutton dressed as lamb has a darn sight more fun than mutton dressed as mutton.' She threw back her head, her shrill peals of laughter echoed around the high ceiling.

'You're only in your thirties, Libs, hardly as old as the hills,' offered Ali reassuringly. 'We are in the prime of our lives.'

Libby sighed. 'I suppose it's nothing to do with how old I am, it's how I feel inside. I must admit I did feel good in my floaty dress and lingerie, for a minute or two, but if you don't feel good on the inside, acres of taffeta and silky lingerie are hardly going to provide the magic cure, are they?'

Rachel lifted her glass to her mouth and took a large sip, before replying. 'I think that it's important to love yourself, because if you don't,' she said, throwing her hands into the air exuberantly, 'sure as hell, nobody else will!'

'But of course *we* love you,' Ali added weakly, realising the implication of Rachel's words.

Libby looked sadly at Rachel. 'I envy you. You're confident and self-assured, witty and intelligent; you shine from the inside. I'm different. I guess I've never really liked myself...' Libby's words trailed away, as she reflected on her many years of suffering with low self-esteem and poor body image. Anorexia nervosa continued to leave a deep and painful scar on her life.

'But why, Libs?' asked Ali quietly. 'You are one of the most beautiful women I have ever met. You're kind-hearted, warm and caring. And, you have Alex; he loves you doesn't he?'

'The thing is, nobody really knows what goes on behind closed doors...' said Libby, as her thoughts returned to her claustrophobic life with Alex.

'What do you mean, Libs? Does Alex hurt you?' Rachel asked, feeling somewhat guilty about her previous comment.

'No, thankfully he has never laid a finger on me.' She paused, nervously wiping her mouth with the twisted corner of her napkin. 'He tells me that I'm the only woman he has ever truly loved... but then he puts me down and ridicules me. He makes me feel useless. It's hard not to believe that he is right...'

'So he does hurt you, Libs,' said Ali sadly, 'maybe not physically, but words can be just as damaging. I'm sorry, I had no idea you were going through a hard time. Perhaps I should have noticed something was wrong.'

'Not at all, Ali, I find it easier not to share my problems, because then I can almost make myself believe it isn't happening. But I do feel better for having shared some of my woes with you,' she said looking from one friend to the other. 'Thank you for listening... but the trouble is I've put a bit of a damper on our girls day out haven't I?' she said with a forced smile.

'Ignore his cruel words, Libs, because Alex is wrong. Emotional put-downs are cheap and cowardly. You need to find the courage from somewhere to believe in yourself, that you are a strong sensual woman.' Ali rested her hand gently on Libby's shoulder. 'You've got this.'

'Let's drink a toast to strong women everywhere,' said Rachel, raising her glass. 'If I were you, I would go to the nightclub on Saturday night, hold your head up high – you are drop-dead gorgeous – and have a fabulous night! And I have the perfect dress for you,' she said, as she reached into her golden bag and pulled out a figure-hugging crimson mini dress with designer diagonal slashes cut through the fabric. 'And I've got a magnificent pair of red killer heels.' She put her hand over her mouth to stifle a giggle. 'My fuck-me shoes – they would finish off the outfit perfectly!'

Sixteen

Everything was red – the bed cover, the curtains, the cupboards; everything. When they first arrived at the hotel, Libby was surprised. She had wrongly assumed that they would be staying in a chic hotel in the heart of Paris; perhaps Montmartre or Place de la Concorde. But she had not imagined a cheap hotel in an industrial estate in the back of beyond. Judging by the constant movement of cars and lorries as they came and went, it would seem that the rooms were available to book by the hour, perhaps for work meetings, but more likely for secret rendezvous, for sex. Alex had reassured her that the hotel would be perfectly acceptable, and it was only €60 a night, without breakfast of course.

Libby lay on the bed, staring gloomily at the small television. She had flicked through at least 120 channels: cookery programmes, children's TV, news, quizzes, countless advertisements, fitness programmes, films, but there wasn't one channel in English. Libby's mother was French; she had grown up in a bilingual household, but she hadn't practised her French for a long time. She had thought that her understanding of the language was pretty good until she tried to follow a fast-moving thriller – the characters spoke at lightning speed, and she could only catch the gist of it.

'What do you expect? We're in France for God's sake. What did you think the language on TV would be, Japanese?' Alex said scathingly. 'I suppose you'd like to see an episode of Eastenders? I give up. I'm going for a walk, not sure when I'll be back.' He curled his top lip in contempt. 'We're meeting Eloise and Roland at the restaurant in the hotel opposite for dinner at seven o'clock. I'm really looking forward to some intelligent conversation.' He threw on his jacket and slammed the door behind him.

Libby listened as the sound of his footsteps faded into the distance. She reflected on her meeting a few days before with Rachel and Ali in MeMe's and their conversation over a glass of wine. It had felt liberating to share some of her unhappiness: of being belittled, ridiculed, the cruel jibes that she had to swallow every day. But there was so much more that she had left unsaid: the initial excitement of planning to have a child, followed by desperate disappointment and the deep sadness of years of infertility; the womanless woman. The loneliness, the suspicion of infidelity: was Alex having an affair?

Something in Libby's consciousness had changed since that day. Over the years, she had become submissive; she would readily bow her head, listen to his unkind words, readily believing that he was right, and she was wrong. But now the balance of her mind was shifting – from submission to determination and resolve – she would no longer accept his insults. She would be subtle, cunning even; she would know when to remain silent and when to speak. She would be assertive, but not confrontational. She was beginning to form a plan.

Libby reached for her suitcase that had been stored above the cupboard. She carefully arranged the slash red dress, black stockings and crimson heels on one side of the bed and stood back to admire the overall effect – striking, sexy, provocative. She then placed the lacy bra and French knickers on the other side, arranging the delicate cream dress with glittery sequins lightly over the lingerie, carefully shaping the full folds of taffeta like the open blades of a fan. This outfit was alluring, elegant, sensual.

She pulled back the faded curtains allowing a warm beam of early evening sun to stream in through the window. It slowly began to dawn on her that she was looking forward to tomorrow evening. She turned to study the two contrasting outfits once again: would she choose to be sexy and provocative, or elegant and sensual?

Feeling weary, she repacked her clothes, placed the suitcase back on top of the wardrobe, and lay on the bed, staring at the ceiling. She knew in her heart that all the beautiful clothing in the world would not make a difference if you feel ugly and worthless on the inside. She must gather her strength and find the courage to make changes.

Opening her eyes, she glanced at the illuminated numbers of the clock just under the television. She realised with horror that it was six forty-five; she must have slept for over an hour. Surprised that Alex had not returned, she had a quick shower and threw on a simple light-weight summer jersey dress, burnt orange, and wedge flip-flops. She hurriedly tied her hair in a messy bun and thought about Ali's words: "You've got this." She strode over to the hotel opposite with her head held high.

***

Libby was shown to a table in a small courtyard leading from the main restaurant area. Alex sat opposite Eloise and Roland, deep in conversation. There was a carafe of red wine, half empty, in the middle of the table, and they were all tucking in to a variety of starters: olives, mixed nuts, sliced salami, mozzarella and sun-dried tomatoes.

'Darling, there you are, we thought you might have got lost.' Alex smirked. 'We've already started on the wine and nibbles; hope you don't mind.'

'Of course not, darling,' said Libby. She beckoned the waiter. '*S'il vous plait, puis-je avoir une coupe de champagne?*' She turned towards Alex. 'Have you ordered yet?'

'No, we haven't…' said Alex, taken aback that Libby had ordered the most expensive drink on the menu, and that she had spoken confidently in French.

'Let me introduce myself,' Libby said, reaching over the table to shake hands. 'I'm Libby. You must be Eloise and Roland, how lovely to meet you.' She looked at the half-eaten snacks in front of her. 'Do we need more nibbles, or should we save ourselves for the three-course *menu du jour*? I don't know about you but I'm simply starving. I see there's steak on the menu this evening. Did you have an easy journey?'

Eloise was a striking woman in her mid-thirties. Her long blonde hair tumbled luxuriously down to her waist in loose curls; chiselled cheekbones and a small, upturned nose defined her features; her generous glossy lips formed a permanent pout. But it was her huge electric blue eyes that caught Libby's attention; her stare seemed to bore into her, hard and emotionless. Eloise was beautiful, detached and as cold as ice.

'Libby, it's good to meet you at last, Alex has told me a lot about you,' Roland said, his dark eyes twinkling above his half-rimmed glasses. 'Charmed, I'm sure.'

'It's good to meet you too,' Libby said brightly. 'I hope you had a good trip; did you get held up on the M4? The traffic from Oxford to the Tunnel was a complete nightmare.'

'It was fine, thanks. Eloise does all the driving, so it gave me the chance to wrap up my marking.' He glanced at Eloise and gave her a friendly hug.

'Are you a teacher?' Libby asked. She quietly hoped that education might be something she could contribute to the conversation.

'Yes, I dabble in a bit of teaching,' he said modestly. 'I'm actually a don at Magdalen College, teaching PPE for my sins: politics, philosophy and economics.' He laughed. 'When I tell folk what I do for a living, I find it can spark fierce political debate, earnest conversations about the meaning of life, or it stops conversation altogether!'

Libby's heart sank; she didn't think she could engage in political conversation with any credibility or articulate any 'meaning of life' debate particularly well, opting instead to focus on some common ground. 'I work in education too; I'm currently taking a short break, but I've spent a good few years teaching lively five-year-olds, rather different from the students I would imagine.'

'Haha, we probably have a lot more in common than you think, Libby. My main aim when I work with my students is to foster a love of learning. Isn't that exactly what you want to achieve with the young children in your care?'

'It is, Roland, but haven't the students already got a thirst for learning? Isn't that why they come to university?'

He vigorously swept a mass of unruly curls from his forehead. 'We are talking about the peaks and troughs of life-long learning. There are so many distractions at university – socialising, drinking, sex – I have to keep my hand firmly on the tiller by providing inspiring teaching and facilitating intellectual, respectful and challenging debate. I like to think that my students leave university as critical thinkers, with enquiring minds and open to an exciting world of opportunities. I am never happier than when I am listening to, and engaging with, young people. We can learn a lot from the younger generation.'

'So much of what you say is relevant to my teaching with young children. I always encouraged the kids to ask lots of questions, to be active learners and to believe in themselves. But, Roland, I bet political debate with your students can sometimes get pretty heated can't it?'

'Oh, Libby, don't get him started,' said Eloise with a deep sigh. 'He can be so boring.' She turned to Alex and raised her eyes to heaven. 'Here we go...'

Dismissing Eloise's comments, he continued. 'The discussion we have in tutorials can be ferocious. My personal views are slightly right of centre but I have to guard against indoctrinating my students with my own personal conservatism. Of course, I can't speak for my colleagues... I find that the media is often uncomfortably biased, so it is important that I encourage my students to think for themselves, to do their own research. We have balanced debates, we respect differing political views, and then the students can reach informed decisions about their own personal political persuasion.'

'It all sounds very admirable, Roland, you must know a huge amount about current affairs. I'm afraid I often feel rather out of my depth when conversation turns to anything to do with politics.'

'Honestly, Libby, you would feel out of your depth in a puddle,' Alex said dismissively. 'Anyway, let's order.'

'I shouldn't worry too much, Libby, there's more to life than politics,' Roland said with a chuckle. 'I enjoy the good things in life, delicious food, fine wine and good company! Oh, and of course, the allure of a beautiful woman...'

Roland wore a tartan sports jacket held together over his large belly by a single button, a pale blue shirt and a paisley tie fastened at a jaunty angle. He had a deeply weathered face, a ruddy complexion and remarkably bushy eyebrows. It was obvious that Roland liked to indulge in wining and dining. Libby watched, fascinated, as he devoured a huge plate of *tartare de cheval* – a dish of raw, chopped horse meat – the meat juices freely dripping down his chin as he ate with relish. He paused, only to take a large gulp of his Merlot, before scraping his plate clean. He removed the serviette that he had tucked into his collar and wiped his mouth. 'I think French cuisine is truly exquisite,' he said with a satisfied sigh. Eloise, on the other hand, nibbled at the edge of her sole, struggling to remove the numerous bones from the succulent flesh, deciding instead to push a few salad leaves around her plate. Libby couldn't help but wonder how some couples end up together. She had only just met Eloise and Roland, but her first impressions were that they were poles apart; she didn't warm to Eloise, but Roland seemed okay. She looked at her empty plate, realising with regret that her ribeye steak, chips and salad had slipped down without her even noticing. She had been too focussed on the conversation to appreciate and enjoy her food. She glanced sideways at Alex, now deep in conversation with Eloise. There was something about their expressions and demeanour that surprised and concerned Libby; were they flirting with each other? She ordered herself another glass of champagne and, as she sipped the cold delicious bubbles, she began to feel rather light-headed, but she knew she must keep her counsel; she must be careful. 'Darling, I'm beginning to feel very tired. It's been a long day, so, if you'll excuse me, I think I'll go and get my beauty sleep.'

'Beauty sleep? That could take a long time,' he scoffed, raising his eyes to heaven. 'It's only ten o'clock, for God's sake. Libs, we didn't come all this way to go to bed early. I fancy a *crème brûlée* and a whisky, how about you two?'

Roland hauled himself up, reached over and planted a wet kiss on each cheek. 'Sleep well, I'm really looking forward to our evening together at the club tomorrow,' he said, his gaze lingering on Libby.

Libby opened her eyes sleepily as Alex returned some hours later, slamming the door loudly behind him. 'Are you asleep?'

'Well, I was,' she muttered grumpily, thinking what a ridiculous question it was. 'It's late, Alex, where have you been?'

'What's it to you? I was frankly embarrassed that you came back so early. Why didn't you make more of an effort this evening, Lib, it's not much to ask is it? And, by the way, your two glasses of champagne cost me a bloody arm and a leg.'

Libby rolled over in bed, choosing to ignore his remarks. She closed her eyes tightly, her body tense and alert. He lay down on the bed beside her and roughly turned her to face him. He placed his hands either side of her head; vice-like, as he inhaled a deep calculated breath, before blowing directly into her face. Libby closed her eyes, and her mind, as she gulped a sickening cocktail of warm alcoholic fumes, garlic and slimy droplets of saliva. Alex knew his breath didn't leave any bruises, any physical damage at all. But he also knew that it sickened her, it damaged her, it was a very effective punishment.

'I'm sorry,' she said coldly. 'Tomorrow is another day.'

Seventeen

Libby regretted her choice of footwear; her pink sandals had already cut deep ridges into the skin on both heels, and her little toe on her right foot rubbed painfully against the unforgiving plastic of her ill-chosen shoes. The journey from their hotel to the centre of Paris by metro had been surprisingly straightforward, and they now found themselves wandering along the left bank of the Seine on a wide boulevard lined with deciduous trees; the tips of their leaves just turning to a muted red, hinting at the first signs of autumn. They paused to watch as a flotilla of boats – some working barges and others crammed with tourists – made their way slowly upriver. Libby breathed in the soft heady air of the morning and began to look forward to the day ahead. 'They say the left bank is where the Parisians first learnt to think,' she said dreamily. 'Many famous artists and writers have graced this area of Paris – Ernest Hemingway, Scott Fitzgerald, Jean-Paul Sartre...'

'Come on, Lib, I'm starving. Let's go and grab a coffee and a pastry before we meet my friends,' he said dismissively. He grabbed Libby's arm and propelled her to a nearby café. 'By the way, what do you think of them, Libs?'

'I think Eloise is a bit of an airhead if I'm honest; she seems rather cold and unfriendly. Roland seems nice enough, obviously intelligent, quite interesting, but of course I don't know him yet.'

'Come on, Libs, this is Paris, live and let live!' Alex retorted. 'Don't be so judgemental.'

'Just because they're your friends, Alex. I don't have to like them,' Libby muttered. 'Anyway, let's get some breakfast.' She hailed the waiter and ordered *deux grands crème* and a generous basket of croissants for dipping. She glanced around the café: most of the tables were positioned on the cobbled street outside to capitalise on the scenic views of the Seine and Notre Dame, an impressive cathedral that rose majestically above the bank on the opposite side of the river. The eatery was buzzing with customers, some enjoying a variety of pastries, cradling cheerful red-and-white striped bowls of steaming coffee; others were already indulging in pre-lunch drinks; extravagant goblets of wine, elegant flutes of champagne, or multicoloured cocktails; many laughing, everyone deep in conversation. She glanced across at Alex, his head bowed, now deeply engrossed in messaging on his mobile phone. She longed for lively conversation and the company of her friends back in Oxford. She wondered idly if she should be jealous of the time and attention he devoted to his phone. Still, it gave her time to soak up the lively Parisian atmosphere of this thriving café. As she scanned the surrounding tables, she was surprised by how many people wore a variety of blue-and-white striped jumpers and T-shirts; she had always thought it rather a clichéd view of the French, but, if the clientele in this café were representative, it was true. Or perhaps they were all tourists? As she dunked her pastry in her coffee, she realised that she preferred layers of butter and jam on her croissant; her creamy coffee was rapidly filling up with islands of soggy pastry. Suddenly a man dressed in the ubiquitous striped top and a navy-blue beret walked towards the table and thrust a red rose into Libby's hands. 'A rose for a beautiful woman,' he said, in a rich accented voice. 'Monsieur, you buy for your wife?' Alex looked up briefly, shook his head and returned to his mobile phone. The man's expression changed from full-on charm to annoyance in an instant. He grabbed the single rose from Libby and turned to the next potential customers; the look on his face altered in less than a second.

'Oh no,' Alex gestured. 'I can't bloody believe it.' He slammed his phone down on the table in front of him.

Libby leaned towards him, worried that something terrible had happened; his mother had died, or that his firm had collapsed. 'Is everything okay, Alex? What's going on?'

'It's Roland, he's been chucking-up all night and isn't coming to meet us today.'

'Oh, Alex, is that all? I thought somebody had died at the very least! Anyway, I'm sorry to hear he isn't well. Oh dear, I wonder if it was anything to do with the raw horse meat he ate last night,' she said, putting her hand over her mouth. 'I don't even want to think about it…'

'Don't be ridiculous, Libby. Horse is a real delicacy here in France. It might be more to do with the amount of whisky we consumed last night,' he said knowingly. 'I hope he'll be okay to come to the club with us tonight.'

Libby nodded. 'He'll probably feel better after some rest; such a shame to miss out on a day in Paris though.'

'We're meeting Eloise at Les Berges de Seine in half an hour, so we'd better get moving.'

As they arrived at the entrance of the riverside park, Eloise was already there to greet them. Libby studied her with envy. She wore a mid-blue sleeveless silk dress that clung to the natural curves of her body, and flowed gracefully from her slim waist, falling away to just above her knees. Her luxurious hair cascaded over her shoulders in a mass of blonde curls. Libby couldn't help but notice her elegant patent leather shoes, which complimented her manicured toenails, shining with crimson polish. Libby sighed, trying to ignore the painful blister that was forming on her heel.

'Libby, Alex, how lovely to see you,' Eloise gushed. She reached over to kiss Alex on both cheeks, lingering slightly longer than was customary. She turned towards Libby and brushed the side of her face lightly with her lips. 'I'm sorry about Roly, he spent the whole night with his head down the bloody loo, heaving like one of his drunken students!'

'I'm sorry to hear this,' said Libby, somewhat surprised that Eloise could look so elegant, and yet sound so sharp and emotionless. 'I hope that he will feel better after some sleep.'

They wandered through the park, admiring the manicured flower beds, carefully crafted to provide an abundance of colour, interspersed with low maintenance beds – areas where carefully selected plants survived without the need for constant watering. Alex gazed at the expansive flower beds. 'They look like a tart's blouse if you ask me.'

'Well, thankfully we didn't ask you, Alex,' said Libby firmly. 'It's hard to believe we're in the centre of Paris, and yet it feels so tranquil here; we are well away from the hustle and bustle of the city, and all the tourist trails.'

'Yes, Alex and I thought it might be a good idea to avoid the main tourist attractions – the Eiffel Tower, the Louvre, the Arc de Triomphe – they would all be hellishly busy at this time of year,' Eloise said, smiling at Alex conspiratorially.

"Alex and I" sounded rather exclusive to Libby, but she chose to ignore a niggling concern that was bubbling up inside her.

'It must be nearly lunchtime, I'm feeling peckish,' Alex said. He linked arms with both women and marched them towards a riverside restaurant. Libby groaned internally; it didn't seem long ago since she had devoured an enormous pastry, it must have been well over her daily calorie allowance, and she was not in the least bit hungry.

They chose a table underneath a tall plane tree, its broad leaves providing welcome shade. Eloise and Alex sat together on one side of the rickety table and Libby faced them.

'I fancy a large glass of Chardonnay and a Caesar salad,' Eloise said decisively. 'I'm glad we're not sitting in full sun, it's far too hot.'

'I think I'll go for steak and chips, and a large beer. I'm going to need all the strength I can muster for our evening at Chez Fleurie,' Alex said, snatching a fleeting glance at Eloise. 'Don't you think?'

'Don't we get a full three course meal as part of the deal tonight, Alex? I'm not sure what I fancy... I think I'll go for something light, perhaps just a mixed-leaf salad and a small glass of white wine.'

'God, here we go, obsessing about your weight again. I really don't know why you bother.' He shot an admiring glance at Eloise.

'Well, I'm pretty sure that beer will go straight to your ever-expanding belly, Alex,' replied Libby angrily.

'Come on, you two, now's not the time for a domestic,' Eloise said with a withering sigh. She reached into her handbag for a tissue, and dabbed the small beads of perspiration that were beginning to appear over her top lip.

The service was slow, but eventually lunch was served. '*Bon appétit!*' Alex said brightly, raising his glass.

Libby studied Eloise as she stealthily stole one chip after another from his plate. Eloise laughed when she realised that her greed had been noticed. She turned towards Alex, fluttered her eyelashes, and carefully positioned a large and rather droopy chip to her lips. Opening her mouth, she took a bite, slowly and seductively, licking her lips extravagantly. 'I'm just thinking about you, Alex... and your waistline.'

Libby looked away, furious by Eloise's blatant flirting with her husband. She slammed her knife and fork down on the table and stood up, scraping her chair back over the cobbled stones as she did so, and followed the signs for the restroom.

As she held her hands under the steady stream of warm water, she studied her reflection in the mirror; she looked tired and drawn, her eyes dull and sunken. She felt unutterably sad that Alex constantly put her down; the more he demeaned her, the more she believed him. Just as she was leaving the building, she glanced through the grubby window at the entrance. Her eyes widened in horror. Alex and Eloise were in a deep and passionate embrace, their bodies intertwined. Her heart plummeted. Suddenly everything made sense. This had to be the blonde woman that Amelia had spotted with Alex a few weeks before in Cafe Calypso. How could she have been so dense not to realise this before? How dare he? Her whole body started to pulsate with emotion: anger, grief, sadness…

She hurriedly splashed some cold water over her face and took a few deep breaths. She willed herself to be strong; hold herself together; pretend she hadn't seen. She strode towards the couple, her head held high. Alex pulled away, quickly averting his eyes. Libby took some pleasure in the guilt that was written all over his face. Tossing her hair back, she asked, 'Are you okay, Alex, you look a little uncomfortable?'

'Yeah, of course I am,' he replied sheepishly. 'I'm just rather hot under the collar, that's all. Shall we pay the bill, or do you want a coffee?'

'Have we got time to visit the Musée d'Orsay? I've read all the rave reviews. It houses a huge collection

Liz van Santen

of impressionist paintings by famous artists: Monet, Renoir… and it isn't far from here.'

'Nah, I don't feel like traipsing round a dusty old museum, I can't be bothered. I want to go back to the hotel this afternoon for a kip, so that I'm wide awake later and ready to dance the night away.'

'I suppose if you don't have the intellect to appreciate fine art and paintings, then of course you'd get bored,' said Libby, directing an icy stare at Alex. 'Okay, I think I might stay a little longer for a coffee and another wander round the park. How about you, Eloise?'

'I think I'll go back to the hotel too, I feel rather tired,' she said awkwardly.

The lunchtime rush was over, and the restaurant was now considerably calmer; most of the tables were empty. Libby sighed, relieved that they had gone; although she did note with annoyance, that neither of them had offered to settle the bill. She sipped her *café allongé* and gazed into the distance. She reflected sadly that she was in one of the most romantic cities in the world, and she had never in her life felt more alone.

143

Eighteen

The wrought-iron gates opened slowly to reveal an avenue of low-level orange lights, casting a warm sensual glow, illuminating the majestic plane trees above. Two Roman pillars, surmounted by golden eagles, defined the entrance to the cobbled courtyard. As they entered, Libby inhaled the heady scent of the bougainvillaea, which clung to the pale grey stone walls of the redundant château.

Small groups of people had started to congregate by the bar for an *apéro* before dinner was served. A young waiter dressed in a dinner jacket greeted them warmly and offered to take their coats. Libby watched in astonishment as Eloise peeled away her poncho to reveal her evening attire; a striking full-length silver chainmail dress which clung to her body and left nothing to the imagination. It reminded Libby of Mithril, a fictional metal described in *Lord of the Rings* – "Mith" meaning grey, and "ril" meaning glitter. She looked like an apparition, an ice queen. Alex stared at her, open-mouthed.

'She scrubs up pretty well, doesn't she?' said Roland with a chuckle, ruining the dramatic effect of her "unveiling" in an instant. Eloise glowered at him, before reaching across the bar to select a glass of Kir Royale, a drink offered to all and included in the price.

'Darling, I wish you'd stayed at the hotel this evening if that is all you've got to say.'

Libby tucked her raincoat tightly around her, all she wanted to do was to disappear. How could she compare herself to the sheer perfection of the woman standing next to her?

'May I help you, *madame*?' the waiter asked as he leaned towards her to remove her coat. '*Vous êtes très belle, madame*,' he whispered quietly, smiling appreciatively.

Glowing with simple elegance and sophistication, her gown was perfectly fitted and looked as if it had been designed just for her. The deep folds of cream taffeta flowed extravagantly from her waist, undulating gently as she moved, the sequins of her bodice glittering and dancing in the soft lighting. The luxurious fabric caressed her body, revealing the merest hint of the gentle curves of her figure beneath. Libby emanated a peaceful, unassuming presence. As she glanced shyly around the semi-lit courtyard, she became aware of a sea of faces gazing at her. Embarrassed now, she glanced nervously at Alex.

'I thought you were going to wear a black slinky outfit. You remind me of one of those dolls with hideous frilly dresses that they used to hide loo rolls in back in the day,' he said unkindly, although Libby did wonder if she caught a brief glimpse of surprise and admiration.

'Oh, Alex, I think she looks quite nice,' Eloise conceded, eyeing her up and down with disdain

'Well, I think you look absolutely gorgeous, Libby,' added Roland with a wide grin.

Libby turned away, feeling dismal. This was going to be a long night.

The two couples were ushered to a table to one side of the courtyard, set with a crisp white tablecloth, shining cutlery, a vase of dried flowers and illuminated by red candles set in decorative holders. They were offered a simple three-course menu – with meat, fish or vegetarian options – and a bottle of wine for each couple to share. Just as the first course was served, a flamenco dancer in a striking traditional costume appeared from behind the bar. She clapped her hands high over her head as she strutted rhythmically to the sound of emotive Spanish guitar strummed by a young man, his jet-black hair greased back to within an inch of its life. As the skilful dancer weaved her way through the tables, she tossed her head back proudly; she was able to convey passion, anger, joy and sadness in just a few chosen moves. Libby, mesmerised by her beauty and artistry, realised with relief that the strumming of the guitar drowned out any attempt at conversation. She thought it rather incongruous that here they were in a French château, enjoying French food and wine, and yet they were being entertained by a brilliant Spanish flamenco duo.

Libby scanned the courtyard, intrigued by some of the women's outfits. A tall willowy woman draped herself across the bar, with almost feline grace, in a sleek all-in-one leopard-skin catsuit, and wearing some of the highest heels Libby had ever seen. Another wore a white satin wraparound dressing gown. Libby was rather puzzled by this; what was she wearing underneath? She discovered, with some satisfaction, that many of the women wore metallic chainmail dresses, displaying their virtually naked bodies, similar – and some identical – to Eloise's outfit. She wondered how uncomfortable this would make Eloise feel; rather common, perhaps? The men, by contrast, were rather colourless in their compulsory dress: chinos, deck shoes and checked shirts.

On the table to the left of them, there were two transexual women enjoying their starters. They looked exquisite: both dressed in glittery ball gowns, slit to the thigh on one side to show an expanse of shapely leg; thick curly hair, tumbling over their shoulders; their faces immaculately made up. They looked comfortable in their own bodies, proud of their sexuality.

She studied another couple on the table next to them. Libby guessed that they must be well into their seventies, their faces serene; remarkably uncluttered by the ravages of time. Libby gazed at the stylish woman, who wore a mini sparkly dress, sheer stockings and elegant high heels; her streaked blonde hair swept away from her face in a stylish French twist. Her partner wore a patterned scarf loosely tied around his neck – reminding Libby of an artist she once knew – his long grey hair falling over his collar in neat curls. His crisp white shirt was rolled up casually at the sleeves to reveal tanned and muscular forearms. He slowly lifted his cigar to his lips, took a deep drag, as he gazed at his wife with transparent love and affection. Libby wondered how long they had been together;

sophistication and style shone through; the number of years they had been on the earth paled into insignificance.

Libby returned her gaze to the dancer, who had now approached their table, taken Alex firmly by the hand, and was now propelling him to the centre of the courtyard to dance with her. As Alex raised his arms awkwardly in an attempt to emulate her Spanish lines, his facial expression conveyed his undisguised mortification and embarrassment, his movements stilted and jerky. Libby could feel the mirth bubbling up from deep within, her shoulders started to shake uncontrollably, and finally, she erupted into peals of laughter, tears streaming down her cheeks. Alex was getting a taste of his own medicine. At last he was experiencing what it was like to be ridiculed; to be undermined; to be publicly humiliated.

The meal had been delicious and now it was time for the headline entertainment of the evening: the French cabaret. The crowds gathered in the main concert hall, an area bedecked with plush scarlet sofas, rich velvet curtains and glittering chandeliers which hung luxuriously from the embossed ceiling. The lights dimmed, the atmosphere electric; the show was about to begin.

A single beam of light focussed on a lone wooden chair positioned in the centre of the stage. As the music began, a young woman wearing a black basque, fishnet stockings and above-the-knee black leather boots slunk seductively from the shadows towards centre stage, her hips swaying provocatively in time to the dulcet tones of Édith Piaf. A hush descended as the audience, mesmerised by this young talented artist, gazed in awe as her body undulated, twisted and turned into extraordinary and seemingly impossible acrobatic poses. She purred and flirted with the carved wooden frame of the chair, stroking and caressing its smooth surface, as she pouted her glossy red lips and fluttered her eyelashes, tantalising the captive audience. She was frivolous and fun, and yet artistic and classy. As the final note sounded, she sauntered towards the audience and selected a bashful man in his early forties. She invited him to sit under the spotlight. He reminded Libby of a four-year-old sitting on the "naughty chair" having done something extremely wicked. He looked shyly towards the floor, the top of his bald head gleaming in the light, his shoulders hunched. There was a ripple of sympathetic applause for the "victim" that she had carefully selected for her next act, many relieved that they had not been chosen. As the music began, she circled the "chosen one" seductively, brushing the side of his face until he raised his head and gazed at her with a coy smile. All of a sudden, she threw herself extravagantly across his knee and, snaking a leg around his neck, she hollowed her back, her sumptuous hair falling towards the ground. His eyes widened in surprise. She stretched her arms downwards and elegantly kicked her legs over her head to standing. Finally she stood with her legs astride in front of him and rose into a headstand, before elegantly stretching her legs into the splits. She skilfully lowered her legs to firmly clamp her calves around his neck in a vice-like grip. His face broke into a wide smile of wonderment. He had just been transported to heaven and back.

After escorting the elated, if a little shell-shocked, punter back to his table, she returned to the stage for the final act. She turned dramatically to face the audience. Drawing her fingers through her hair, she attached a tall red plume to the side of her head. Statuesque, she listened to the opening lines of "La Vie en Rose", an anthem of love, tapping a single foot in time to the sultry voice of the Édith Piaf. As she danced, the line of her movement mirrored the rise and fall of the exquisite love song. She slowly, suggestively, unbuttoned her basque and peeled it away, revealing her shapely breasts, covered only by two small glitter circles. Placing a foot on the chair, she walked her fingers seductively towards her thighs and unzipped her leather boots, pausing only to tease and tantalise. Finally, she undid the clips of her suspenders, and rolled each stocking down her leg, like a snake shedding its skin. She circled each stocking gracefully around her head, before tossing them into the hands of one of the many hopeful onlookers. As the last words of the song faded away, she bowed to the audience, blew a single kiss and sauntered back into the shadows, her red plume quivering in the fading light.

'She was simply unbelievable,' said Libby, shaking her head in amazement. 'How on earth did her body contort into those incredible poses? I thought it was a striking performance; stylish and classy.'

'Well, I'm utterly speechless,' Roland said. 'What say you, Alex?'

'I don't know about "stylish and classy", I thought she was bloody…'

'Okay,' Libby interrupted. 'Would anyone like another glass of vino?'

As the audience started to disperse, Alex turned to face the two women. 'Do either of you fancy a dance? I think there's a disco with a DJ in the marquee.'

'I think I might go and get a breath of fresh air, I'm feeling rather light-headed,' said Libby as she drained her glass. 'You go ahead, and I'll catch you up.'

Libby wandered outside into the courtyard, now empty of people, and sat on a wooden bench. She spread the taffeta folds of her dress like a fan on either side of her and breathed in the fragrant air of late summer. The evening had been surprisingly enjoyable so far, but now she was feeling rather nauseous, the wine was slipping down rather too easily.

'May I join you, Libby?'

'Of course, Roland, I just needed to clear my head,' she said brightly, although she would really have preferred some solitude. 'Did you enjoy the show?'

Roland sat down heavily beside her, catching one side of her gown under the weight of his body. Libby made a mental note not to move, otherwise she would be in danger of ripping the fabric.

'I did very much, Libby, but I came out here because I wanted to ask you something.'

'Ask away, but I may not have any answers. I fear I'm rather squiffy already,' she said, with a sigh. 'I really ought to know better.'

'Do you know what's going on?' he asked bluntly, as he shifted uncomfortably on the folded taffeta. 'I mean with Eloise and Alex   '

Libby's body stiffened. 'I found out yesterday,' she muttered quietly. 'I saw them together, they were kissing. Are you telling me that you knew all along? Aren't you furious with Eloise... or Alex? You agreed to come away with us. What's going on?'

'I'll try to explain, Libby. We look at things in a different way. Eloise and I have an open marriage. I have known about their relationship since it began, because we are honest with each other, extramarital relationships are consensual. I'm sorry you've been drawn into this by Alex's behaviour, his deception. This isn't right. It is unfortunate that you had to find out in this way. I persuaded Eloise that we should organise this trip in order to get things out in the open. You never know, Libby, you might end up with a stronger marriage with more openness and honesty... Oh dear, I feel like a marriage guidance counsellor,' he added with a wry smile.

'It's all a bit of a shock, Roland. He does nothing but put me down all the time, and now, to add insult to injury, he's having an affair.'

Questions were spinning around in Libby's head. *Do I want my marriage to end, with all the trauma and upheaval it would entail, or is there a way of working through this? Perhaps I need to broaden my mind?*

'Do you think that all the couples here have the same views as you?' Libby asked nervously.

'Probably. I think people are more open-minded in Europe. Have you ever heard of Muditā?'

'No, I haven't, but what's this got to do with anything?'

'It's an emotion which is more or less the opposite

of jealousy. Buddhists believe it is one of the hardest emotional states to achieve. It literally means finding joy in someone's happiness. The English word is "compersion". In other words, Libby, if Eloise wants to have a liaison with someone else and it makes her happy, then I am happy. It gives *me* pleasure. Does that make sense?'

'It feels a bit one-sided to me; how about Alex does something nice for me for a change? And anyway, aren't you afraid she might leave you?'

'I think she would be more likely to leave if I stifled her.'

'That's very generous-minded of you…'

'Well, Libby, if you could look at it the way we do, you might find that things get better. Most of the couples we know who have adopted this lifestyle have been together for years and are very devoted to each other.'

They sat together in the semi darkness; the silence only broken by the relentless hum of the cicadas and the distant throbbing of the dance music.

Nineteen

The dim lighting cast a shadowy pink and purple hue across the dungeon. Libby paused at the entrance as she scanned the unbelievable scene unfolding before her. The thick stone walls were beset with a myriad of restraining equipment for adult amusement – elaborate chains, body harnesses, dog leads, masks and rope. A naked woman – embellished with an array of symmetrical knots, arranged strategically around her body – reminded Libby of the prey of a spider, cocooned in an intricate silken web. Towards the far end of the dungeon, a man captured in mediaeval stocks, gazed in awe as his partner and another woman teased and tantalised him, their bodies joined together in an exquisite and erotic dance.

She turned towards the left wall and drew a sharp intake of breath as she stared unblinkingly; despite the mask he was wearing, there was no mistaking that it was Alex – spreadeagled and naked, and lashed to the stone by buckled hand and ankle cuffs. Eloise, wearing a snakeskin bra and thong, was deeply engrossed, tying an intricate pattern of rope around his torso; neither noticed that they were being observed.

'I can't believe what I've just seen...' Libby whispered urgently. 'Please tell me that he's okay.'

Roland gently removed Libby's hands from her face. 'I know this is bound to be a shock for you, Libby, but this is just adults at play. It is fully consensual, and nobody gets hurt. Lots of couples enjoy this kind of role-play; it's usually about control and submission, the active partner likes to experience power and control, and the passive partner likes the feeling of helplessness and submission.'

Her mind was racing. She found it ironic that here was Alex indulging his fantasy of being controlled, being submissive, and yet in real life, *he* was the one who sought power; *he* was the one that controlled her. The seed of an idea was forming in Libby's head.

'Shall we go and get a drink, Roland? I'm parched.'

'Are you absolutely sure you don't want me to tie you up?' he asked, raising his eyebrows quizzically. 'Or perhaps you would like to put me in the stocks?'

'I rather think not,' she said firmly, but with a small smile forming on her lips. She propelled him up the well-trodden stairs to the bar.

'What are your thoughts, Libby?' Roland asked, as they shared an enormous vodka cocktail made for two to share and garnished with a bright pink orchid. 'I do admire the French style, elevating the taboo to a pure art form, don't you think?'

'I really don't know. I thought I'd led a relatively unsheltered life, but now I'm not so sure. What do you mean by an "art form"?'

'The club provides a great venue for couples to explore their fantasies, providing top-quality equipment. It's a place of limitless possibilities, a rich palette of opportunities,' he said, throwing his arms into the air with enthusiasm.

Libby wasn't sure if it was the effect of the huge cocktail, or Roland's words, but she was beginning to understand his sentiments. 'So when you watched Eloise and Alex, did you feel any compersion?'

'I did, Libby. They were both freely acting out their fantasies, in a safe space.'

'But do you think it is really safe, Roland? I wonder if some people, particularly women, feel rather vulnerable in this situation.'

'The rules are very clear in the club; they don't allow single men, and no means *no*, it doesn't mean *maybe*. People are very respectful of this. The club is carefully monitored and anyone not respecting the rules will be asked to leave. And couples engaging in role-play usually agree on a safe word. They might scream "no, no, stop" but this is all part of their play, but when they use the agreed word, it actually means *stop*.'

'I suppose I do respect the open, honest atmosphere; there is no pretence, people are free to express themselves with no judgement. But a lot has happened, Roland. I've just discovered my husband is having an affair, and now, I've seen him handcuffed to a wall and being tied up by his lover. It's a lot for me to process.'

'Yes, I do understand, but I have to say…' Roland hesitated. 'I'm more than a little disappointed with Eloise.

She has chosen to have a liaison with someone outside the lifestyle, and for this, I am very sorry. We don't ever intentionally put marriages at risk. I can assure you though, that Eloise is not looking for a long-term relationship. Alex is just one in a long line of liaisons. Does it feel any better for you now that it is out in the open?'

'Yes, I think it does,' Libby replied pensively. She sighed. 'I wish I could be as open-minded as you, Roly, but I was brought up to uphold very different values. My parents had a strict moral code, no sex before marriage, that kind of thing…'

'Yes, there has always been pressure in society to conform but, for now, I think you should just relax and enjoy the evening. New experiences can really enrich your life in quite unexpected ways.'

'Excuse me, may we join you? I'm Stéphane and this is my wife, Carmelle,' he said proudly. He put his arm affectionately around the elegant woman standing next to him.

'Please do!' Roland drew up two chairs beside them. 'I'm Roland and this is my good friend, Libby.'

'I think you come from England?' Stéphane said. 'I met Carmelle a few years ago when we were both studying English at college in Toulouse. I think English is a very difficult language to learn!'

Libby glanced at Stéphane. He had an impressive mass of blond curly hair held back with an Alice band, revealing a tanned and rugged face; his pale blue linen shirt, chinos and shiny deck shoes cut a handsome figure.

'I think French is more challenging; all the "*le*" and "*la*" and "*tu*" and "*vous*". Tell me this: why is a table feminine?' Roland asked, creasing his brow. 'I believe it is, "*la table*".'

'Because it just is,' Stéphane replied, shrugging his shoulders. 'And if you think that is funny, how about *le vagin*? Can you believe that a vagina is masculine in French?'

They roared with laughter. Stéphane had successfully broken the ice.

'Have you been to this club before?' Libby asked, interested to find out why a handsome couple would frequent a French club such as this one.

Stéphane smiled. 'Yes, we have been here a few times. We love the fine dining and the cabaret… and of course we enjoy all the… I think you call in English, the "fringe benefits"!'

'Fringe benefits?'

'We adore each other. Carmelle is everything to me. I want, more than anything in the world, to make her happy. And I know that she likes women as well as men. So we come here so that she can enjoy the freedom and pleasure of some physical contact with other women.' He paused to gaze at Libby. 'You are beautiful. You caught my eye as soon as you arrived; you are chic and elegant. If you and Carmelle want to have a bit of fun together, then this would make me very happy.' He chuckled. 'And it would certainly make her happy too…'

Libby reflected on his words and glanced at Roland; this is exactly what he meant by compersion. But it was not the answer she was expecting; although she enjoyed the company of her girlfriends in Oxford, she had never considered anything more with any of them.

'Don't get me wrong, I like to dabble too. We are not seasoned swingers in our everyday lives, but this is a fine club, and we always enjoy our evenings here. It's a very classy venue, the food and entertainment are top quality, everyone is welcomed and accepted for who they are, and, importantly, all the hygiene and safe sex practices are strictly adhered to. And you don't have to do anything you don't want to do. We have a lot of friends who love coming here.' He paused to look around. 'Carmelle, I did think that Pierre and Chantelle were going to be here tonight, but I haven't seen them yet.'

'Perhaps they decided to stay at home, Stéphane, Bordeaux are playing Nantes tonight!' Carmelle answered with a grin. 'They do love their football!'

'Do you have clubs like this in England?'

Libby glanced shyly at Roland. 'Do we? I'm not sure. I haven't been to any clubs at all to be honest, this is certainly a new experience for me.'

'*Vous êtes débutants…*' Stéphane acknowledged quietly, pausing to wait for Roland's reply.

'Yes, I think there are a few exclusive clubs that offer this kind of experience in London, and maybe in other big cities, Birmingham or Manchester… but Eloise and I haven't been to any of them. I may well be wrong, but I think the French have a more open-minded approach to sex and relationships, which is why we like to pop over to France…'

'How interesting. The English do seem to be very different. I think I'd like a drop more wine,' said Stéphane, 'I'll order a litre of rosé and some ice. I hope you will do us the honour of sharing it with us.'

Libby nodded. She was beginning to enjoy the company of this delightful French couple, although she did wonder what Alex and Eloise were up to, and she was feeling rather unsettled by the suggestion that Carmelle might enjoy a "bit of fun" with her. But, as the cool wine slipped easily down her throat, she was beginning to feel that nothing really mattered anymore.

'Libby, let's go and dance,' Carmelle urged. 'Stéphane is a terrible dancer; he is like a block of wood on the dance floor!'

'*Ma chérie*, you are wrong, I am a marvellous dancer… but yes, you go. I suppose Roland and I can talk about football,' he said, turning to Roland with a wide smile.

As the two women walked towards the small dance floor, the throbbing disco music faded away and the DJ had now selected to play a slow French ballad, full of emotion and passion. Libby swayed dreamily in time to the music, absorbing the rich melody and the sensuality of the French language. Carmelle drew Libby closer, gently exploring and caressing the gentle curves of her body. It all felt very surreal to Libby. Here she was in a French club on the outskirts of Paris, dancing with a French girl she had only just met. And what her husband was doing, she could hardly imagine. Libby placed her hands either side of Carmelle, stroking the soft smooth flesh of her upper arms, and inhaling the heady floral scent of her perfume. It reminded Libby of a gift given to her by her first boyfriend, was it Chanel No5 or Miss Dior? She wasn't sure, but it transported her to a bygone era; a time when she was happy. Tingles of pleasure coursed through her body, as Carmelle brushed her fingers lightly over her breasts, following the line of her waist, towards her thighs. Libby found herself relaxing into the arms of a beautiful woman; everything felt right, natural, exquisite.

As the final words of the song faded away, Libby found herself longing for more.

Twenty

It was as if they were sitting in the gallery of an ornate theatre, watching a ballet performance. The playroom was shrouded in semi-darkness; luxurious four-poster beds were placed around the room, some surrounded by translucent lacy curtains, others not. Some occupied by single couples, some in use by multiple groups. The new-found friends sat on a padded settee in the balcony, side by side, and watched the proceedings silently.

Libby's eyes widened as she glanced at a stage area at the back of the room, to see the shadowy outline of a mass of naked bodies all writhing together, like the tempestuous waves of the sea. She was reminded of photos of erotic figures carved into the stonework of Indian temples that she had admired in one of Alex's "coffee table" books. The silence was interrupted only by the frequent cries and whimpers of ecstasy. Her head was spinning, everything becoming a blur. She watched, mesmerised, as the multitude of naked bodies twisted and turned into a magnificent moving and ever-changing sculpture; it was as if she was watching a black-and-white movie from years ago – a truly exquisite study of the human form. As she peered through the dim light, she could feel her heart beat hard against her ribcage. There he was, buried deep in the midst of the throng of bodies, lying on his back being ridden by a woman, her left hand cupping the breast of another woman. All of a sudden she remembered the picture displayed on their sitting room wall in Oxford, the graphic image of an orgy. Suddenly everything made sense. But where was Eloise?

She placed one foot firmly on the floor to try and control the dizziness building inside her head. 'Come with me, Libby,' said Carmelle, calmly taking her by the hand. She glanced over her shoulder and beckoned to the two men to follow. She led them to one of the recently vacated beds, in a quiet secluded corner. Stéphane gently whispered in her ear, 'Remember, Libby, you don't have to do anything you don't feel comfortable with.'

Carmelle slowly unzipped the back of Libby's taffeta gown to reveal her silken underwear and sighed with contentment. 'You really do have a perfect body,' she said, as she slipped her own dress from her shoulders. Libby stretched herself luxuriously across the bed and gazed upwards; nobody had said these kind words to her before and, although she struggled to believe it, Carmelle made her feel special, valued. Roland gently removed her shoes and began to massage her toes, one by one, and then he pushed his thumbs deep into the balls of her feet, expertly relieving the tension after the efforts of the day. Stéphane drew his fingers through her hair, firmly massaging her scalp in circular movements, intermittently stroking her brow to erase the worries and stress of her life. Libby breathed in the warm comforting air and felt liberated and more relaxed than she could ever remember. Carmelle worked on Libby's body with her hands and her mouth, pleasuring her in ways that Libby had never experienced or imagined were possible. She could hardly process the six hands that were working as one, devoting themselves entirely to her pleasure. The time passed in a blissful haze and finally they came to rest, lying together in companionable silence. She couldn't believe what had just happened. She felt strangely powerful; none of it had made her feel ashamed; she had no regrets. The only thing that was playing on her mind was that she didn't feel that she had given much, she had simply accepted all that was offered. Would her new friends think she had been very selfish, or did they freely give pleasure, without expecting anything in return? Perhaps the simple fact that Libby enjoyed herself was pleasure enough for them.

As Libby glanced to one side, she realised that the solitary man who had been quietly watching them, was her husband. He caught her eye, a smile forming on his lips, and then, without a word, he walked towards her, leant over the reclining body of Carmelle, and kissed her gently. He then turned and walked away.

'Who was that, Libby? I think you have a lot of admirers,' Carmelle asked.

'That, Carmelle, is my husband.'

As her eyes slowly became accustomed to the light, she noticed Eloise who was on her hands and knees on a rug with two men, engaging in an activity, the likes of which Libby had never seen before. 'What are they doing?' she asked Stéphane.

He smiled. 'Ah yes, in our country we call this the Eiffel Tower, three bodies form the shape of the iconic Parisian landmark. Maybe we could try it sometime?' he suggested provocatively.

As they walked over the cobbled courtyard towards the exit, Stéphane stopped. 'It has been a pleasure to meet you. Perhaps we could meet again tomorrow. It's great here on a Sunday. The outdoor pool is open all day – naturist, of course – and the staff provide a delicious al fresco lunch. There is access to "*Le Bois*" a beautiful woodland area designed for adult play and, believe it or not, they even have a foam party by the pool sometimes. Does that sound good?'

'I think it sounds great,' said Libby enthusiastically, although she wondered whether Alex would agree. Eloise and Alex had not spent much of the evening together.

'It sounds pretty good,' said Alex rather tentatively. 'Are you up for it, Eloise? Roly? Okay, how about we meet you at the front gates at ten o'clock?' he asked, turning to Carmelle.

'Perhaps we should make it more like eleven thirty. I don't think you'll be awake at ten, Alex,' Libby suggested confidently.

Stéphane's face broke into a wide smile. He leant forward, cupping Libby's face in both hands and kissed her lightly on her lips, before bidding the others a good night. 'Until tomorrow...'

Carmelle brushed Libby's lips seductively, and whispered, '*à demain*...'

As they drove by taxi back to the hotel, everyone was calm and peaceful, sated after a full evening of entertainment. Suddenly the driver slammed on his brakes as a herd of wild boar appeared out of nowhere and ran across the road in front of them, blinking in the flickering headlights. They looked like cardboard cutouts. 'Wow,' Libby mused, 'it all happens in Paris.'

It was nearing four o'clock in the morning and the roads were now deserted. As Libby reflected on the evening, she studied Alex, now fast asleep, his mouth open and his head resting on the plush leather seat. As she gazed at the sky, etched with deep pink and navy blue, she wondered if there would be a new understanding between them; she would no longer be controlled by Alex. She could feel an inner strength and resilience developing within her, a new-found confidence, like the warm glow of the sunrise heralding a new day.

***

'Shut the curtains, for God's sake!'

Libby looked at Alex, his hair dishevelled, his face grey and creased by sleep. This morning he looked much older than his years. He rolled over angrily, pulling the covers over his head. 'I said, shut the bloody curtains…'

'We agreed that we would meet Stéphane and Carmelle at eleven thirty, and it takes half an hour to get there,' Libby said brightly, 'so we'd better get moving.' She glanced out of the window, the sky was deep blue, promising a hot day ahead. She selected a simple halter-neck floral sundress and a pair of flip-flops to wear to the club and then jumped into the shower.

As the water trickled comfortingly over her body, she realised she was looking forward to the day ahead. The evening at the club had been enlightening and empowering. She had had the privilege of gaining a brief insight into the wonders of human nature. She was aware that, for some people, it would be unthinkable; they would be highly critical of a club like this, considering it immoral, distasteful and degrading. Libby understood these views, she would have agreed with them before this trip, it is all too easy to criticise something that is outside your experience. Sex is, without question, a powerful driver, but Libby's experiences the previous evening had been so much broader than this. It was more about showing respect for each other; giving as well as receiving; it was all about consideration and generosity within a loving partnership. She would still wrestle with ingrained moral beliefs, but she had become more open-minded to a new world of possibilities.

She realised that she had also gained more understanding of herself and of how low her self-esteem and self-image had become. With Alex, she had become subservient, submissive. She believed him to be right, that she was insignificant and worthless. She knew that success in life has so much to do with self-belief; if we believe we can do something, then we are halfway to success. Stéphane and Carmelle had given her some confidence that she was a significant and unique being in her own right, a strong independent woman. But she recognised that she had a long way to go before she wholeheartedly believed in herself.

'Alex, would you prefer to stay in bed today? If so, I am happy to go with Roly and Eloise,' Libby said, frustrated that he had not moved a muscle since the beginning of her shower. He roughly threw the covers off and pushed his way past her into the bathroom.

Suddenly gloom descended. Would Alex ruin everything?

Twenty-One

'*Bonjour, mes amies!*' said Stéphane cheerfully. They all greeted each other with hugs and kisses. 'I was a little worried that you would still be asleep!'

Libby smiled. He might not have known it, but he was dangerously close to the truth. Alex had brightened up considerably since meeting Roland and Eloise earlier in the car park. He could change his mood in an instant, but Libby was relieved that, for the moment, he seemed okay. So far, so good.

'It's a beautiful day; shall we go for a swim?' suggested Carmelle. 'The unisex changing rooms are over here.' She took Libby's arm and together they wandered towards the small stone building near the swimming pool. She giggled. 'I don't know why they bother with changing rooms here; we are all naked. Don't you find it funny that we have to go into a cubicle to take our clothes *off*?'

Libby laughed. She had been feeling a little nervous about seeing Carmelle and Stéphane again, but they had immediately put her at ease with their relaxed manner and conversation. She felt that they had already forged a special connection between them, which she found quite surprising. It normally took her far longer to form friendships. Maybe it was to do with the intimacy of their first meeting.

Libby peeled off her sundress and draped a large towel around her to hide her body. She had not really considered how she might feel walking around naked in broad daylight. Carmelle strode out of the adjacent cubicle, wearing nothing but gold-rimmed designer sunglasses, and an overflowing carry-all that she draped effortlessly over her shoulder.

'Libby, shall I put your towel in my bag? It's a hot day, you won't need it, I promise,' she said as she carefully relieved Libby of her covering. 'One of the first things I learnt about naturism is that, if you are naked, you don't draw attention to yourself, but if you wear something, anything at all, everyone stares.'

They selected six sunbeds by the perimeter wall of the swimming area and carefully positioned sun umbrellas to protect them from the heat of the day. 'Libby, this is a wonderful place isn't it?' They leant on the wall and Carmelle pointed to a row of small tents in the distance. 'We are in one of France's famous naturist campsites. Naturism is very popular here in France. This particular campsite is adult, couples only, but there are many beaches across Europe that are more family orientated. I love to see young families enjoying the freedom, and the feeling of the wind, the rain and the sun on their bodies.' She smiled. 'There is so much I could tell you about the wonders of naturism, I could talk all day about it!'

Libby gazed across the dry scrubby land to the line of small tents and understood the draw of a campsite such as this, and she realised that she was becoming less self-conscious with every minute that passed. 'The trouble is, what do you do if it is cold?'

'Haha, then you put your clothes on. I'm certainly not a cold naturist!' Carmelle answered with an exaggerated shiver. 'But I must let you know that there are rules within the campsite that everyone must adhere to. People must be allowed to enjoy the quiet peaceful atmosphere, so no wild parties here! Everyone must be naked, and no sexual activity is allowed. In all the years that we've been coming here, we have never seen anyone break these rules.' She paused. 'Not all lifestyle people are naturists, and vice versa... is that how you say it?'

'Yes, I understand what you're saying. So, although we are in the grounds of Chez Fleurie, not everyone here would go to the club?'

'That's right, some people here might not approve but, generally speaking, Europeans are open-minded and non-judgemental. I believe that many of our textile friends mistakenly think that, because naturists like to be naked, it is automatically all about sex, but this is not true. Sometimes I don't tell them that we're naturists, it's simpler that way...'

Libby glanced around. People were now pouring in to enjoy the facilities and claim their sunbeds. Carmelle reached into her holdall for a bottle of factor-fifty sun cream. 'I don't want to get old and wrinkly before my time,' she said, smoothing a generous amount of the white cream onto her thighs. 'Would you like some, Libby?'

Just then they spotted Stéphane, Alex and Roland paddling through the foot bath at the entrance. Stéphane stood confidently with his towel draped around his neck, looking tanned and stylish – rather like a French aristocrat. Roland and Alex stood behind him, their shoulders bowed, looking embarrassed and uncomfortable. Their startlingly white skin stood out in a throng of sun-bronzed bodies. 'I love and adore men…' Carmelle said dramatically, before whispering conspiratorially in Libby's ear, 'but their private bits… now they are surely an accident of nature!'

Libby laughed. She loved the direct and refreshing way Carmelle spoke in her irresistible broken English. 'But, Carmelle, you've just told me about naturism – surely your comments don't quite fit in with the ethos?' Libby asked, slightly tongue-in-cheek.

'You're right,' she said, putting her hand over her mouth, her eyes smiling. 'But isn't it just human nature to observe?'

The two women watched as Alex and Roland negotiated their way past all the reclining bodies and scurried towards the safety of their sunbeds. Alex, usually so confident and self-assured, now looked like a rabbit in the headlights. Libby, although she took some satisfaction from his discomfort, found herself almost feeling sorry for him.

'Roland, where is Eloise?' Although Libby had not warmed to her, she cared enough to be concerned.

'Don't worry, she's in the shop by the reception. They sell a huge selection of clothes, sarongs and other beachwear… quite bizarre really, considering this is a naturist campsite, but ask not the reason why! I'm sure Eloise will have no trouble spending a few euros.'

Libby smiled. She was beginning to like Roland; he was caring and considerate, and he gave an expert foot massage. She closed her eyes and relaxed as the warm sun caressed her body, everything felt like a dream. Here she was in the outskirts of Paris, in a beautiful setting in the grounds of a French château, lying naked in the sun beside a stylish French woman who had given her a lot of pleasure the night before. She glanced admiringly at Carmelle, who was now flicking through *Vogue* magazine, looking very alluring and attractive. It had come as quite a revelation – an awakening of a hidden desire that she didn't know existed – that she would find intimacy with another woman exciting. This weekend was turning into a voyage of discovery.

Her peace was suddenly interrupted by Alex dive-bombing into the pool and laughing raucously as he struggled to mount a lime-green inflatable crocodile in the middle of the pool, toppling backwards into the water several times before clumsily capsizing the float. Libby cringed, feeling embarrassed by his loud laughter. Why did he have to be so annoying?

'I think it's time for a pre-lunch apéro,' Stéphane suggested thoughtfully. 'It's just past midday, would anyone like to join me? We can leave everything here, except towels to sit on, and perhaps a few euros. Our stuff will be quite safe while we have lunch.'

Carmelle dug deep into her bag and pulled out a red-and-turquoise beaded necklace 'I'm coming, just give me a minute.' She carefully arranged the striking item of jewellery around her neck, brushed her hair, and flamboyantly sprayed herself with cologne. 'When I go out for a naturist meal, I have to look my best,' she said with a salacious wink.

Eloise was already sitting by the bar sipping an Aperol Spritz, deeply engaged in conversation with a ruggedly good-looking man in his early sixties. 'She looks as if she's having a good time doesn't she? And I find that if Eloise is happy, then life is good,' Roland said contentedly. 'Now, what can I get you all to drink? It's definitely my round.' Just as he was ordering the final drink Alex arrived, dripping wet and rather flustered. 'Alex, my old mate, do you fancy bubbly or a beer?' he asked, throwing a friendly arm around his shoulder.

Lunch was a friendly affair. A bronzed member of staff with rope-like dreadlocks and a friendly face served up individual plates of paella from a huge cast-iron pan balanced on the open flame on the grill. Everyone queued patiently, inhaling the tempting aroma of saffron, seafood and fried chicken. They then carried their plates piled high with food and sat at one of the many rustic long tables, shaded by green parasols, that comprised the outdoor dining area. Large carafes of rosé were placed on each table, with jugs of ice, and olives to nibble. Roly filled their glasses and proposed a toast; '*A nous et à la liberté*,' he said with a flourish. The surrounding couples raised their glasses in unison. '*Bon appétit!*'

'Alex always spills his food; at least we won't go home with a load of washing!' Libby said. 'I just hope you don't burn any delicate areas, darling!' Alex, who was sitting at the end of the table, raised his eyes to heaven but said nothing.

Libby sipped her cool wine, quietly absorbing the calm relaxed atmosphere and the gentle hubbub of French conversation, enjoying their spirit and *joie de vivre*. She was surprised at how easily the conversation flowed, considering the challenging dynamics between them all. As she savoured every mouthful of the delicious Spanish delicacy, she was reminded of the fabulous flamenco dancers in the courtyard the previous evening; so much had happened in such a short space of time. She glanced across the table. Eloise and Roland were deep in conversation. She couldn't hear what they were saying, but they seemed so close and loving. Roland teased her with a large prawn before popping it into her open mouth. Eloise gave him a fishy peck on the cheek, and they both giggled. How can it be that last night Eloise was having wild sexual adventures with two strange men, and today here they are a happy couple, content in each other's company? They had an open marriage, and, for them, it obviously worked. She turned her attention to Alex who was also observing the couple, his expression desolate. Perhaps he realised in the cold light of day that his affair with Eloise was nothing more than a fleeting moment in time. How Libby longed to have a close loving relationship with her husband, but Alex was different; he had been deceitful and dishonest.

'Libby, what do you think?'

She jumped, realising that she had not heard a word of the conversation. 'I'm sorry, I was a million miles away. Say again?'

'Do you fancy some gâteau?' asked Stéphane gently. 'It looks creamy and very chocolatey.'

'If I eat or drink any more wine, I will sleep all afternoon,' said Libby with a satisfied sigh.

After lunch they returned to their sunbeds. Libby found herself unavoidably lying next to Eloise. She gave her a withering look. Eloise was really nothing special; she happened to be around at the time when Alex was available. She consoled herself with the fact that she had no physical attributes that compared to Carmelle or herself. In fact, her midriff was rather going to seed, and her bottom was considerably less than perfect.

'Well, Libby, did you enjoy yourself last night?' Eloise asked rather sheepishly. 'I didn't notice you in the playrooms. Roly is such a sweetie, I'm sure he kept an eye on you.'

Libby decided that the time was right to confront Eloise. 'It has taken a while to sink in what's been going on between you and Alex, but I have to accept it. What alternative do I have?'

'You've probably gathered by now that Alex and I aren't mutually exclusive. We didn't mean any harm, it's really just like a hobby for me. Roly and I thought this trip would be a good chance for you to see the lifestyle we enjoy. You never know, you and Alex might like it too.'

'You are assuming an awful lot, Eloise. I'm nothing like you. Much as I enjoyed last night, I'm finding it difficult to snap into this new way of life; it's a huge amount for me to process. I have experienced nothing but kindness from Roly and our new French friends. They seem to be a little more honourable than you, Eloise, more open and honest. I have had nothing but deception and emotional turmoil, verging on bullying, from Alex for months so, although you have good intentions, I can't just forgive him and pretend that nothing has happened. He needs to change.'

'I completely understand, Libby. He wasn't like that with me, so I can see where you're coming from. I realise that Alex and I made a big mistake; we got carried away in the heat of the moment. I'm afraid Alex didn't need a lot of persuasion.'

'I can see how it happened,' said Libby sadly, 'we've been married for a few years now and perhaps we have become rather mundane and set in our ways. He was a libertine at university...'

'Don't take it to heart, Libby, we're only human, and life is short. Roly and I find pleasure in this lifestyle. Even if you decide it's not for you, we planned this trip with the best of intentions. Is it really worth breaking up your marriage for what is realistically only a passing phase? I do hope we can be friends. Roly is a very kind man and he'd never want us to hurt anyone. But maybe, Libby, you will have to accept that Alex has a different outlook to you and, in time, this is something you might be able to enjoy together. Sex is only a small part of a relationship; maybe this weekend will help you to rebuild your marriage, now that you realise that I am not a threat to you.'

Libby's mind was overwhelmed: Alex was involved in a tangled web of deception. Perhaps Eloise wasn't so bad after all.

Twenty-Two

They followed the narrow path which led into the mixed pine and oak forest, appreciating the wide canopy of trees above them, relieved to be protected from the harsh glare of the sun. They walked a while, enjoying the peace of the forest, all feeling subdued after a substantial lunch. Eventually they came to a clearing and discovered a settlement of military-style tents, half wooden and half canvas, all with beamed wooden ceilings and covered with olive-green canvas. Libby was struck by the ethereal atmosphere and magical quality of this small area, hidden deep in the forest. At the entrance there was a single log inscribed with the words, *Le Bois*. This was an area where adults could freely indulge in any fantasies they could ever possibly imagine.

The group sat on a long bench to one side watching quietly, keen not to disturb or distract anyone. In the hut in front of them, there were three couples freely enjoying each other's bodies, on a huge round bed. They were all laughing and chatting together, talking in a language Libby didn't understand – perhaps German or Dutch. As she watched, one of the happy band of revellers beckoned to her to join them. Libby put her hands in prayer position and bowed her head in thanks but declined his invitation. She felt quietly satisfied to have been singled out as a desirable addition, but in reality she felt more like running a million miles away. 'Wow, they're a friendly bunch aren't they, Stéphane?'

'They are, Libby... the more the merrier!' he said, shrugging his shoulders. 'And why not?' he added with a grin.

Libby creased her brow, deep in thought: it was one thing to be together with her friends, but quite another to join a group of strangers. She smiled inwardly. Eloise would probably have jumped at the chance, but they didn't ask her...

'I've brought a few toys with me,' said Eloise, producing a velvet collar and chain from her bag. 'Alex, I thought you might enjoy this. I've also brought a blindfold and a few other bits and pieces for us to enjoy if we would like to.'

'Shall we go in that tent over there, it's empty now,' Stéphane said, putting his arm around Eloise.

'I'll be there in a minute, Stéphane, there is something I must do first.' Eloise faced Alex.

He gazed at her with large doe eyes and whimpered, 'Do with me what you will.'

She slowly attached the deep purple collar around Alex's neck and led him by the chain to the side of the tent where she tied him securely to one of the wooden uprights. 'Stay there, and maybe if you're good, you will get a reward.' With that she hopped onto the soft leather bed with Stéphane.

I can't just be a taker from the wood pile, I have to give something back, Libby thought inwardly. She found herself drawn to Carmelle. She wondered if it was simply because she felt safer with another woman, or if it was more than this?

The afternoon passed in a blissful haze; there was an interchange of bodies, of freely giving and receiving, all the friends enjoying each other in this mystical place where they could explore new boundaries, where creativity and imagination were truly unleashed.

Alex stood silently, watching, statuesque throughout. Libby couldn't help but wonder what was going through his mind as he observed her being a powerful individual: a sensual woman, freely engaging with other people.

Just as they were about to leave, Eloise and Carmelle turned to Alex, still chained, and they finally gave him the reward that she had promised him.

A single cry of ecstasy rang out through the forest, muffled only by the dense foliage.

As they followed the dappled path back to the swimming pool, Libby breathed in the balmy moist air; her whole body tingled with delight and pleasure – a heightened awareness – the likes of which she had never experienced before.

A kaleidoscope of colour greeted them on their return: blue, violet, yellow, green and red beams of light darted across a myriad of bubbles that formed the surface of a high wall of foam. The pulsating beat of disco music filled the air. An array of heads and shoulders bobbed up occasionally, some looking like Father Christmas with beards of foam, others more like mysterious moving snow sculptures, all with wide grins.

'Shall we join in? It looks like so much fun!' Libby said, skipping into the bubbles, without so much as a backward glance. She grabbed the waist of the last person in the conga, and they shuffled around the foam area in a snake-like parade, until almost everyone had joined in. She found herself sandwiched between a tall redhead and her friend in a wheelchair, everyone swaying to the beat of the drum. The atmosphere was intoxicating, electrifying. All at once, the leaders formed two lines, linking arms, and the stragglers wriggled their way between them and joined the end of the line, with all the light-hearted fun of a barn dance. As Libby negotiated the narrow gap between the rows, she slithered past Stéphane, Carmelle and Roly, but she couldn't see Alex or Eloise, but, at this moment in time, Libby didn't have a care in the world. She laughed as she absorbed the delights of another new experience – slippery human connections – in this truly amazing adult playground.

The pink and pale blue tinge of early evening spread across the sky, reflecting a soft pastel glow over the bubbles. Libby realised with sadness that it was nearly time to leave this magical place and return to the hotel.

'It's Happy Hour; time for one last cocktail?' she asked the others as she reluctantly stepped out of the foam, her body still covered with bubbles. 'I think I'd do well to go and rinse off first.' As the jet of hot water streamed deliciously over the nape of her neck, she sighed with satisfaction. It had been a magical day – a wondrous weekend – full of unexpected pleasure, new-found friendships and rich experiences. Some of her beliefs in life had been challenged in transformative ways; she had discovered so much about herself. She knew it would all take time to process, but she now felt stronger; empowered to make changes for the better.

But that was all for another day. For now, she felt truly happy.

When she returned, the atmosphere was calm and peaceful, the air filled with a gentle hubbub of conversation, all enjoying the company of friends after a long and enjoyable day.

'I wonder where Alex and Eloise are,' Roly said quietly as he placed a large tray of mojitos on the table. 'They've probably gone for one last dip in the pool.'

As she sipped her cool drink, Libby noticed Alex and Eloise wandering towards them in silence. They both looked exhausted.

'Come on, you two, did you go into the foam? We didn't see you there… actually it was almost impossible to see anything… especially without my glasses,' Roly added with a chuckle.

Alex stared at the rapidly diminishing foam. 'No, we just went for a walk and a chat,' Alex replied. 'I needed to clear my head,' he said, directing a cold stare towards Eloise. 'Didn't I?'

Libby, anxious that Alex did not put a dark cloud on proceedings, turned her attention to Stéphane and Carmelle. 'Thank you for suggesting that we spend the day here; I've never been anywhere like this before. You're very lucky to live nearby, will you come here again soon?'

'But of course, we love it here,' Stéphane said, touching his lips extravagantly and throwing a kiss into the air. 'It has been such a pleasure to meet you all.'

Carmelle took Libby's hand in her own. 'You are beautiful, Libby. You light up a room when you walk in, like the brightest star in the night sky.' She stroked the side of Libby's face. 'And I'm not just talking about physical beauty – this is only skin-deep and fades in time – I'm thinking about you; your body and your mind. You really are a very sensual and powerful woman; one in a million, and – I think you say in English – drop-dead gorgeous!'

Alex stared at Carmelle, opening and shutting his mouth as if to say something.

'*Ma chérie*, here is my mobile number,' Carmelle whispered, pushing a crumpled piece of paper into Libby's hand. 'Message me,' she urged. Stéphane and Carmelle drained their drinks and said their fond farewells. Stéphane paused. 'Treat her well, Alex, she is very special.' They turned and walked together hand in hand towards the château. The others sat in silence watching as the couple disappeared from view.

'Oh dear, back to the humdrum world of work and chores tomorrow,' Roly said, bringing them all back down to earth with a bump. 'I think we should meet up again before too long. We could always go to The Boudoir in the City, it's reputed to be a brilliant club!'

'I've had a great weekend, and I am relieved that everything is now out in the open,' Eloise said as she gently squeezed Libby's hand. 'I would really like us to be friends. What say you, Libby?'

Libby gazed into the distance. She had learnt so much from her experiences here in this beautiful place: she appreciated the openness and honesty, but the jury was out as to whether the lifestyle choices were for her. She needed time to consider this. She had really enjoyed Roly's company, and she was even beginning to warm to Eloise. 'I would love to meet up again, perhaps we could go out for dinner? There are so many great restaurants in London with Michelin stars, and maybe we could even combine an early supper with a show – I would absolutely love to go to Covent Garden,' she suggested.

A flicker of disappointment registered on Roly's face, before he said kindly, 'That sounds like a great plan, Libby.'

Alex sat in silence; he had been completely disarmed and on the back foot. The excitement of his illicit affair with Eloise had been completely defused, and now that everything was out in the open, it didn't seem to have the same appeal.

Libby studied her husband, his head bowed, and his shoulders hunched; he looked exhausted, broken. She acknowledged that she still had feelings for him, but was he worth fighting for? He would have to change; he would have to be more like Stéphane or Roly; he would have to care. Her mind returned to the seed of an idea that she had had in the dungeon, as she watched his pleasure at being restrained. The idea had now germinated into a plan which she would soon put into action. She resolved to rebuild herself stronger, more resilient. She would no longer be content to hide in Alex's shadow.

Twenty-Three

'I can't believe it; my stupid brothers have played right into my hands,' Alex exclaimed in disbelief, clutching a letter that had just been delivered. 'How can they be so dense? You should read this, Libs, it's totally absurd. They are both demanding to resign as joint power of attorney for our mother, accusing me of all kinds of things: lying, cheating, bullying, harassment. God, I could go on…'

Libby poured coffee into two cups and passed one to Alex. 'Good grief, this doesn't sound good, Alex. Are the accusations fair? Have you been unreasonable?'

'What do you think?' he asked, spitting out his words. 'How could you even think that? You have absolutely no idea how hard it is to manage my useless brothers on top of everything else. I have to check that all the legal systems are in place, deal with endless health and financial stuff on my own, and not only that, but I've also had to sort out her house, sell a lifetime's accumulation of junk and liaise with property consultants and estate agents, all giving different advice over how to sell that old ruin of a house. I don't know why I bother; I know a darn sight more than property consultants for God's sake!' He paused for breath. 'And Matt and Andrew are about as useless as a chocolate teapot.'

'Why do you think that they have played right into your hands, Alex? Surely this isn't what you really want is it? Aren't you going to end up with more hassle if you go it alone? Wouldn't it be better to apologise, and find positive ways of working more constructively together?'

'The point is, Libby, I am a solicitor,' Alex shouted, banging his fist angrily on the table. 'I know what I'm doing. I could have asked a colleague to take on the work, but why would I do that? I'm an expert in the field; this is what I do! Matt is nothing but a waster, strumming his wretched guitar, and swanning around America pretending to work – he really hasn't got a clue – and as for Andrew, and that bloody wife of his... I give up! I wouldn't care if I never saw either of them again.'

'You don't mean that, Alex, family is important, they're your flesh and blood,' said Libby firmly.

'Believe me, Libby, I do.'

'So, what are you going to do?' she asked coldly.

'This morning I'm going to draft two official letters for my secretary to complete, accepting their resignations with immediate effect. They'll have to fill out the appropriate paperwork, and I suppose I'll have to inform the authorities. I trust it won't affect my reputation.'

Alex drew his fingers roughly through his hair. 'But, if I'm canny, I just might be able to work this to my advantage,' he said, looking at Libby with a glint in his eye. 'I need to make a plan; I'll be working late at the office tonight.' Without hesitating, he grabbed his briefcase and stormed out of the house, banging the door behind him.

Libby poured herself another cup of coffee and gloomily stared out of the window into the greyness of another day. A week had passed since they had returned from Paris, but it seemed like a lifetime ago, more like a dream than reality. She had come back full of good intentions to be more assertive: she would not accept Alex's constant put downs, and she would find ways of feeling better about herself. But, so far, nothing much had changed. She just felt tired and lethargic. She had hoped that Alex would have changed his attitude towards her. Perhaps there was a flicker of hope; he did seem more caring when they were together, but the trouble was, he was spending more and more time at the office, and when he was at home, he was usually asleep. And now, she knew he would be totally obsessed with power of attorney issues, but she contented herself with the fact that at least he would be doing something useful rather than chasing after impossible dreams.

Holding the letter in front of her, she read the words again – lying, cheating, bullying, harassment – the words went round and round in her head. Was he a bully? Her heart sank. Matt and Andrew were voicing what she already knew. Alex had to be in charge, he didn't suffer fools gladly and he controlled her every move. He had taken her credit card away, taken her name off the joint bank account and, as she glanced round the sitting room, it was as if she was visiting a bachelor pad. And now she had a growing suspicion that he was tracking her movements on his mobile phone. As she read the words on the page, she wrung her hands in despair. But what did Alex mean by implying that the two brothers were doing just what he wanted? That he could turn this to his advantage? That he would make a plan? The dark suspicions forming in her head were unthinkable.

Her mind suddenly returned to Chez Fleurie. It puzzled her that, in that setting, Alex wanted to be passive, submissive. Did he enjoy the humiliation of being restrained, of watching his wife and lover engaging with their new-found friends, of being powerless? It would have made more sense to her if Alex had been the dominant partner, holding the chains.

Her train of thought was suddenly interrupted by the shrill ring of her mobile phone.

'Hi, Libby, Roland here. How are you doing?'

She smiled, pleased to be taken away from all the worries coursing through her head.

'I'm okay, thanks, how about you?' Libby said, rather flatly.

'I'm ringing because...' He cleared his throat. 'We were a bit worried about you. Alex seemed...' He took a sharp intake of breath. 'He didn't seem to treat you well, Libby. We just wanted to check that you are safe.'

The word "safe" resounded in Libby's head. She had always associated "being safe" with being *physically* safe but this was only one form of abuse. Alex did not physically abuse her, he *emotionally* abused her. She did not feel safe with Alex.

'I'm fine, thanks, Roly...' she answered, not feeling ready to share her anguish.

'That's good,' he said. 'We wondered if you and Alex would like to come for a walk with us in Wytham Woods on Saturday afternoon. It looks like it's going to be a sunny day and it would be great to see you both again.'

'That would be wonderful, Roly. I'm not sure Alex will make it, but I am definitely up for a walk.'

'Okay, shall we meet at two o'clock at the car park?'

'You're on,' Libby said with a smile.

'Got to dash now, Libs, things to do, people to see. Look forward to catching up on Saturday. Bye for now.'

The idea of a walk in the woods lifted Libby's spirits; she looked forward to seeing Roland and Eloise again.

***

Saturday dawned bright and clear. As Libby pulled into the Wytham car park she felt happier than she had done for a long time. Although she hadn't known Roly and Eloise long, there seemed to be a connection between them, which was surprising to Libby, considering the lies and deception of Alex and Eloise's affair. Perhaps it was because of the open and honest way that Eloise had approached the subject with her and also, in some way, the physical connection that they had enjoyed altogether in *Le Bois*.

As Libby stepped out of the car she saw Roland standing at the opposite side of the car park. But where was Eloise? She watched as he placed one foot on the bumper of his car to put on his thick green walking socks and sturdy boots. He looked every bit the country squire, wearing green corduroy trousers, a fleecy checked shirt and a Barbour jacket – not the trendy extra-expensive kind, but the original well-oiled quality product, made many years ago. He placed a tweed cap over his unruly curls and strode towards her with a bounce to his step.

'Libby, how lovely to see you. I'm afraid it's just me today, Eloise couldn't make it, she's flat out under the covers with a streaming nose and a hot-water bottle. I think she was quite glad of the peace this morning!' His eyes softened. 'Poor darling.'

'Alex is working today so he couldn't make it either…'

'I really don't believe they're having a steamy encounter somewhere,' Roly said, his face breaking into a wide smile. 'I don't think Eloise would be up to much today!'

'That's not funny, Roland!' Libby remonstrated, before bursting out laughing, any potential tension between them dispersing in a second. 'Which way do you fancy walking? Up the field, round the circuit past the lodge back to the car park, or this way,' she said, pointing to an inviting gravel track lined with oak and birch trees. 'We will end up where we start whichever way we decide to go.'

Roly turned towards the field in front of them. 'Let's get the steep bit over with first, I really wish I was fitter,' he said, running his hands over his rotund belly. 'Too much of the good life I'm afraid.' Roly opened the wooden gate and waited for Libby to pass. The ground was damp from the rain that had fallen a few days before, so they kept to the single track that ran beside the small fence that separated farmland from the designated footpath. They paused to admire the impressive view of the Oxford spires in the distance and the giant white structure of the John Radcliffe Hospital rising up behind them.

'I'm glad we're on our own in a way, Libs, because it gives us a chance to have a good old chinwag. I rang, partly because we wanted to see you both again after our wonderful Paris extravaganza, but mainly because I was worried about you, Libby. I've known Alex since we were at university together. He is a very good friend, but I am under no illusion, I know only too well what he's like.'

Libby looked at Roland in surprise. 'You went to university with Alex? I had absolutely no idea, why didn't he tell me?' Libby gazed into the distance, realising that there was so much about her husband that she didn't know.

'We were great friends back in the day, but after university I got married, and then I applied to do a doctorate in Chicago and continue my academic studies. We stayed there for a few years whilst I completed my course. We loved everything about America, it was here that we learnt about alternative lifestyle choices, and we adopted an open marriage. Alex and I drifted apart during these years; our lives went in different directions. We reconnected in Oxford quite by chance, when I accepted a teaching position at Christchurch College, and we moved back to this country.'

'How interesting, Roly. This explains why you didn't come to our wedding! So, you were at university together?'

'Yes, we were both at Oxford. Alex was a law student, and I was studying PPE, so our paths didn't cross academically, but we certainly hit the social scene together.'

'What was Alex like at university?' Libby asked, intrigued to find out as much as could about what Alex was like before she met him.

Roland hesitated. 'Well, I guess you could say that he was like a heavily peated single malt: you either loved him or you hated him. Alex was the life and soul of the party. He took everything to the extreme, he could drink us all under the table, convince us all – hook, line and sinker – with all his nonsensical ideas, and he had the enviable art of seducing even the most unlikely suspects! Not only this, but he also managed to be a brilliant student. We all expected him to get a first, but it was not to be.'

'His mother told me that Alex was a libertine at university…'

'The libertine club in Oxford was more of a drinking club. It was for the rich privileged kids who could afford to drink champagne. They went round trashing bars and restaurants and then paid for the damage caused with their rich parents' credit card, or with huge bundles of cash. It was called the Bullingdon Club. We weren't actually part of this club, but we were definitely libertines in outlook. We drank freely, pushed all kinds of chemicals up our noses and, let's be honest, we had a lot of sex. We were like-minded freethinkers who made up our own rules. We were hedonists, seeking pleasure in whatever way we thought best, and I like to think that no one got hurt in the process.'

'It all sounds very full-on to me, very different to my college days. I think I worked too hard and didn't have enough fun. You say that the students either liked Alex or hated him. What was it about him that made people dislike him?'

'Alex was militant. He was renowned in the Oxford Union for being outspoken, aggressive and bullish. He ruthlessly ran roughshod over anyone that dared to disagree with his radical beliefs. He was certainly a force to be reckoned with.'

'Alex likes to be in control, that's for sure,' Libby muttered under her breath. 'So why did some students like him?'

'Because we always knew where we were with Alex. He was always scrupulously fair, he had an amazing sense of humour, and many stories to tell. But if you had a pretty girl on your arm, Alex never failed to flirt outrageously with them. The girls seemed to like that. He did manage to upset a few fellow students, but that's life when you're a youngster. We men, being hunters, thought the girls were fair game, but it did result in a few skirmishes, and one or two bloody noses,' he said, with a wistful smile.

'It all sounds terribly sexist to me, Roly, but I guess everything was different back in the day. In my experience, men take terrible risks with women in life don't they? More than once I've been at a dinner table and had my thigh stroked by a man who was married to one of my friends. They risked everything for a fleeting moment of excitement. So tell me, why did you end up being such good friends?'

'It's a good question. During our first year we played rugby together. He was a great fly half, and I was a prop forward. The after-match bath was riotous, and we certainly consumed a pint or two. We also started to play squash together, and there is nothing like squash for revealing your personality; you literally strip away the veneer of civilisation from your opponent and reveal the raw aggressive personality that lies beneath. No quarter was expected or given on court, but afterwards we always ended up having a laugh over a jug and a club supper.'

'Do you think Alex was having too much fun to get a first?'

Roly stopped in his tracks and looked directly at her. 'Something terrible happened to him in his final term at university. Alex changed from being confident and happy-go-lucky, to being quiet and introverted. I don't know what it was, Libby, but it must have been pretty serious. He was never the same again.'

Twenty-Four

'Let's follow this path further into the woods,' said Roland. 'It's more interesting than keeping to the main drag.'

As they turned left turning onto a small muddy path, Libby's head was full of questions. *What happened at university to change Alex?* It must have been significant – life changing – to affect him in the way that it did. She recalled his mother's description of him as a child, as being a perfectionist. Surely he would have been fiercely determined – driven – to achieve a first-class honours degree at Oxford? He would not have been satisfied with anything less. His mother said that he had had his head turned. By what? Or by whom?

'A penny for them, Libs…'

The light was slowly fading, and the chill of early evening was beginning to permeate her clothes. The wood was strangely quiet; all the walkers had gone home, even the birds seemed to have disappeared. All she could hear was the sound of her boots squelching in the mud, and the rhythmic beat of her heart as it pumped in her ribcage.

'Roland, it's funny how you sometimes think you

know somebody, but then it turns out you don't know them at all.'

Roland tutted. 'The number of times I've made friends, assuming they are good people, only to find out as time goes on, that my first impressions were completely wrong.'

'Yes, but I married him…' Libby said sadly. 'I wonder what happened that fundamentally changed him. It must have been quite serious.'

'The brain is a very powerful tool. I honestly believe that whatever happened to Alex, was so terrible, so torturous, that he might have blocked out the nightmare. I have tried over the years to encourage him to talk about it. I have no doubt that it would be cathartic for him to open up, but he just changes the subject. It's as if his whole body and mind puts up a barrier, Libs. He is undoubtedly damaged.'

As they walked, the wind started to rustle the leaves in the uppermost branches of the trees. 'We're nearly at the car park, shall we motor down the hill and finish our walk with a pint at the pub?'

Libby smiled. 'Good plan, Roly.'

Twinkling lights shone from the tiny diamond-paned windows of the welcoming country pub. Libby breathed in the distinct scent of wood smoke as they approached the entrance. They chose to sit on two large wooden rocking chairs, positioned on the uneven flagstones in front of a huge roaring fire. 'What can I get you, Libby? I think I'm going for a pint of Hooky, a delicious Oxfordshire brew! How about you?'

'I'll have the same please, Roly.' Libby reflected on their conversation. She hadn't known Roland for long, but she warmed to him. The special circumstances in which they met, and the respect he had shown her was very special. She hoped that her first impressions were right.

'Here you go,' Roland said, handing her one of two drinks. The golden liquid spilled over the rim of his glass as he raised it to his mouth. 'We used to come here occasionally when we were students. I remember it felt a welcome relief from the wilder venues we frequented!'

'Tell me more, Roly. Did you enjoy Oxford?'

'I did enjoy most of it although, quite frankly, I don't remember some of the crazy parties we went to. I feel rather ashamed now, but I think we had some fun at the time.'

Libby put her beer on a small table beside her and stroked her chin. 'Do you think Alex doesn't talk about what happened to him because he can't remember? Perhaps he was too drunk and high on coke?'

'I think he remembers all right. He just chooses not to tell.'

'But, Roly, this isn't what you suggested earlier. You said that he might have blocked the nightmare from his mind, because it was just too awful. Knowing what happened and deliberately refusing to disclose the details is a very different thing.'

Roland nodded. 'How perceptive, and you are right. The trouble is, I really don't know what has happened or how his mind is working. In the first two years of uni we used to tell each other everything; there wasn't much about

Alex I didn't know! I could certainly tell you a few juicy stories, Lib…' He hesitated. 'I feel sad and disappointed that he has never confided in me about whatever the problem was. Isn't this what friends are for?'

'It is quite a mystery. His mother told me that he was always a perfectionist and he liked to be in control. I would say that these personality traits are still with him today. How has he changed since that final term at Oxford?' Libby asked softly.

'Alex was always bubbly and full of life. He had radical views. He was either dearly loved or sorely hated by his tutors and fellow students alike. He impressively took command of any situation. He had charisma, intellect and charm; everyone listened to him. Yes, he was always in the midst of a throng of people, always in control…' His eyes glazed over as he absentmindedly lifted the glass to his lips.

'He still commands attention and likes to control,' Libby mused.

'But Alex loved and devoured women. He was drawn to women like a moth to a flame. He adored strong intellectual women, attractive women and spirited women with alternative viewpoints. He would use women mercilessly to satisfy his own carnal pleasure, and then, with no apology, he would reject them. He was truly hypnotised and beguiled by women.'

Libby listened with interest. She couldn't help but wonder why Alex had ever been attracted to her. She wasn't particularly intellectual or attractive, and she certainly didn't have radical views; she always thought herself rather a conformist. 'Why were you friends with him, Roly?'

'I guess I looked up to him. I was proud to be a friend of such a popular guy, a live wire. He was an influential presence, a free spirit. I longed to be like him, he seemed to have everything. But I was quietly confident about my intellectual superiority, and my stabilising influence. I was his best friend and his minder.'

'Gosh, Roly, this is fascinating.' Her back straightened as she gazed at her new-found friend with interest.

'And as for all the women, I hoped that some of his success would rub off on me. I was envious of all his conquests; he had hundreds of notches on his bedpost.' He peered at Libby over his half-moon glasses. 'But women often wrong-footed him. They could strip him of his control – and his clothes – in an instant.' He paused. 'The extraordinary power of women.'

'Some women are powerful, but some just pretend to be meek and mild to preserve the status quo, keeping their head down so as not to rock the boat.'

Roly stared into the distance, in a world of his own. 'But then it happened. In his final term he suddenly became withdrawn. He lost his appetite for speaking his mind in the Students' Union or for partying. He locked himself in his room for days on end. I became seriously worried about his mental health. I consoled myself with the notion that he wanted to spend more time studying, because exams were approaching. But when he did appear, he was angry and bitter about so many things. The most striking was his abject dislike of women. He distanced himself from everyone, particularly women.' He shook his head sadly. 'Maybe he was being affected by the drugs he was stuffing up his nose, or too much booze, but he scared me.'

'Why did he scare you, Roly?'

'Because when he was under the influence, he would talk about death and dying. I felt out of my depth. He would describe in graphic detail how he planned to jump off St Mary's tower onto the street below, in broad daylight. Even in the event of his own death, he wanted to be the centre of attention, he wanted to be in control. He had lost the will to live. I had no idea what to do, Libs.' His face creased with the painful memories. 'I loved him like a brother, and all he wanted to do was destroy himself. His followers and friends deserted him. I was the only person that would listen.' He reached over to cup her hands in his own. 'I'm sorry, Libs, this is not what you want to hear.'

Libby was shocked by his words. 'I need to hear this, Roly, to understand why Alex behaves in this way. How did he survive the final few weeks at Oxford?'

'He's probably never told you this, Libs, but he took his final exams in a local hospital specialising in mental health. He did extraordinarily well to achieve a second-class degree and to become a well-respected solicitor. That must have taken such grit and determination.'

'I had no idea.' Libby bit her lip nervously. 'What on earth could have happened?'

'Since our days at Oxford, Alex has regained some of his old spirit, but it is as if he has had the stuffing knocked out of him. He is still a perfectionist, and he likes to be in control…' He paused, locking eyes with Libby. 'But not in every situation…'

Libby drew her fingers through her hair. Suddenly her mind flashed to their recent weekend in Paris, and more specifically, to the dungeons of Chez Fleurie. 'Roly, you're right. In the dungeons at the club I saw a completely different side to Alex. He didn't want to be the person in control, as I would have expected, he chose to be submissive. He chose to be vulnerable, captured. And Eloise wielded her control. In *Le Bois* Eloise tied him up like a dog. He was passive and obedient.'

'I found this interesting, Libby, somewhat mystifying. I heard him say to Eloise, "Do with me what you will.".'

'I expected him to be the one with the chains, not with the collar and lead.'

'Alex has definitely changed over the course of the years. Perhaps in time he will be able to say the words we are curious to hear. He may never speak. Who knows? All I do know is that he is a good friend of mine, and, for all his faults, he will always be an important part of my life.' As if to draw a line under the conversation, he offered her another drink. 'And I feel the need for some pork scratchings,' he added with a grin.

He lent over the bar and crossed his legs. He reminded Libby of landed gentry, a Dickensian figure. But what he had said worried her. She knew so little about Alex, and these revelations did nothing to comfort her.

Roland crunched his pork scratchings noisily and with relish, his face becoming increasingly ruddy with the gentle heat of the fire and the effect of the ale as it slipped easily down his throat. 'It is good that we are alone this afternoon. It has given us a good chance to talk openly.'

Libby nodded, her mouth full of a large chunk of salty crackling.

'Alex seems to have become more erratic in his behaviour since he left university. We don't meet up as often as we should, but when we do get together, he seems increasingly bitter and less tolerant of people than he was. He has a hard edge to him. But I do see glorious glimpses of the old Alex too. I believe he is a good person, Libby; he has just been damaged by circumstances. Fate has clouded his judgement.'

'I have a lot to think about, Roly. What you have told me explains a lot about why Alex treats me the way he does, but it doesn't make it right,' Libby said, rounding her shoulders. 'I need to understand what happened to him. I will find out in the fullness of time.'

'Hang on in there, Libby. He is worth fighting for.'

Libby had nagging doubts, but she looked up and gave Roland a weak smile. 'I'll do my best to save our marriage, but it won't be easy.'

'I don't believe it,' exclaimed Amelia. She strode over to Libby and Roland, carrying a small baby in a colourful sheet of material strapped to her waist. 'Long time no see,' she said, her eyes fixed on Roland.

Libby almost jumped out of her seat in surprise. 'How are you? How is life with a baby?'

'How long have you got, Libs? I didn't realise that a tiny baby would be so exhausting. It's a 24/7 job, with no break for good behaviour.' She sighed extravagantly. 'But

Jack is pure heaven. Are you going to introduce me to your friend, hun?'

Libby was lost for words. It felt like two sides of her world had collided, and it felt rather uncomfortable. 'Amelia, this is Roly. We went to Paris together.' Her hand flew to her mouth. 'With his wife, Eloise, of course… and Alex.' Her body tensed with embarrassment.

'I am very pleased to meet you, Amelia,' Roland said cheerily as he shook her hand. 'Would you like to join us?'

'We won't disturb you,' she said, 'Tom and I are just grabbing half-an-hour while Jack is asleep, to remind ourselves that life goes on in the outside world.' She groaned. 'The nights are just the worst nightmare, Libs…'

'Let's catch up soon, Amelia.'

'Definitely.' Amelia eyed Roland up and down. She made no attempt to conceal her curiosity. 'I need to hear all about Paris.' She sauntered away to join her husband.

Roland smiled. 'Well, I'm mighty glad we're not having an affair. I've a feeling the gossip would be flying in the local "mum and babe" circles.'

'It might anyway,' said Libby dryly. 'Actually, Roland, I meant to say, I had a text message from Carmelle yesterday. We have an open invitation to stay with them in Paris. I think they enjoyed our company, and she was particularly flattering about me.'

'She did take a shine to you, Libs. I'm not surprised,' he said with a smile. 'What do you think? Would you like us all to meet up with Stéphane and Carmelle again?'

Libby looked pensive. 'I'm not sure. Don't get me wrong, I had an amazing time and I learnt so much about human nature, and about myself. But I'm not totally convinced that the lifestyle is quite "me". I certainly don't judge others who are libertines, in fact, I admire the openness, honesty and freedom that I witnessed first-hand. The whole experience has been transformative, life changing. It really has opened my eyes to a new world of possibilities. Looking back on it, it feels like a dream, completely surreal. There were so many surprises. I suppose it all depends on how things work out with Alex. But I think I would like to meet up with Stéphane and Carmelle again. Let's wait and see.'

Looking at his watch, he sighed. 'Unfortunately I must dash, Libby. Eloise will probably think I've run away from home.' He paused. 'I have so many good memories of our weekend together. I want you to remember that you are not just beautiful, but you have an inner depth of character that I am only just discovering.' He gave her a kiss on both cheeks, and a gentle kiss on the lips. '*A bientôt, ma chérie.*'

Twenty-Five

Alex sat on the settee amidst a sea of paperwork. 'I intend to visit Mum first thing tomorrow morning,' he said gruffly.

'She will be really pleased to see you, Alex. You haven't visited her for months.'

'I have some important business I need to discuss with her. A colleague is joining us for the meeting.'

Libby's heart sank. 'So, this isn't just a friendly visit?'

'Don't be daft, Libs. I have better things to do with my time than visit the old bat, but this is important.'

Libby studied Alex. Since they arrived back from Paris three weeks ago, Alex had been sullen and ill-tempered. This was due, in part, to his sudden and inexplicable impotence. Libby dreaded the feeble attempts at lovemaking, because it always ended in failure and a barrage of expletives. Afterwards he would cling on to her and sob, pleading for reassurance that she still loved him.

'What is the meeting about? I'm sure she would prefer to have a nice chat with you.'

'Never you mind, Libs,' he said firmly. He stood up, shoved his papers randomly into his briefcase and drained his whisky. 'I'll go to the spare room tonight, it's important I get a good kip, I will need my wits about me tomorrow, that's for sure.'

He stormed up the stairs without a backward glance, leaving Libby worried about what the meeting entailed with his mother. She was apprehensive about what he intended to do.

After a restless night, Libby awoke to the sound of the car pulling away from the driveway. She peeled back the covers and padded over to the window and drew back the curtains. The sky was dark grey and low clouds scudded from west to east. One or two windswept passersby lent into the wind as they made their way towards town. Libby felt dismal. She glanced around as Dusty trotted in, his claws clattering on the polished wooden floor. He jumped lazily onto the bed and found the warm patch where she had lain. He flopped his body luxuriously across the bed, yawned, and looked sleepily at his mistress.

'Oh, Dusty, life's good for you isn't it.'

After taking a quick shower and a bite to eat, she decided to take Dusty for a walk. Everything was grey: the sky, the street, even the people's faces. A walk usually lifted her spirits, but not today. She felt bleak. At least Dusty was enjoying the exercise. She passed through the wrought-iron gates at the entrance of the Oxford University Parks and strolled towards the river. The trees were starting to shed their leaves and grey squirrels were darting from branch to branch with impressive agility. She let Dusty off the lead for a quick run and he headed straight towards a clump of long grass. He looked rather comical as he trotted through the undergrowth, lifting his paws high off the ground. Libby smiled. He reminded her of horses performing dressage. 'Come here, Dusty, we're nearly at the duck pond.' She slumped down on a damp wooden bench by the side of the pond and watched a family feeding the ducks, with unrecognisable food out of a plastic bag. Libby remembered feeding the ducks with chunks of bread when she was a child, devouring most of it greedily, before the ducks could have it. But bread is apparently no longer considered a healthy option for ducks. She wondered why. Have ducks got more delicate stomachs these days? A young child squealed with delight as a duck waddled towards him, before he turned tails, and fled, screaming in terror. One of his parents rushed to comfort him. Libby envied them; she longed to be part of a loving family.

Her mind drifted to Alex. *What can I do to lift him out of his misery?* She had a bold idea that had first come to her whilst observing Eloise and Alex in the dungeons at Chez Fleurie. She would enlist a couple of her more broad-minded friends to help; it would take a bit of explaining, but she would cajole them; she would convince them. She would entice them with gifts of exotic lingerie, and a large glass of Chardonnay. She was confident that these two strong women would be willing to play a vital and exquisite role in her ambitious plan. It would be the best birthday treat Alex could ever wish for.

The rain was just beginning to fall so Libby decided to retrace her steps back home instead of walking the full circuit of the park. Thinking about Alex and her plan had helped to lift her spirits, and her pace quickened. She must select her friends carefully if her plan was to work. A lot had happened since she had last met up with them. Her weekend in Paris had opened her eyes to alternative ways of living. She contemplated sadly that her life at present was more about existing from day to day, rather than making the most of every day.

Her experiences in Paris had given her a different outlook on life; she couldn't stop thinking about it. Roly had posed the question: is it better to be in an open relationship, with mutual consent and honesty, or is it better to have an unsolicited affair, with all the deceit and dishonesty that goes with it? It was quite a conundrum for Libby, because, in her rulebook for life, neither sat comfortably with her. But, if she were to put aside her own moral stance, she was convinced that the open partnership was more honourable. She thought about Alex and his seedy affair and felt nothing but contempt for him. She wondered if, by bringing the relationship out in the open, it had lost its shine. Roland was thoughtful and kind, and he had been disappointed with Eloise; her behaviour had not been part of their lifestyle. She liked him and respected his views.

She realised she had just walked all the way home, and she hadn't registered anything about the journey at all; her mind was fully occupied. The afternoon stretched before her. She made a quick snack of cheese on toast and poured a glass of milk, turned on the TV and slouched on the leather settee. She realised that she was missing work and felt at a loose end. Even the draw of *Neighbours* and *Home and Away* didn't distract her from the thoughts that were churning in her mind. She wondered when Alex would return from his meeting with his mother. What mood would he be in? Desperate or jubilant? She drew her knees up to her chest and sighed.

She must have drifted off to sleep. She woke up with a start to the sound of the key turning in the lock. She didn't want Alex to know how lazy she had been. He strode into the sitting room and threw down his briefcase. She could detect a glimmer of triumph in his features. His eyes glinted darkly, and his lips curled into a tight smile. 'Mission accomplished, Libby. Our future is in the bag.'

'What on earth do you mean, Alex? What have you done?' she muttered.

'We had a successful meeting, and it was very well timed too. She is on the brink of losing her marbles completely.' He smirked. 'If we'd left it for more than a matter of weeks, she would have been declared medically unfit, so she would have been prevented from making decisions about her own affairs.'

'What about Matt and Andrew? What have they got to say?'

'Libs, keep up! They resigned their roles as powers of attorney so they don't have any right to voice an opinion on anything. I am in charge, and I make the decisions.'

Libby wrung her hands together. The tips of her fingers were icy. 'I hope you know what you're doing, Alex. I really don't like the sound of it.'

'Lighten up, for God's sake, everything is coming up roses.' His face broke into a smile. 'I did it for us, Libs.'

She lapsed into silence. She now knew without doubt what he had done. He had abused his position. This wasn't about "us". She looked at him with utter disdain. At that moment he looked evil. She hoped that, in time, his two brothers would contest the will, challenging the injustice, but she realised that, at the moment, there was absolutely nothing she could do except continue to visit his mother to brighten up her day.

There is a fine line between love and hate, and Alex was in danger of crossing that fragile divide. But she was not ready to give up on him yet. She remembered Roly's description of Alex's desire to take his own life at university. She would uncover what had happened to him, because it might explain why he is as he is. Things are often best laid bare. She had a glimmer of hope that, if he did find the courage to talk about the past, he might accept therapy to come to terms with everything, and to eventually find some peace and acceptance. Their marriage might survive.

***

It was close to midnight and the muffled sound of Alex's mobile phone sent shivers down Libby's spine. She strained her ears to hear the low mumbling and intonation of his voice through the closed door of the spare room. She wondered if he was having another affair.

'Libs, are you asleep?'

'Well, I was…' she said. She pulled the sheet under her chin, dreading what he was going to say.

'It's Mum, she's pegged it. I can't believe it.'

Libby could hear a hint of pleasure in his voice. Her eyes brimmed with tears. 'I was planning to go and see her tomorrow. I put it off because I had things to do. God, I wish I'd gone earlier. What happened? How did she die?'

'I have no idea. I didn't ask.' He stood like a statue at the end of her bed, his eyes fixed on the ground. Libby thought for a second that he was actually sad about the death of his mother. 'It's only been a week since my meeting with her.' He paused. 'This is just what I need,' he said furiously. 'There is so much bloody admin surrounding a death. I'll have to register the death, put a death notice in the paper and organise the flaming funeral. And how much will that cost?' He hesitated. 'But then there is the reading of the will,' he added.

'Alex, take a minute to mourn the loss of your mother. She was significant in your life; make time to remember her. All the other tasks can wait. I'll make a cup of tea.'

'Why the hell does the whole bloody world think that a cup of tea will fix everything? I'm going back to bed.' He turned, slamming the door behind him.

Libby's shoulders shook with emotion. She felt alone in her grief.

The next few days passed in a depressing flurry of activity. There was so much to do. Libby wondered if the system of vast quantities of legal documentation was put in place to distract them from their grieving and profound misery. But this was not so for Alex. He hardly mentioned Flo, or his feelings of loss – if he had any – he just soldiered on with the paperwork. He didn't mention his brothers or any relatives at all, but he efficiently put notices confirming her death in the local newspapers, and one in *The Times*.

Clutching her steaming coffee to her chest, Flo came into Libby's mind. She never enjoyed visiting Blackmore Rest Home; she could almost smell the institutional stench and the urine. But Flo was a survivor, a determined soul. She didn't suffer fools gladly, and she didn't think much of her daughter-in-law. She was always fearful of Alex, scathing about his life, disappointed in his achievements, but Libby believed that Flo loved Alex unconditionally.

Perhaps her fear had enabled Alex to carry out his final defiant act of control.

Twenty-Six

November is a bleak month for a funeral. All arrangements had been made, except for one thing: it was impossible to plan for the weather. Sheets of rain were lashing against the rough stone walls of the crematorium. Libby sighed deeply. Today was a day to endure; she knew it would be emotional; it would be stressful. There were a lot of unknowns; how many people would turn up; how long the ceremony would last; which family members would come. Alex had arranged a humanist service led by an independent celebrant. Flo had little interest in religion when she was alive, and she probably would have little faith in death either. The blurb that Libby had read about the service seemed a fitting tribute.

As individuals, couples and small groups arrived in dribs and drabs, Libby waited at the entrance to welcome them and show them to their seats. The atmosphere was sombre, and the small chapel was freezing cold. Libby pulled her black woollen coat tightly around her and shivered. Although she had an umbrella, the rain had hit the back of her calves, and the damp was seeping into her bones. She looked around for Alex, but he was nowhere to be seen.

Finally everyone settled on the unforgiving benches
and the note of the first song sounded: "Always Look on
the Bright Side of Life" by Monty Python. Libby's eyes
widened. She had, perhaps unwisely, left the choice of the
musical selection to Alex. She thought how incongruous
the choice of the first song was. It had a wonderful message
of optimism, and she loved the cheerfulness of the song,
but did it reflect Flo and her rather cheerless outlook on
life?

An elderly lady struggled to the front to stoop by the
coffin and read a poem. She was tiny and engulfed in
an extravagant fur coat and hat. Her face was lined and
wrinkled by the years, set in misery.

'Pardon me for not getting up.
'*Oh dear, if you're reading this right now,*
'*I must have given up the ghost.*
'*I hope you can forgive me,*
'*For being such a stiff and unwelcoming host.*'

Kelly Roper

As she spoke, everyone listened attentively, except for a
young man at the back who erupted into a loud coughing
fit, blowing his nose like a trumpet and spluttering at
frequent intervals. The words of the poem were quirky
and humorous, but the woman's face was like thunder.

As Alex stood up to talk about his mother, Libby
turned, her attention drawn to a lone man sitting on
one the benches towards the back of the chapel. He sat

stiffly, bolt upright, his head cocked to one side, listening to the words of the eulogy. He had fine oriental features, immaculate black hair greased in position and he wore a dark pinstriped suit that looked extremely expensive. He had a pale complexion, and Libby felt distinctly unnerved, as his eyes darted nervously from Alex to lock eyes with her. He looked totally out of place. Who was this mysterious stranger?

Libby turned her attention back to the funeral proceedings and realised, with some regret, that she had not listened to a word of Alex's tribute, it must have been very short and to the point, and now the strains of "My Way" rang round the chapel. Libby pondered the irony of this choice of song. She was not convinced that Flo had successfully lived her life *her* way. She thought it better suited to Alex. He certainly did everything, *his* way.

As the celebrant stood to make his closing remarks, Libby turned to study the smart-looking oriental gentleman once again, but the bench was empty. He had gone. Her face creased in puzzlement; who was he, and what connection did he have with the family? The spluttering person at the back interrupted Libby's thoughts. All in all, the service had taken place without a hitch. Finally the iconic sound of Simon and Garfunkel singing "Bridge over Troubled Water" filled the chapel with sadness, as the lyrics described the struggles of working through a trying time in life, and the sacrifices that have to be made along the way. Libby glanced at Alex, and she felt bitter. They were going through turbulent times, but she was the one that was having to sacrifice everything

Alex had booked the local pub, within walking distance of the crematorium, for the wake. The gathering was small and select; some of the people attending the service had decided to give the wake a miss. Libby envied them.

The pub was small and hot, muggy with damp clothing and stale breath. One of the guests plied her with a huge and welcoming glass of red wine. It was Alex's brother, Andrew. He had grown a beard, perhaps to compensate for the rapidly thinning hair on the top of his head. He looked older than his years. 'Libby, lovely to see you, even under these circumstances. How are you?'

Before she could answer, his wife, Jane, butted in. 'Well, I must say, what a strange service. There wasn't even one mention of God, or any hymns at all. Very odd if you ask me.' Her voice was thin, her face bland and expressionless. 'And using a sound system instead of the organ is just crass. Did you plan the service?'

'No, that was Alex's responsibility. I was in charge of organising the free bar and the buffet for the wake.'

'That explains it then,' she said, pursing her lips. 'Trust Alex to ruin his mother's send-off.'

'Darling, Flo wasn't particularly religious. I think the service was... okay.' His voice trailed off. It was obvious who was the boss in this relationship.

Libby's shoulders tensed with shame, thinking how Alex might have manipulated the will to his advantage. She disliked Andrew's wife, but she held a flame for Andrew: he was downtrodden, a victim, but he was genuine and kind. She felt guilty, as if by being silent, she was colluding with Alex in some way. Thankfully just at that moment she was approached by one of Alex's aged aunts, mercifully saving her from a potentially awkward conversation with Andrew and Jane.

'Libby, pretty good shindig, huh? The free bar is bloody brilliant.' To Libby's horror, Alex was already slurring his words. She dreaded to think what unguarded and careless sentiments might pass his lips. 'God, have you seen Andrew? He looks like death.' His hand shot to his mouth. 'Probably not the best description at a funeral is it?' He threw his head back and laughed. 'Just wait until he realises…'

Libby quickly propelled him to the other side of the room well away from Andrew's earshot. 'Alex, go and sober up. This is not the time or the place to make a fool of yourself,' she hissed.

He looked at her in astonishment. 'Don't tell me what to do. Get lost.' He turned abruptly towards the bar, his empty wine glass swinging high over the heads of the mourners.

A woman approached in the other direction, balancing a tray of gin and tonics precariously on the upturned palm of her hand. She wobbled, and all the drinks slid gracefully from the tray to the floor – as if in slow motion – with an almighty crash. 'Oops-a-daisy,' she bellowed, 'never fear, there are plenty more G and Ts where they came from.' She staggered her way back to the bar. Libby silently vowed never to offer a free bar at any party ever again. Everyone seems to be intent on getting pissed these days. She had noticed that Alex had been drinking more in recent months.

Libby glanced at her watch, willing the time to pass. She put her wine down on the nearest table and walked to the door, deciding that a blast of fresh air might give her fortification to get through the rest of the day. The chill of the early evening hit her cheeks with force; she gulped the cold air. The rain had now stopped, and water poured freely down the drainpipe behind her. She listened to the distant sound of traffic on the A34 and stared desolately into the distance. Suddenly she became aware of a figure standing silently in the shadows. Her eyes narrowed as she tried to focus. She couldn't be sure, but she thought she saw a glimpse of a man she recognised: pale, oriental, smartly dressed. She blinked and peered into the darkness again. He had gone. She shivered.

Returning to the wake, she was relieved to find that most people were finishing off a last vol-au-vent or samosa, draining their glasses, and were preparing to leave. She scanned the room. Alex was deep in conversation with two attentive women, but thankfully not with his brother. She breathed a deep sigh of relief; it was at last time to return home.

After the last mourners had gone, Libby thanked the staff of the pub and bundled Alex into the car. He had had far too much to drink; he was disgruntled and morose. 'Thank God that is over.'

It wasn't often that Libby agreed with Alex these days, but, over this, she did. She was pleased that the funeral was all done and dusted. 'It was a shame that Matt couldn't make it, but I guess it would have been hard to fit the funeral around his American tour.'

'I'm bloody glad he didn't come, he's such a waste of space.'

Libby glanced sideways at Alex who had now fallen asleep; his body awkwardly doubled up, his head bowed and swinging haphazardly with the bends in the road. Blinking against the oncoming headlights, Libby hated driving at night, and she felt out of practice. Alex rarely let her drive these days. She was relieved that he was not awake to criticise her or her driving ability.

She yawned, her body ached and she felt drained and miserable. Planning a funeral had felt busy and productive, and they had worked hard to ensure that it all went according to plan. And it did. But, as the rain lashed relentlessly against the windscreen, Libby worried about her future: tomorrow, next week, next month. She knew she must find positive focus in her life. She shot another glance at Alex. She felt love and hate for him in equal measure. But the balance had altered. She stared blankly into the darkness. Alex's birthday fell in mid-December, the beginning of the winter. She jutted out her jaw with grim determination: she would put her plan into action.

The time was right.

Twenty-Seven

It was Amelia that suggested a girls' day out. She always cooed to everyone how much she adored being a mum, and that Jack was the most perfect angelic baby. She was a "yummy mummy" in every sense of the word. But she also craved time out, to be herself. Amelia, rather than "Jack's mum". She longed to discard her baby-stained clothes, throw on something classy and sexy and pamper herself in the luxurious facilities of the spa, and have a good natter with her friends. Her husband had bought her a voucher on the internet: a day pass to The Carlton Hotel, Health and Well-being Centre. The pass included two guests. Libby wondered wryly whether Tom might have longed for some welcome relief from his wife too.

Rachel was very quick to accept the invitation. She was looking forward to a well-earnt break from her high-powered executive job. She often frequented spa clubs; pampering herself was an important part of her extravagant lifestyle. She believed in fostering her mental and physical well-being. She was footloose and fancy-free and she thought she was worth the investment.

Libby had considered the invitation carefully. An outing such as this seemed rather frivolous and self-indulgent, but she had never been to a spa before. Perhaps it was just what she needed.

The three friends walked through the main door into the high-ceilinged entrance hall of the spa, and were warmly greeted by a smiley receptionist, who handed them each a bath sheet, a fluffy white dressing gown and some towelling slippers. 'The changing facilities are over there. Just bring back your belongings to me when you're ready, and I'll store them safely for you.'

Before long they were in their bikinis and reclining on loungers by the side of the indoor pool. The centre was very quiet today. The pool was empty, and the water looked cool and inviting. Jets of water blasted out from one side, causing an intricate pattern of bubbles on the surface of the water.

Amelia breathed in the warm perfumed air. 'This is pure heaven, and there's not a blooming baby in sight.' She laughed. 'Come on, Libs, spill the beans about your trip to gay Paris! I can't wait to hear all about it. Who's idea was it? Was it an anniversary or birthday treat?' She looked pointedly at Libby. 'Or did Alex feel guilty about something?'

'Oh yes, tell us all the juicy gossip, Libs.' Rachel beamed with anticipation.

Libby was prepared. She knew her friends would want to hear all about her trip. 'Well, you've heard that fact is stranger than fiction. If I tell you the truth, you'll never believe me. Maybe I'll just make something up, and you can decide for yourself.'

'Libs, we want all the gory details,' Rachel said. She

stretched out luxuriously on the lounger, showing off her skimpy black-and-gold designer bikini and her washboard abs.

Libby took a deep breath. 'We didn't go on our own to Paris, we went with another couple. They seemed okay and we had a few things in common. Amelia, you might remember the guy I was with at the White Hart?'

'Ah the mystery bloke! I did wonder who he was. Come on, Libs, you can trust us. We will be very discreet.'

'Okay, this is when you're going to think I'm diving into the realms of fantasy. Roland's wife, Eloise, was none other than the blonde woman that you caught a glimpse of with Alex in Cafe Calypso, Amelia.'

'You are joking…' Amelia opened her mouth in surprise.

'She was having an illicit liaison with Alex.'

'Oh, Libby, how on earth could you go to Paris with your husband's lover?' asked Rachel. 'It sounds to me like a recipe for disaster!'

'I didn't know at the time that she was his lover,' Libby reminded them.

'When did you twig what was going on?' asked Rachel.

'It all seems so obvious in hindsight; the clues were all there. Alex was always late home from the office, he never wanted sex, I could even smell perfume on his collar. I questioned him, but he vehemently denied it. And I believed him. I was rather naïve wasn't I?'

'I'm sorry, Libs, it must be awful for you,' Rachel said sympathetically. 'How did you find out what was going on?'

'Well, on the first full day in Paris we did the normal touristy things. We wandered along the Seine, had lunch in a waterside restaurant and drank French wine. Roly had overindulged the evening before, so it was just the three of us. Well, you know what it's like, I had drunk far too much coffee, I was dying to go to the loo. The trouble was, I had horrible memories of French loos, standing on footprints over a hole in the ground. I dreaded going, but I braved it. I happened to glance out of a window of the washroom, before returning to the table, and what do you think I saw?' She paused for dramatic affect. 'Alex was kissing the waiter!'

'Oh, come on Libby, now you're fantasising.' They both giggled.

Libby suddenly became serious; her eyes welled up with tears. 'You can guess who he was really kissing, can't you?'

'Poor you, Libs. What on earth did you do?'

'I took a moment to compose myself, and then I walked out as if nothing had happened, although my mind was in turmoil.'

'You're a strong woman. I'd have thrown my coffee over both of them.' Rachel scoffed.

'This is nothing. Wait until I tell you about the evening.'

She closed her eyes, giving a clear signal that she was ready to relax. 'I'll tell you more later. But now I fancy a swim.' She was well aware that she had left her friends desperate to hear more about her Parisian adventure. 'Anyone going to join me?' Libby gently eased herself into the pool and covered her shoulders. The water felt silky and warm, but she felt uncomfortable in her bikini; having swum in the pool in Paris naked, she never wanted to swim in a costume again. She swam slowly towards the other side of the pool and positioned herself in front of one of the jets of water, sighing with pleasure as the bubbles caressed and massaged her skin. She felt the tension gently ebbing away from her body, but she knew it would take longer to relax her mind. 'It's blissful in here, come on you two,' she urged.

Amelia and Rachel were deep in conversation, and Libby enjoyed a moment of solitude. As she moved silently through the water, she wondered how much of the weekend she should share and how much she should keep a secret. It wasn't because she felt embarrassed or ashamed, she just preferred to keep a few things to herself. There was a small part of her that wondered if they would view her in a different light if they knew everything.

'Libs, do you fancy a steam?' Rachel asked. 'It's a great steam room; it's huge with marble benches, and we can hose each other down with icy water if we get too hot and sweaty.'

They sat in a line; the steam was so dense they could hardly see one another.

'Libs, don't keep us in suspense. We can't wait to hear more. I was just telling Amelia about our trip to MeMe's to buy sexy lingerie. I remember the beautiful cream taffeta dress covered in sequins that we selected for you. You looked stunning in it, Libs. Did you wear it to the French nightclub, or did you choose to wear the scarlet outfit with the red high heels?'

'In the end I chose the cream frock, because it went better with my basque. I must admit I did turn a few heads.'

'Well, you really got into the swing of it, Libs!' Amelia enthused. 'Did everyone dress up? And, more importantly, what did Eloise wear?'

'I thought she looked rather plain next to some of the chic French women. There were some fabulous outlandish outfits. The château where the club was based was like a setting from a period drama – breathtakingly beautiful with an abundance of bougainvillaea, pine and Cypress trees in the grounds. And they sure knew how to make a good aperitif! We sat in a walled courtyard to enjoy our meal. You should have seen Alex trying to dance with the flamenco guitarist and the dancer, who were there to entertain us. He was well out of his depth. Eloise couldn't even bear to watch! I rather enjoyed her discomfort. And his,' Libby added mischievously. 'Wow, you should have seen the cabaret, it was an amazing spectacle. If I tell you that all our eyes were on stalks, you can just imagine what the dancing was like. Well, eventually we ended up dancing in the disco marquee. Alex and Eloise had disappeared somewhere, but Roly was good company. He took me on a tour of the facilities, and you would never believe it. Downstairs there was a setup like you've never seen before, outside a film set.' She breathed deeply. 'It's boiling, I'm going to get some fresh air.'

Rachel suddenly grasped the hose and doused Libby's body with freezing cold water. It took Libby's breath away, but then her body tingled all over

'Let's go and have a shower and cool off before lunch. I can't believe how the time has flown,' Rachel said, peering at her Rolex watch. 'Libs, I'm dying to hear the next part of your story.'

Lunch was a pleasant affair. They sat round the small table in their dressing gowns. The menu was varied and full of healthy options. Libby chose strips of chicken from the protein list and a fragrant stir-fry from the vegetable selection. A glass of sparkling mineral water from the Highlands complimented her meal. As she ate, she resolved to take better care of herself and her health. The morning had felt very detoxifying. Her body was beginning to relax, and she was relishing the attention of her friends. She felt powerful in her choices: what she would eat and what she wouldn't; what she would share and what she would not. As they ate, the story unfolded.

'A question has been playing on my mind, Libs,' said Amelia, 'how did you feel when Alex and Eloise disappeared?'

'Do you know what, by this time I didn't care. I'd had enough champagne and wine to dull my senses. And I enjoyed Roly's company.'

'What did Roland think about Alex and Eloise's disappearance?'

'He wasn't fazed at all. He explained the open nature of their relationship, which is more flexible than we're used to.'

'What do you mean, Libs? Are they swingers?' Amelia froze, her fork halfway to her mouth.

'Yes, although that's not how they would describe

themselves. They have been married for a long time, and they find a more open and honest approach works for them. But Roly was disappointed with Eloise for involving Alex – someone who isn't part of the lifestyle.'

'Good grief, Libby, it sounds like you've stepped off the world into some kind of fantasy land. I saw something like this on Channel 4 last week.'

Libby continued her story, oblivious to Rachel's remark. 'But then we went downstairs to explore the dungeons…'

'What do you mean dungeons? Don't you mean a cellar, Libby? Is that where they stored the wine?'

'If I told you, you wouldn't believe me. But what I will say is that Alex and Eloise enjoyed the equipment. And if I mention chains, leather handcuffs and mediaeval stocks, I might be giving you a clue. I'll leave the rest to your imagination.'

'Now you're really having us on, Libs.'

Libby raised an eyebrow. 'I'll leave you to decide.'

'Did you enjoy the equipment too?' Rachel was curious.

'No, but it was fascinating to watch adults enjoying themselves, but in the end Roly and I decided to go back up to the bar, where we met a lovely French couple. We enjoyed the rest of the evening with them, chatting and doing this and that.' She hesitated. 'It was a memorable evening, and I learnt a lot about myself. I will never forget it.'

'But, Libs, weren't you angry and jealous, seeing Alex and Eloise together? You must have felt something?'

'I had very mixed feelings: anger, jealousy, but in a funny sort of way, I took pleasure in seeing Alex enjoying himself. It was as simple as watching children having fun in the playground, nothing more, nothing less. Does that make sense?'

As she was speaking, she had an image in her mind of Alex lashed to the stone wall: submissive, vulnerable, passive. This was part of Alex's personality that she didn't understand or even know existed. She wondered what had happened at university that had changed him.

Rachel scraped her plate clean and licked her lips, savouring the last tasty morsel. 'Well, I must admit that I've never experienced anything remotely close to this, and I thought I was the broad-minded one.'

'Shall we go back to our loungers to digest our lunch and have a snooze?' suggested Amelia.

'Actually, guys, I've booked a treatment for myself, I hope you don't mind. I've had an annoying ache in my left shoulder for a few weeks, and I thought a deep-tissue massage might shock it back into action!' She looked at her watch. 'I'll have to go to the treatment room now, so I'll see you in about an hour.'

'That sounds like a good plan, Rachel. We'll see you beside the pool later.'

Libby and Amelia peeled off their dressing gowns and lay on the loungers. The centre seemed deserted today, and Libby enjoyed the tranquil atmosphere.

'I'm glad we have some time alone, because I really want to check in with you. Before you went away, I was worried about you. I saw how unkind Alex was towards you when you came to dinner with us. Things aren't going well for you, are they, Libs?'

Libby closed her eyes. She knew that she could tell a good story, but Amelia was right: she was in a bad place.

Twenty-Eight

'I guess things haven't been good between us for quite a long time, but I still hold a candle for him, Amelia, despite everything.'

'I know I've said this to you before, Libs, but is love enough? Isn't marriage about treating your partner with respect, about being friends, about being companionable?'

'It is,' agreed Libby sadly, 'but love runs deep, and I'm not sure that we can apply logic to love. But it doesn't mean to say that I like him.' She put her head in her hands. 'Most of the time I hate him.'

Amelia placed her hand lightly on Libby's shoulder. 'I'm struggling to understand, Libs. How can you ever forgive Alex for being unfaithful to you?'

'In Paris, everything was out in the open about their affair, and this defused the situation. I think Alex realised that everything seemed less attractive in the cold light of day. The excitement and intrigue of a secret rendezvous, or a chanced kiss, had vanished. And without the thrill of deception their relationship meant absolutely nothing.' She paused. 'The strange thing is, I hate him for deceiving me, but a small part of me feels sorry for him. He was just one of Eloise's many conquests.'

'Libs, you are too kind to him. His deception is not acceptable. If Tom ever strayed, God forbid, I would kick him out into the street with all his belongings and hope never to set eyes on him ever again. Do you think you can ever trust Alex again?'

Libby sighed. 'No, I don't think I can. They say that once a partner strays, they are likely to stray again.'

'Has Alex apologised to you? How has he helped you come to terms with this? Is he interested in keeping your marriage alive?'

'He almost pretends it never happened. He refuses to talk about it. I have to move on. But he has learnt things about me too. It is almost as if we have accepted that we are not quite the people we thought we were.'

'Have Roly and Eloise converted you into their lifestyle, Libby?'

'I think the jury's out on this one, but we have been invited back to Paris. I'm not sure that Alex would be interested though…'

'Did you confront Eloise?'

'I did, but I ended up quite liking her. She was open and honest about her way of life, and sorry for the hurt she had caused. She didn't want Alex as a long-term prospect; she is no threat to me, Amelia. But when I met with Roland at the White Hart, he told me a few surprising things about Alex.'

'I remember seeing you together, deep in conversation by the fire. What did he have to say?'

'They were at the University of Oxford together. Roland studied PPE and Alex studied law. They were socialites. Do you remember me telling you that Alex was a libertine, after my visit to Flo at Blackmore Rest Home?'

'I do, Libs. Carry on.'

'Alex was always in the midst of any social whirl, and he was a leading light in the Oxford Union. He had radical opinions, the students either loved him or hated him. He had to be the centre of attention, always in control.'

'Isn't he like that now, Libs?'

'Well, something happened in his final term which pushed him off the rails completely. It still affects him to this day. It must have been something really traumatic, but Roly had no idea what it was. Amelia, he even became suicidal.'

'Good grief! I've heard about this happening with high-flying students. He seems so normal, holding down a demanding job, but perhaps it explains his behaviour towards you Libs.'

'Perhaps it does, Amelia. I am determined to find out about the trauma that he suffered all those years ago. The trouble is I hardly see him at the moment, because he's busy sorting out his mum's estate and probate, and all the other stuff us mere mortals don't understand.'

'Hello, you two.' Rachel strolled up to them, looking calm and glowing after her treatment.

'How was the massage, Rachel?'

'It was painful, but I feel good now. He advised me to relax for a couple of days. Some hope, huh? He went on about chakras and acupressure points, but I was in a world of my own.'

Libby looked across at her two friends; they were perfect for the activity she had in mind. She briefly wondered if she should include her friend Ali – the creative fiddle player – but she didn't think Ali would go along with anything like this. Rachel and Amelia both looked relaxed and satisfied after a delicious lunch, and Rachel radiant after her massage. She gauged this would be a good moment to discuss her plans with them.

'I've been thinking about ways that I can build bridges with Alex, and I've had an idea. His birthday is in a few weeks' time, and I wondered whether you both would help me to arrange a special treat for him. Something which I know he will love, after watching him at Chez Fleurie.'

'But are you absolutely sure that you want to save your marriage, Libs? There are more fish in the sea. And, you never know, maybe you'll find someone who is more loving and respectful than Alex,' Amelia suggested quietly.

Libby nodded; her features fixed in grim determination. 'Yes. I want to give him one last chance. So, are you ready to listen?'

'I don't know why but I feel rather nervous, Libby. What have you got in mind?'

Rachel and Amelia sat up, their backs straight, and listened attentively as Libby laid out her plans.

'Before I begin, I want you to set your minds free. So often our thoughts and actions are constrained by the rules and regulations that society places on us: *they* tell us what is right and what is wrong. *They* tell us what we should be doing. We are so often limited by invisible rules.'

'What are you saying, Libs?' Amelia asked, feeling rather out of her depth.

'I would like you to listen with an open mind, free of constraints, free of judgement.'

Amelia and Rachel shot glances at each other. 'Okay, we're all ears…'

'I have a choreographed role-play in mind, and each of us will have a crucial part to play.' She drew breath and turned towards Amelia. 'You will be the temptress. You will draw Alex in with your beguiling, provocative moves and your piercingly blue eyes. You will tease and tantalise, all through gesture and movement, but no contact will be made. You will wear red satin, and your face will be partially covered, revealing only your eyes. You will be mysterious, erotic, sexy, but discreet, detached. You will keep your distance, leaving Alex vulnerable, longing, begging for more. You will be the rook on my chessboard – You are stronger than a bishop or a knight. You have the power to outwit the king, should you so wish.'

Amelia's eyes widened, unblinking. She remained still, alert.

Libby turned her body to face Rachel. 'And you will be the seductress. The strong woman, sexy, erotic, the lady in black. You will use your seductive powers to lure and catch your prey, like a spider encasing a fly in an intricate web. You will taunt and coax, you will touch, only fleetingly, as light as a feather, and then you will withdraw. You will whet his appetite, leaving him desperate, wanting, panting and drooling for more. You will be the knightess on my chessboard. You are powerful and dangerous; you are there to seduce and protect.'

Rachel's mouth formed a smile, her eyes shining. 'And you, Libby, what part will you play?'

'I will be the humble pawn on the chessboard.'

Amelia's face creased in puzzlement. 'This is not the part I expected you to play.'

'The pawn is a lady in waiting, she is a mere servant – a peasant.'

'I thought you might want a more powerful part in the drama, Libs, you have to be the central character. Surely you want to be the spider who catches the fly?'

'Ah, but you see, the pawn is potentially the most powerful piece on the chessboard. Many a king has been overpowered by a mere peasant. I will wear a simple cream taffeta gown, and, if I am able to overcome obstacles, if I lure Alex into submission – it would only take a few inspired moves – then I will be queen. I will be the dominant one.' She drew her body upwards, statuesque, regal, and stared, trance-like, into space. 'I will be the victor.'

'But, you haven't told us what part Alex plays in the chess game,' Rachel said, now fully immersed in Libby's fantasy.

'Alex is the fallen king. He will be submissive, passive, constrained by leather hand and ankle cuffs, lashed to the bed. He will have a studded velvet collar around his neck, attached by a chain that will be locked to the bedpost. I will hold the key. His head will be carefully positioned so that he can enjoy the spectacle to the fullest.'

Rachel pursed her lips. 'Libs, I'd never have thought it of you. A bit weird… Interesting, but definitely weird.'

'Remember what I said about keeping an open mind, Rachel, with no limitations or fixed judgements. This is simply role-play, theatre, play acting, no more, no less. It will be entertaining, and I know it will be a very special birthday present for Alex.'

'But will it, Libs? Or will it just be a prick tease?' Rachel asked bluntly.

'I must finish my story. We will complete our performance, and then we will leave him to indulge in his own erotic fantasies.' She paused to breathe in the fragrant air. 'And we will go and have a large glass of Chardonnay!'

Amelia looked aghast. 'And then what? We can't leave him imprisoned forever.'

'And then I, as the queen, will return and give him his long-awaited special treat. I can assure you without question, that it will be the most exquisite experience he has ever had.'

'Spare us the details, Libs. He's a very lucky man.'

Amelia looked unsettled. 'But Alex hardly knows us. This could go horribly wrong.'

'Now you're in fantasy land, Amelia. Of course he will. Alex is a simple soul; he will be easily excited and manipulated by three gorgeous sirens.'

'Okay, Libs, I think this is a very creative idea. I suppose it's rather like buying him a token for a cruise on the River Thames with cocktails thrown in, or a meal in a country pub somewhere. Alex will have the priceless token of live entertainment in his bedroom.'

'Rachel, you are right, it's just a present with a difference,' Amelia said with a sigh of relief. 'I always find that experiences given as presents are more meaningful than material goods that you often don't want or need. And we're saving the world's resources.'

'I suggest we go to MeMe's again. I will treat you to an erotic outfit each. And after that, I will bribe you further with a cocktail or two. So, what do you say?'

'Sounds good. You only live once. I'm up for it. How about you, Amelia?'

'I do wonder what Tom would make of it all…' She paused, her eyes darting from one friend to the other. 'Ah for goodness sake, it's just a birthday treat after all, and I'm helping out a friend. Yep, count me in.'

Twenty-Nine

Libby peered out of the window. A broad ribbon of deep crimson and purple brushed the sky, heralding the hope of brighter days to come. She sighed. A week had passed since her day in the spa with Amelia and Rachel, and the time had dragged ever since. She had been excited about her plans for Alex's birthday, but today her head was full of gloom. Alex's attitude towards her was worsening; his cruel and thoughtless comments affected the way she thought about herself. She felt worthless. Useless. Suddenly she was brought back into the moment by a tentative knock on the door. She hesitated. Who could it be? She wasn't expecting Alex home from work for at least another hour. She waited and listened. There it was again, a knock on the door, louder this time. She placed her newspaper carefully on the coffee table and opened the door. She was surprised to see a young man of about eighteen, tall, angular, dark-haired with oriental features, standing in the porch.

'Hello, can I help you?' asked Libby, looking at him intently. He seemed familiar. Where had she seen him before? She racked her brain.

The stranger looked down at the tiled floor and mumbled, 'My name is Tai.'

Libby waited, expecting him to give a reason for his visit. 'What can I do for you, Tai? Are you selling something?'

'I have come to see Mr Alex Wilkinson. I believe he lives here?' He shuffled nervously on his feet. 'I would very much like to meet him.'

'I'm afraid he is not home from work yet. Have you come from far? Would you like to come in and wait for him? He shouldn't be long now.'

'Thank you, I would like that very much. I have come by train from London.'

Libby opened the door wider to invite him in. She instantly regretted her decision to allow a complete stranger into her house, but it was too late to turn him away. She took his raincoat and his folded umbrella and showed him into the sitting room. He sat on the edge of the armchair, his hands clasped in his lap, his knuckles white. He looked awkward and uncomfortable.

'I'm Libby, would you like a cup of tea or coffee while you wait?'

'That would be kind. A cup of tea would be very welcome, thank you.'

As Libby prepared the tea, it did cross her mind that he could be a burglar, or anyone, and he could freely help himself to anything while she was out of sight. But he seemed a very polite young man with smart clothes, and immaculate and formal manners.

She poured two cups of Earl Grey and they sat in silence. The ticking of the clock rang in Libby's ears as she struggled with the awkwardness of the situation. 'So, Tai, are you a student in London?'

'Yes, I am a medical student studying at Imperial College.'

'How exciting, you must be very intelligent. It is commendable to want to be a doctor.'

'But I didn't want to do medicine, I wanted to study music. I play classical violin. I would like to be a solo performer, and play in a prestigious orchestra, but it was never to be.'

His head dropped, his eyes staring steadfastly at the floor.

'It sounds to me like you have many talents. So why are you studying medicine, Tai?' Libby asked softly.

'It was my mother's dying wish. She wanted the best for me, and for the family. She believed that becoming a doctor was a fine upstanding profession. She came from Korea. I loved and worshipped her.' He paused, wringing his hands. 'But now, I don't know anymore.'

Libby reflected on his words. Why was this young man opening up to her, and what had happened to make him question his love and devotion for his mother. 'I'm sorry to hear that your mother passed away, it must have been very hard for you.' There was something deeply sad and forlorn about Tai. 'Will you continue to study medicine, or are you tempted to transfer to a music degree?'

Tai looked defiantly at Libby. 'It was my mother's last wish, of course I will respect and honour her decision. I will study hard, and I will become a doctor.' He jutted his chin out stubbornly.

The ticking of the clock continued to scream in Libby's ears. 'I admire your determination,' said Libby, willing Alex to come home and relieve her of this stilted conversation. 'Do you play in an orchestra? I know that medical students are often very musical, but I'm not sure why…'

'I hope to join the college symphony orchestra early next year, but the coursework takes up so much of my time.' His shoulders slumped.

'I hope you do play in the Imperial College Symphony Orchestra; they have a great reputation, and a wonderful leader. He is the son of a friend of mine.'

Tai looked up; the hint of a smile etched on his face.

'What does your father think about you becoming a doctor? He must be very proud of you.'

Tai became silent, his eyes darting around the room nervously. Libby offered him a ginger biscuit which he nibbled. Libby was already eating her second biscuit; eating seemed to relieve the tension.

Now listening to her own breathing, her mind searched for another topic of conversation. Suddenly she remembered. 'I knew you looked familiar. You were at Flo's funeral weren't you? You stood at the back of the chapel… and then you disappeared. I saw you again at the reception, outside the pub.'

Tai bowed his head and mumbled something inaudible.

Libby smiled. 'I guess you knew Flo. She was quite a character wasn't she?'

At that moment the key turned in the lock. 'I've still got shedloads of work to do, I'll be in the study,' Alex called sharply from the hallway.

'Alex, you have a visitor. Tai is keen to meet you.'

'I haven't got time, for God's sake. Why the hell didn't he make an appointment? I can't just see any Tom, Dick or Harry on a whim.'

'I'm sorry,' Tai stammered.

Alex threw down his briefcase and glared at the young man in front of him. 'I suppose I can spare a few minutes, but I haven't got long. Follow me.' He glanced at Libby and shrugged his shoulders. 'Couldn't it have waited until I could see you in the office? I'm assuming you are here to talk about legal stuff?' He held the door for Tai to enter the study and then followed him in and slammed the door behind him.

Libby stared at the closed door, feeling sorry for this polite young man, who had already been rebuffed by Alex. She wondered why he was so keen to meet her husband. Perhaps he needed a solicitor to sort out family matters following the death of his mother. But, if this was the case, why hadn't he made an appointment during office hours? Why was he at Flo's funeral? Was there some tenuous family connection? Alex didn't seem to recognise Tai. It was all rather odd. She listened and could hear muffled conversation interspersed with long periods of silence. Her head was buzzing as she went to the kitchen, pulled the cork of a bottle of Shiraz and poured herself a large glass. Dusty padded up to her and laid himself heavily across her legs. He looked up, his brown eyes pooled with love. 'Ah, Dusty, what on earth would I do without you?' She stroked him lovingly and sipped her peppery wine. She sat and waited.

Sometime later, she looked at her watch. An hour had passed; she was surprised that Alex had not already shown him to the door. What could be so important? She studied her glass, now nearly empty and considered that another half a glass wouldn't do her any harm. As she returned to the sitting room, nursing her wine, she could hear movement. They came out, one after the other, no one said anything.

Libby looked at Alex. His face was waxy, ashen, his eyes in a fixed trance-like stare. A deep chill ran through her body. What could possibly have been said to evoke this ghostly and extreme reaction from Alex?

Tai, crestfallen, turned towards Libby, offered a limp and sweaty hand, discreetly passing a crumpled piece of paper into the palm of her hand. He mumbled his thanks for her hospitality, and scuttled out of the door, leaving it ajar behind him. Libby folded her fingers around the note, and turned towards Alex, who was now rooted to the spot. She waited for an explanation. His eyes bored into hers, leaving her feeling disconcerted. 'I am going to the spare room, and I don't want to be disturbed,' he said bluntly. He turned towards the stairs and didn't look back.

Libby tossed and turned in bed that night, worries whirling around in her head. She had no idea of what had happened, but she knew it was very significant. Alex usually brushed things off, hard and off-hand in his approach, but last night he looked shocked and vulnerable – terrified even.

Early the next morning, Libby padded downstairs to get a drink of water. As she passed through the hall, she noticed a neatly folded black umbrella, stored in the ornate brass storage rack to one side of the front door. She remembered the crumpled note that Tai had pressed into her hand as he had left the previous evening. She had hidden it in a pile of newspapers on the coffee table. She shuffled through the papers until she found the insignificant piece of paper. Curious, she unfolded the note. It simply said "Ring me" with a scrawled mobile phone number written underneath his words. She carefully put it in her dressing gown pocket and returned to bed to think.

The next few days passed in a blur. Alex was morose in his silence. Libby coaxed him with comforting words, food and wine, but nothing she did would lift him from his deeply troubled state.

'Alex, we can't go on like this. Whatever Tai said, we can work through this together, but I'm powerless to help if you won't talk to me.'

Alex let out a deep sigh, his head bowed. 'There is something that I need to tell you. I can't believe it's come to this.' He drew his fingers roughly through his lank hair. 'I've been so stupid.'

Libby drew up her chair to face Alex. 'Whatever it is, everything will be okay.'

'How the hell can you possibly know that?' he muttered.

Choosing to ignore his rudeness, she replied, 'You are right, I don't know for sure, but tell me Alex. I'm here and I'm listening to you.'

'It's something that happened a long time ago when I was at Oxford.'

Libby recalled Roly mentioning a serious incident that had happened to Alex in his final term.

'I loved everything about Oxford: the studying, the Students' Union, how everyone seemed to idolise me for my radical views and daring ways. I was wild.' His eyes lit up briefly. 'My friends and I all enjoyed the high life, getting sloshed, taking drugs, sleeping with all the girls – they used to circle around us like bees round a honeypot.' He paused, his eyes now dull and lifeless. 'We used to brag about how many women we slept with, how many notches we had on the bedpost. I used women mercilessly for sex, for physical pleasure, and then I literally spat them out, with no regard for their feelings or their welfare.' He made a fist and started to bang his head repeatedly. 'But I thought they wanted it as much as we did. How could I have treated women so badly?'

Libby studied him, puzzled and angry that his attitude towards her, and women in general, was still degrading and dismissive. Had he learnt nothing? And what had this all got to do with Tai?

'We behaved like this for most of our student days. The coursework was easy for me; I could get top grades even when I was drunk or heavily influenced by cocaine. I was flying high, Libs, I was on top of the world. I had everything.'

'So what happened, Alex?' Libby asked softly.

Alex screwed his face in anguish and pain. 'We'd had a good night. The Students' Union was buzzing with excitement, following my rousing speech on freedom and equality. I was on fire that night.' His back straightened with the memory of the thunderous applause that he had received from his fellow students. 'Afterwards, we all crowded into the pub for several pints and snorted cocaine. I was euphoric, in ecstasy. I was in heaven. I adored being the centre of attention. The girls circled around me, offering their bodies, or so I imagined anyway. How could life get any better?'

Silence followed. Libby's body was taut, waiting for what he would say next.

'I suddenly felt strange, discombobulated, so I decided to go back to my room and sleep it off. I vomited several times on the way back, I felt wretched. I lurched from side to side unable to control my limbs. I was alone, all my friends were still celebrating and socialising, I don't think they even noticed I had gone.'

Libby put her hand tentatively on his knee, hardly daring to move.

'Miraculously I made it back to my room. I stripped off and threw myself on the bed, still feeling strange but less sick than I had done. My mouth was parched; I couldn't swallow, I could barely breathe and my limbs felt heavy. I stared up at the ceiling. The harsh light shone painfully into my eyes, and everything was going round and round. I craved comfort and normality. But then...' He scratched his face roughly with his fingers, leaving streaks of red in their wake. 'The door opened, and two women walked towards me. I recognised one of them, I had had sex with her, I couldn't remember her name, or any of the details, she was an insignificant conquest.' He shook his head in despair. 'I can't find the words...'

Libby hardly dared to breathe. Everything taut.

'They teased me and taunted me. They ridiculed me, they treated me with utter contempt. They spat out their words with hatred, while they teased my cock, one holding me down, the other riding me, bearing down, her hands tightly round my throat. She made me do it.'

Libby breathed in the horror of his words. 'She made you do what?'

His body twisted with pain and agony. 'She rode me. She forced me to enter her. I retched, but the second woman had her hand clamped over my mouth. All I can remember was her writhing body, her oriental features twisted in a curious expression of ecstasy and sadistic pleasure, and her relentless rhythmical grinding over me, destroying me and destroying my life.' He looked up and stared steadfastly at Libby. 'They told me I deserved everything they had done to me that evening. I had treated women as second-class citizens and this was my just punishment. They stared, their eyes boring into me. And then they left.'

Thirty

The air hung heavy between them, as Libby absorbed the significance of his words. 'She raped you.'

'As the law stands, men cannot be raped by women. She violated me, she sexually abused me, she morally raped me. And the other woman looked on and allowed the abuse to happen, she must share the guilt.' Alex gulped the air, his body weak with exhaustion. 'But, in reality, I am the guilty one. I abused women for years, I deserved to be punished. They were right and I was wrong. Since that day I have felt dirty, used, humiliated. At the time, I considered taking my own life. I felt I had nothing left to live for. I have never recovered. Everything changed.'

She absorbed the severity of his words. 'Did you ever think about having therapy?'

'Oh, Libby, they would have laughed me out of the surgery. I had a reputation; they knew all about me. They would have thought I would revel in being pleasured by two young women.'

'I suppose they were different times then,' Libby acknowledged, 'there was a different attitude towards mental health... sadly.'

'So no, Libby, I didn't seek help. I thought I was man enough to deal with this on my own.'

Libby did not gauge the time was right to challenge him on his attitude towards her, and indeed, all women. 'I just don't know what to say, Alex, I need time to process it all. But I am sorry that it happened.' She paused. 'But I can't understand what all this has got to do with Tai?'

Alex paused, taking a deep breath. 'He came to the house last night to tell me that he is my son. I am his father.'

Her jaw dropped in shocked surprise. 'Your son?'

'Tai was conceived on that night.'

Libby covered her mouth and stared out of the window. The oriental features, her ecstasy and sadistic pleasure; she is... was Tai's mother. 'The poor boy, how much does he know about what happened?'

'Don't you care about me or my feelings, Libby? How could you care more about a stranger than you do about your husband?' A vein in the front of his forehead bulged with anger.

She looked at him coldly. It wouldn't take long before he returned to the Alex she knew, with his cruel, unfeeling comments. 'Are you sure he is your son? This could just be a coincidence. How did he find you?'

'His mother died two years ago from cancer. Whilst sorting out her belongings, he found a journal that she had written during her time at the University of Oxford. In it, she described her bitter hatred of me. She was a feminist, fighting for equality and the rights of women. She hated me, she thought I was a chauvinist pig of the worst kind. Her journal described how she became obsessed with me, how she followed me and observed my every movement

But she finally broke when she discovered how I had disrespected her best friend. She planned her revenge in intricate detail. It worked.'

'But you still don't know for sure. It might be all lies and deceit. You will have to take a DNA test. How did Tai finally trace you?'

'Tai told me that his mother's name was Binna. She brought him up single-handedly, but she never mentioned to him who his father was. He believed his mother was perfect, he adored everything about her. But her continued refusal to talk about his father, fed his curiosity, he had to find out more. He listened, he watched, he read, but he could find nothing to help him with his search. He knew that he would have to wait until he was eighteen to start his quest in earnest.' Alex took a deep breath. 'But his mother's death precipitated everything, and her journals told him all he needed to know, including my full name. He was born and raised in London, and, quite by chance, he scanned the death notices in *The Times* a few weeks ago and spotted the small insignificant notice announcing my mother's death and funeral arrangements. He made the connection and came to the funeral. And then it was relatively easy to find out where I lived.'

Libby stroked her chin in thought. 'Could he be after the inheritance, Alex? You do hear stories like this about distant family, or even strangers, turning up out of the blue, hopeful to secure wealth following the death of someone they didn't even know.' She felt instantly ashamed of herself. Her first impressions of Tai was that he was a polite and trustworthy young man, but she had to acknowledge that first impressions can be deceptive.

Alex's face flashed with anger. 'I hope that is not the case.'

'So, how have you left it with Tai?'

'I said that we should let the dust settle, and he agreed to contact me again in the near future. I hope to God I never hear from him again.'

***

Sunday morning dawned bright and clear. There was a distinct chill in the air signalling the oncoming of winter. Alex was still asleep in bed, but Libby had let him know the previous evening that she was meeting friends in town for lunch, so he wouldn't be wondering where she was, or what she was doing. She hated lying, but she had no option. She clutched the black umbrella firmly in her right hand and strode towards the centre of town. She loved Sundays because, although the shops now opened every day of the week, Sunday still seemed to be quieter. She could hear the church bell pealing in Cornmarket, enticing people into the church for the morning service. Most of the time the sound of the traffic drowned out the sound of the song thrush, but today she paused to listen to the cheerful tune. She breathed in the cold air and wondered if she was doing the right thing.

When she had found the courage to ring Tai, he was obviously delighted to receive her call. He suggested that they meet in the Randolph Hotel at midday. Libby was surprised, because the Randolph seemed a very grand place to meet, and beverages or food of any kind would be very expensive, and, more surprising still, he had offered to pay. She agreed to the meeting. As she walked through St Giles, she felt less confident than she had felt when she agreed to see him. Tai was a complete stranger, and she had no idea why he would want to meet her. Surely he would rather meet Alex again, but perhaps not. Alex had not been very hospitable, in fact he had been rude and morose. But if she had thrown his number away, she would have always wondered what might have happened. She quickened her pace. Yes, she was doing the right thing. And she had to return his umbrella.

Oxford looked beautiful today. Groups of tourists had gathered on the steps of Martyrs' Memorial, its proud spire majestic against the blue sky. Libby's mind wandered to the history of the three martyrs, Thomas Cranmer, Nicholas Ridley and Hugh Latimer, who were tried for heresy and burnt at the stake for their religious beliefs in 1555. It didn't seem quite right that youngsters were tucking into Kentucky Fried Chicken on the steps of this ancient monument which honoured three significant men in history who sacrificed their lives.

As she approached the red-carpeted steps of the Randolph, her heart was beating hard in her chest. She felt nervous and unsure of herself. Passing the hotel doorman at the entrance, she was greeted by one of the restaurant staff and shown to the dining room. Her eyes were drawn to the elaborate chandeliers that hung from the ceiling and the sheer grandeur of the setting. She had never been in the hotel before, but she had often wondered what it would be like.

'Mrs Wilkinson, I am so happy that you agreed to meet with me today.'

'Hello, Tai, and please call me Libby.'

Tai was immaculately dressed in a navy-blue suit, a light blue shirt and a floral silk tie. But it was his shoes that drew Libby's attention. They were luxurious black leather with a seam across the front, pointed like a sword, and shone, not a scuff mark in sight. He held out his hand and gave her a dry and firm handshake, bowing as he did so. He pulled Libby's chair back for her to sit down, and then he sat down opposite her. 'Libby, I have ordered a champagne cream tea, I hope that will be okay for you? I know that it is a rather strange time of the day to drink champagne and eat cake, but this is a significant occasion for me.'

Libby nestled into the comfortable chair and began to relax. There was something very endearing and old-fashioned about Tai; she warmed to him. She gazed out of the window, enjoying the spectacular view of the pillared entrance of the Ashmolean Museum on the opposite side of Beaumont Street.

'I did consider meeting you there,' he said, as if reading her thoughts. 'They have a wonderful rooftop cafe, but I thought it might be a bit chilly today.'

At that moment the waiter placed a silver cake stand, piled high with sandwiches on the top level, scones on the second level and huge chunks of cake at the base. Libby looked at it in amazement. 'There's enough to feed an army here,' she said cheerily, although her anorexic mind started to count the calories of such a rich feast. A second waiter placed two flutes of champagne on the table. And a third waiter brought a large floral teapot, and a china tea set to match. Libby helped herself to a crustless cucumber sandwich.

Tai raised his glass and offered a toast. 'To my father and his good wife.' As they clinked glasses, Libby had a lot of questions.

'So, Tai, you have told me that your mother brought you up in London. Do you have fond memories of your childhood?'

'My mother was very intelligent – she got a first-class degree in English literature from the University of Oxford. Binna was fiercely driven by her political and moral beliefs, particularly the rights of women. She was renowned for her passionate, controversial presentations, and was invited as a keynote speaker at conferences all over the world. She wrote many books about women. I am proud of her achievements.' He nodded his head to affirm his pride. 'In fact, she was ruthless.'

Libby tilted her head to one side. 'But what about you, Tai? Was she kind and caring to you when you were a young boy?'

'I loved and adored my mother; she was my world. But sometimes she was too busy to notice.' He sighed. 'She gave me everything I needed, I had a good education and I do believe she loved me in her own way.'

Libby gave a small smile. He had given her a helpful impression of his mother, as much in what he hadn't said, as in the description he gave. 'I'm sure she was very proud of you, Tai.'

'But, Libby, when I read her journal after her death, I was mortified and ashamed. It shattered my perfect image of my mother. She held high moral beliefs, she was passionate in her fight for women's rights, but her hateful and sadistic revenge…' He hung his head in shame. 'I have no choice; I have to disown her.'

Libby sat quietly, thinking about the desperation of this poor young student. All his love and devotion had been erased in an instant by words on a page. 'Tai, there are always two sides to every story. Alex believes that he was the guilty one at university, treating women badly, using them, disrespecting them. I can't deny that he has been damaged by what happened, but he believes to this day that he deserved to be punished.'

Tai creased his face in pain. 'No, I can't condone what my mother did. It was sexual assault.'

Thirty-One

Libby lifted the chilled champagne flute to her lips, studying the young man in front of her. She must find the right words. 'I'm sorry, Tai, this must be very hard for you to process. But you and I were not there, we can't possibly understand what actually happened without the full context.' Libby's eyes rested on the impressive architecture of the Ashmolean, desperately trying to draw inspiration from its dramatic structure. 'Can you find it in your heart to forgive her, or at least find some peace and acceptance, knowing that she was fighting for the cause she so passionately believed in?'

'I'm not sure I will ever forgive her, but it did strengthen my resolve to find my father. Unfortunately our meeting didn't go as well as I had hoped.' He wiped the corner of his mouth lightly with his napkin. 'I knew it would be a shock for him to hear that I was his son... but I didn't expect him to be so angry. I knew he would need time to think, but he instantly dismissed me. I'm not even sure he believed me.'

Libby's face reddened. 'Tai, I have a practical suggestion, and I hope I won't offend you.' She reached into her handbag and pulled out two small plastic boxes.

'I personally believe that you are Alex's son, but there is a way that we can prove it beyond doubt. Alex has this annoying habit of cutting his toenails in the bedroom, so I collected a few clippings,' she said, pushing one of the boxes towards him. 'And, just to be sure, I have also collected some hair from his hairbrush. Would you be prepared to take a DNA test?'

Nodding, Tai took both containers, unclipped his briefcase and placed them carefully inside. 'I was going to suggest the very same thing myself, Libby. I will organise this first thing tomorrow. There is not a shadow of doubt in my mind that Alex is my father, but I do understand any suspicions that he might have.'

Libby let out a huge sigh of relief.

'My concern is that, because I have appeared just after his mother's death, that you both might think that I am just after inheritance money.'

Libby averted her eyes. He was voicing exactly what had already crossed her mind.

'I can assure you that this is not the case. My mother was extremely wealthy. When she died, she left me a large coastal property in Devon, and a great deal of money, more than enough for me to live a very comfortable life.' He smiled. 'Even after all the inheritance tax I have had to pay.'

'I'm pleased to hear this, Tai. So, what would you ideally like from Alex?'

'It's quite simple really. I would like a positive relationship with my father. This is something I have longed for all my life. I just want someone I can call "dad".'

Libby's heart sank. Would Alex be able to fulfil the role of a loving father? Would he want to? She somehow doubted it.

'I can foresee that this will be challenging, especially after the vile way I was conceived, but I am an eternal optimist, perhaps unwisely at times, I believe everything is possible.' He paused. 'But, Libby, there is something playing on my mind. Can I ask you something very personal?'

'Of course, Tai.' She fiddled nervously with her hair.

'When I came to your house, you welcomed me. But when I met Alex, he scared me. He was aggressive and intimidating, I thought he was going to lash out at me… This was not how I imagined my father to be, Libby, but I am strong in mind and body, I knew I could defend myself if the need arose. But you…'

Libby remained silent.

'Are you safe, Libby? Please forgive me for asking. I don't know you very well, but I have been worried about you.' His eyes widened with his concern for her.

Libby was not sure how much she should reveal to Tai about the turmoil of her marriage and the fear she held close to her heart. 'All marriages have peaks and troughs, Tai. I must admit that things haven't been easy over the last few years.' The corners of her mouth turned down. 'But, like you, I try to hold on to some hope that things will get better.'

Tai looked at her, unconvinced by her hopeful words. 'Have a scone, Libby,' he said, passing her the strawberry jam and the pot of cream, piled high in generous swirls.

They lapsed into silence as they negotiated their way from the sandwiches to the coffee and walnut cake on the bottom layer of the cake stand in front of them.

'If I eat any more, I think I'll burst, Tai. What a feast! I'll be glad of the walk home to digest all of this,' Libby said, feeling her bulging midriff.

'Will you tell Alex about our meeting today?'

'No, I think it might be wise to wait until you confirm the results of the DNA test with me. In the meantime, I will find out from Alex what his true feelings are, now that he has had more time to think. We have been trying to conceive without success for many years. You, Tai, could be the answer to our wildest dreams.'

They left the hotel and walked in opposite directions, Tai towards the station, clutching his briefcase and umbrella, and Libby back home. 'I'll be in touch with the results as soon as I receive confirmation. Take care,' Tai shouted as he strode down Beaumont Street.

Libby wandered back through St Giles, enjoying her freedom. Alex would be home, and she didn't particularly relish the idea of seeing him. It had been a pleasure to meet Tai properly, but some of what he had said left her feeling rather uneasy. Opening the front door, she was greeted by Alex. He looked unusually cheery, younger even. His face radiated pleasure.

'Libs, I've got great news. I've had email confirmation of something that I've known for a while, but I have had to keep to myself.'

Libby poured water into the kettle and switched it on. 'What is it, Alex?'

'As you know, I've been horrendously busy sorting out Mum's estate. God, the legal work is never-ending...'

'And?'

'Do you remember when I went to see Mum at her ghastly care home with one of my colleagues?'

'Yes, I do.' Her heart was beginning to sink.

'Well, between us, we managed to persuade the old bat to change her will.'

Libby's face darkened.

'Her house is sold; the value of her entire estate is worth a mint, Libs. We are rich. I think we should open a bottle of champagne. I have a Dom Pérignon in the fridge. I've been waiting for the right moment to pop the cork. We can now live a fine life forever.'

Libby remained silent. 'How much will you receive when the inheritance is split three ways with Matt and Andrew?'

Alex threw his head back and laughed, his Adam's apple bobbing up and down. 'They resigned as powers of attorney; they just walked away; they didn't deserve anything. I did everything. And besides, Flo didn't love either of them. It was a piece of cake to persuade her to take them out of the equation. They will receive nothing.'

Libby stared at Alex with contempt. 'How could you, Alex? You abused your position as power of attorney, and you took advantage of your mother at her most vulnerable. Matt and Andrew are entitled to their inheritance. You have only considered yourself. You disgust me.' Without waiting for a response, she turned her back on him, marched out of the room and slammed the door behind her. She had her suspicions that he might do this. She slumped down on the bed, tears streaming down her face. Did he have no conscience? How could she continue to love and live with anyone who could cheat on their own flesh and blood in this callous way. He had no regard for his own brothers, or for the memory of his mother.

Her thoughts were interrupted by Alex carrying two glasses of champagne into the bedroom. He offered her a glass, looking at her with a blank expression, and eased himself onto the edge of the bed. 'Celebrate with me. Don't you understand? I did it for you,' he insisted.

Libby took the glass, her hand shaking uncontrollably with anger and with fear. She took a sip, but she could taste nothing but the bitterness of her own bile.

'We could buy a house on the Riviera surrounded by bougainvillaea, we could swim with dolphins, we could go on a world cruise, Libs. I've always wanted to go skiing. Don't you understand, this money gives us the passport to freedom? We can do anything in the world we want to do…'

'Money – especially dirty money – can't buy happiness,' Libby mumbled under her breath.

'You just listen to me for a minute,' he muttered through clenched teeth. 'I've planned this carefully; I have opened up a world of possibilities. But, if you don't want to go along with it, I will leave you behind. I will divorce you, citing adultery.' He smirked. 'I've got evidence – photos of you at the club with Roly, and that awful French couple. Not only will I divorce you, but I will also circulate the photos to all your contacts. Your life will never be the same again.' He put his face close to hers. 'And don't try and steal my phone because the evidence is fully backed up.'

The blood drained from her face. Alex was blackmailing her. She knew that his behaviour was getting worse, but she didn't think it would come to this.

Libby was trapped, like a rabbit in the headlights.

Thirty-Two

Her fingers gripped the wall, her body paralysed with fear.

'How dare you,' he sputtered, 'you have abused my trust.' His body clamped against Libby's, pinning her to the wall. 'I did not give you permission to give that fool any part of my body.'

Libby breathed in the stench of his breath. 'I did it to protect you. Tai might have been an interloper...' She felt a sharp pain as the flat of his hand struck her on the side of her face. She felt her neck wrench sideways with the power of his blow.

'But you should have discussed this with me first. How dare you do this behind my back?' He stared at her, his eyes fixed and crazed.

'Alex, stop... please. Can't we talk calmly about this?' Her voice shook.

He clamped his hands around her throat. 'You don't know what you've done.'

The veins in her neck started to pulsate, she struggled for air.

'You have proven beyond doubt that Tai is my son.'

'But that is good news, surely?' she stammered.

'In the small print, it states that any surviving grandchildren are to receive ten per cent – ten bloody per cent – of the estate.' His hand came down forcibly on the side of her face, her neck still gripped by his other hand. Her skull ricocheted against the unyielding plaster. 'I have to hand over a wodge of hard-earnt cash – my money – to a complete stranger. And it's your fault.'

Libby tried to focus on a hook on the picture rail above his head, but, as she stared, the image altered from colour, to grey, to black. A piercing whistle rang in her ears, her body became limp and lifeless, her legs buckled, and she slowly slid down the wall to the floor.

Alex stood and studied the limp body and sucked in a deep breath. 'Serves you right.' He turned towards the door and walked out into the night.

One of Libby's eyes blinked against the harsh light, her body was cold and stiff. She froze in a foetal position, terrified that Alex was towering above her. A dark shadow blocked the light. His head came down and pushed the side of her face relentlessly until her head turned. He whimpered, his wet nose leaving a slippery trail across her face. She realised with relief that it was Dusty attempting to revive his mistress. In her haze, she marvelled how a simple creature could have the knowledge and sensitivity to feel her pain. He was trying his best to help her.

She levered herself up, her back slumped against the wall. Her eyes darted nervously around the room. She listened. Everything was silent except for Dusty's open-mouthed panting. Her breathing was shallow. She drew her hand tentatively over one side of her face and winced.

Her cheek felt raw and bruised. She closed one eye and peered out of the other. She could detect a faint mound of her swollen cheek, but everything else was blurred and watery. She sat still, composing herself. Time passed, until she was able to heave herself up to standing, stagger over to the coffee table and clutch her mobile phone. She eased herself gingerly onto the settee and scrolled her contacts until she found his number.

'I'm sorry to ring so late but I need to see you urgently.'

'Libby, are you okay? You sound as if you're crying,' Roland asked, his voice full of concern.

'No, not really...' Her body heaved with deep sobs. 'Can we meet first thing tomorrow morning? I need to see you.'

'Of course, Libby. But I need to ask, are you safe? Is this about Alex?'

'Yes,' Libby whispered.

'Then you should call the police,' said Roland firmly. 'I can call them for you if it would be easier. You need to be in a place of safety.'

'Roly, it is more complicated than you know, and the police can't help me. I will be okay until tomorrow. Please don't do anything...'

'All right, Libby, but I am going against my better judgement. Shall we meet at a coffee shop? Brothers in the Covered Market? Nine-thirty?'

'Thank you, Roly. I'll see you tomorrow.' Eager to finish the conversation, she ended the call abruptly and stared into the darkness. She now knew with certainty that the balance had shifted from love to hatred. It had taken months, but she knew now, tonight, that she hated him. She loathed him for his selfish greed, his controlling power, and the way he dismissed her as an insignificant being. She must think.

Alex did not come home that night.

After a sleepless and painful night, Libby peeled herself out of bed and looked in the mirror. She winced. The extensive bruising on her face had turned bluish-purple and black. One eye was completely closed, swallowed up by her swollen cheek, her eyelids on the other eye, purple and red. She looked like she had done ten rounds in a boxing ring. Her skin looked waxy and pale. She reached into her makeup bag and smeared the brown liquid onto her face. She might be able to temporarily mask the wounds, but the damage inside would be with her forever.

It took longer than usual to walk into town – her whole body ached – but she eventually stepped into the moist warmth of the coffee shop. Roland stood up to welcome her as she walked towards the corner table where he had chosen to sit. He put his arms around her, his lips brushing the side of her face. Her body recoiled in pain. 'Libby, what has he done to you?'

Libby eased herself gently into the wooden chair and bowed her head. 'Roly, I'm not in a good place.'

'I can see that, Libs. You don't need to tell me anything if you don't want to, but it might help if you talk to me.' He peered over his half-rimmed glasses and clamped her hands in his. 'You poor darling…'

Libby felt the comforting warmth of his touch seep into her body, giving her strength to find the right words.

Her eyes welled with tears. 'So much has happened since I last saw you, it's hard to know where to begin.' She took a deep breath. 'I know what happened to Alex in his final term at university.'

Roland looked at her in amazement. 'How on earth did you find out, Libby? I've been trying to persuade him to confide in me for years.' He stared beyond her into space. 'I will never forget the agonising look of despair in his eyes, and the way he withered away into a mere shell of his former self. What happened to damage him so badly, Libs?'

'You described to me the highlife that you both enjoyed at university: drinking, socialising, taking drugs and sleeping around...'

'We were wild, Libs, we had a great time...' He covered his mouth with his hand. 'But I'm not proud of some of our behaviour, we ran roughshod over everyone, over women in particular. Alex was like a handsome stallion; women were attracted to his dashing features and radical views. He was always surrounded by adoring women. But there is one particular woman that I will never forget. She fell head-over-heels in love with Alex. He slept with her a few times, giving her false hope, and then he unceremoniously dumped her. The gossip in the halls of residence was rife when she started to spread malicious rumours about Alex and his strange, outlandish, sexual preferences. I don't believe any of it was true, but we never did find out. Anyway, Libs, carry on.'

'I wonder if this was the woman in question,' she mused. 'One evening after a wild party, two women broke into his room and took their revenge.'

'How? What did they do?'

'One of them held Alex down. Remember he was drunk, Roly, so he was not able to defend himself. The other woman…' She bit her lip. 'She teased and tantalised him until he was excited… and then she forced him inside her.'

'My God, he was sexually assaulted by two women?' His body stiffened. 'They were giving him a taste of his own medicine…' His face reddened. 'I would never have guessed, Libs. He must have been devastated, mortified, to be violated in this way.'

'But this isn't the end of the story. Alex has a son.'

Roland's eyes widened. 'What?'

'A baby was conceived on that night. His son turned up at Alex's mother's funeral. His name is Tai.'

'You are joking, Libby. It all sounds rather more like fiction than fact. I just can't believe it. What did Alex say when he realised he had a son?'

Tears overflowed and forged beige rivulets down her cheeks. 'He wrote his two brothers out of his mother's will, Roly. He is despicable. He manipulated Flo when she was at her most vulnerable.'

'I always knew that Alex could sink pretty low, but this is unscrupulous, despicable. I hope his brothers contest the will.'

'I agree, Roly. But there is a twist in the tale. In the small print there is a clause that states that any surviving grandchildren – Tai – receive ten per cent of the inheritance. Roly, he is so angry about this, about everything.' Her shoulders slumped and she put her head in her hands. 'There is so much more I have to tell you, but I'm exhausted. I haven't got the words…'

They sipped their coffee, now tepid, in silence. Customers came and went. The barista brought another two Americanos to the table. He smiled generously. 'These are on me. You look like you could do with them.'

'He's been treating you badly for a long time hasn't he?' Roland said, breaking the silence.

'Alex is so unpredictable. He can be really loving one minute and fly off the handle the next. I never know where I am with him… It is like treading on thin ice.' Libby's limp hair fell over her face. She slowly nodded her head. 'I've got to try and resolve this with Alex; it's all so complicated. Suddenly we've got a son that we've always wanted. I don't want to walk away without giving us a chance to be a proper family.'

'I see what you mean, Libby, but you've got to think about your own self-preservation. If you're not prepared to go to the police, how can you be sure that he won't harm you even more seriously? If you are really determined to go back home and confront him, we should arm you with pepper spray or some other means of defending yourself.'

'I've got to be careful, Roly, because he is blackmailing me. If you cast your mind back to the club in Paris, you might remember you and I were together with Stéphane and Carmelle when Alex left the playroom. He must have got a phone from somewhere, because he's got photos of us in compromising positions, and he has threatened to send them to all my contacts unless I cooperate with his plan. If he releases the photos on social media, it will make my life very difficult. What a nightmare... I'm trapped, Roly. I can't do anything.' Her eyes welled up. 'And of course you're implicated as well.'

'How dare he? Don't worry about me or Eloise Libby, because we are open about our lifestyle, we have nothing to hide.' He hesitated. 'I can totally understand how difficult this would be for you though, with work and your friends.'

'I will get pepper spray, and make sure I keep my phone on me ready to speed-dial the police. But, Roly, I do wonder if this is my fault. I collected some toenails and hair from Alex for a DNA test without his permission, and this helped to prove beyond doubt that Tai is his son. It was after this when he finally flipped and lashed out at me.'

'Stop right there, Libby. None of this is your fault. There is no justification for physical or emotional abuse. You are the victim. He is the perpetrator.' He shot her a glance. 'I think you should consider packing your bags and taking shelter in a women's refuge.'

'I don't know if I could do that, aren't they all drug addicts and radical feminists?'

'No, absolutely not, they provide a place of safety for vulnerable women. You should seriously consider this as an option.'

'Okay, I won't rule it out if it happens again.'

'I have another suggestion. Why don't you leave him and disappear without a trace? I could help you do this, there are ways and means. I read a book about this recently. It was fictional but I'm sure it was well researched.'

'I couldn't possibly do that, Roly. What would I do for money? I couldn't leave Dusty behind. Where would I go? It would all be too difficult.'

'I'm going to have a word with Alex. I can't stand by and watch him destroy you. And himself.'

Thirty-Three

She stared into the rich crimson liquid as she swirled her glass. Was she becoming too reliant on the comfort that she gained from pouring herself several glasses of wine every evening? She consoled herself with the thought that it was a temporary measure, a crutch to help her through the darkest days. Alex sat on the other side of the room, hunched over his computer, his eyes fixed on the screen. These days he would either be shouting or, worse still, belittling her; or he would be deeply absorbed in something on his computer – she had no idea what. But, more often than not, he was at work, leaving Libby to think. And thinking hurt.

She jumped with the sound of the front doorbell. She glanced nervously across at Alex.

'Well, are you just going to sit there?'

She slowly stood up. Her unhappiness brought with it inexplicable pain raging through her joints. She felt old and tired. She reluctantly opened the door and stared blankly at the gentle compassionate face of her friend. Her mouth formed the word "no" and she shook her head, her bottom lip quivering.

'Hello, Libby,' he said, kissing her on both cheeks. 'Is Alex around? I'd like to have a chat with him.' Roland stroked the side of her arm. 'Don't worry, Libs, I won't rock the boat,' he whispered.

A week had passed since she had met Roland in the coffee shop, and she had fervently hoped that he had decided against visiting Alex. But here he was. Although the evening was unseasonably warm, her whole body shook, the tips of her fingers white and numb.

Roland pushed past her into the sitting room. Alex looked up from the computer. 'What the hell do you want at this time of the night, Roland?'

'Well, that's not very friendly, Alex, and by the way, it's only eight o'clock, the night is but young. Would you like to come to the pub for a drink with me, or shall we chat here?' He glanced at Libby. 'Over a glass of wine perhaps?'

Libby couldn't help but admire how Roland had taken control, not offering Alex the third option of not meeting at all.

'Okay,' Alex agreed, 'but I've a full day at the office tomorrow so I need an early night. Libby, pour Roland a glass of wine. We'll be in my study.'

Roland stared at the glowing wood burner, pumping out comforting warmth. 'We could stay here. I'm quite happy for us all to have a drink and a chat together. There is nothing that I'm going to say that I wouldn't want Libby to hear.' Alex shook his head vehemently and marched to his study without a backward glance.

Libby clutched her glass, watching the liquid quiver, like the restlessness of the sea before a storm. This was the second time she had not been party to a conversation. She must listen and wait. Her mind wandered to the unsettling conversation that Tai had had with Alex a few weeks ago, and now she dreaded to think what Roly would say, and how angry Alex would be. The muted conversation ebbed and flowed as Libby listened. She knew that Roland was intelligent, highly skilled in the art of debate and, most importantly, he was empathetic and compassionate. She must have faith that he would be subtle and say and do the right thing. But Alex was cruel, lacking in compassion. How would he react?

She listened to the intrusive sound of the clock ticking, marking each painful second; the hands moved slowly, time seemed to drag. After what seemed like forever, the door opened, and the two men appeared in the sitting room.

'Libby, we must all meet for a drink and a meal sometime.' Looking at Alex, he suggested a French restaurant that served delicious French cuisine. 'We could imagine we were back in France, I'm sure Eloise would love that,' he said, with a mischievous glint in his eye.

'Perhaps,' Alex answered gruffly. 'As I said, I'm going to have an early night so, if you don't mind…'

Libby looked from one to the other, both calm and smiling. This was not what she had been expecting. She walked towards Roland and gave him a peck on his cheek. 'Thanks for coming,' she whispered.

Left alone, Alex poured another glass of wine and slumped on the chair, watching the flames flicker from behind the glass, now semi-obscured by black soot. 'Libby, Roland and I talked about many things. And, for the most part, he was entirely wrong, meddling in things that don't concern him. But he did say one thing that has made me think.'

'What is that?' Libby asked nervously.

'Roland underlined how fortunate I am to have you as my wife, and that I should nurture and love you. I should cling onto you for dear life.' He turned his head and their eyes met. 'I know I'm really difficult, Libs, but I can't help it. And I do love you.'

Libby let out a deep sigh. 'We can't go on like this. I want our marriage to stay the course, but you have to treat me with respect, Alex.'

'I will try, but so much water has gone under the bridge, I'm not sure there is a way back.' He stood up and locked eyes with her. 'It's as much your fault as mine.' With that, he turned and climbed the stairs to the spare room.

She sat in the darkness, deep in thought. The fire had died down now leaving just the glowing embers. What should she do? Her mind was in turmoil. This evening, it felt like there was a small chink of light at the end of the tunnel. Roland's words had made a difference. Alex had acknowledged, in part, that he was lucky to have her as his wife. She thought he had anyway. He had also acknowledged that he knew that he was difficult. But there had been no apology. He had not taken full responsibility for his behaviour. But he had taken partial responsibility for the problems in their marriage. She put her head in her hands and wondered if the meeting with Roly had actually achieved anything at all.

Should she still organise Alex's birthday treat, considering everything she now knew? She cast her mind back to the description that Alex had given her about the sexual assault that happened in his final year of university. It had been an atrocity, which had undoubtedly damaged Alex, and he was still suffering from the events of that night. But would the birthday treat that she had planned, which involved restraining Alex to the bed, and being tantalised by three women, be a ghastly re-enactment of his worst nightmare? Would it be torture, reliving an act that plagued his life? Then her mind turned to the dungeons of Chez Fleurie, and in the forest the next day. She had witnessed Alex, tied up, restrained, in ecstasy, as he hungrily observed the sexual activity in front of him. He craved the role of subservience, submissiveness. She considered their sex life now, when – if – it happened. Alex always made her clamp his hands to the bed and ride him, insisting that she took the lead. She was in control.

The treat could go one of two ways. He could be completely broken. She would finally have her revenge on him. She hated him, but there was a part of her that still cared. But, on the other hand, the whole experience might be cathartic, it might help him to turn a corner. He might want to save their marriage, especially when he realises that his wife cares enough to organise such a thoughtful birthday present.

She should go ahead with her plan.

***

Alex's birthday drew near. Libby had a week to ensure that everything was in place. So much to do, so little time. She had already met with Rachel and Amelia, and they had thrashed out the plan in meticulous detail.

The drama had been choreographed; the critical and distinctive role of each character: the lure of the temptress, the magnetism of the seductress, the sheer power of the humble pawn; the transformation to the supreme power of the queen, ruler of all things. The timings worked out within a millisecond. The costumes: red to tempt, black to seduce and cream to overpower. All had been purchased and stored. And finally, the strains of Édith Piaf would provide the perfect backdrop. Everything was in place.

The stage was set.

Thirty-Four

He propped his breakfast tray precariously on his knees, partially covered by the crumpled duvet. His greasy hair fell across his face, his eyes puffy from the overindulgences of the night before. Libby turned towards him, breathing in the intoxicating fumes that seemed to emanate from every pore of his body, every orifice. This was not a promising start to the day.

'Happy Birthday, Alex...' she said softly. 'It's going to be a very special day.'

'It's just another day,' he said grumpily, as he absentmindedly drew circles with spilt orange juice across the surface of the tray with the tip of his index finger. 'I'm just another year older, another year nearer the grave.'

Libby drew back the curtains. The sun streamed in, bathing the room in a warm pool of light. She smiled inwardly as she thought about the treat that Alex had in store later. She looked at her watch: nine hours and thirty minutes to go. The event was due to begin at six o'clock sharp. This would allow time to perform their routine, slip away for some refreshment, and then she, alone, would return to Alex to perform the final act.

Alex screwed up his eyes against the harsh glare of the early morning sun. 'God, last night was a mistake,' he groaned.

'You'll feel better when you're up and about,' Libby soothed. 'More toast?'

'No, go away, leave me alone. And close the bloody curtains, it's too bright.'

Libby padded downstairs, pulling her towelling dressing gown tightly around her waist. She poured herself another cup of coffee and went back upstairs into her bedroom. She knew Alex wouldn't appear for the next couple of hours, so she would make the most of the time. She reached into the wardrobe and pulled out three costumes, immaculately pressed and stored on coat hangers. She spread them across the bed and breathed out a deep sigh of pleasure; the carefully chosen lingerie was exactly what she had envisaged.

The red basque, held by stiff whalebones into the curvaceous shape of a woman; extravagantly detailed with lace and satin, and trussed together under the breast by crossed black laces. The light from the sun enhanced the smooth satin, making the lingerie drip with elegance. This outfit could not fail to tempt even the most feeble of beings.

The black basque, bold and sexy yet subtle and alluring. This was the perfect outfit for seduction; it revealed and yet left just enough to titillate the senses. This will surely leave any mere mortal drooling, begging for more.

Finally her eyes alighted on the cream robe: it was simply perfect in every way. The sequins sparkled, casting a myriad of tiny stars that shimmered and danced across the ceiling. She had no doubt in her mind. She will shine. She will rise and conquer.

She thought about Amelia, her irresistible charm and her piercingly blue eyes. Perfect in her role as the temptress. Rachel is different. She is bold, confident in her body, content in her womanhood. She will draw in her subject with her irrepressible sensuality.

And then she thought about herself, undoubtedly the most vulnerable, but strong and committed in her resolve to carry out her plan. Today. Whatever the consequences.

***

It was five to six. The stage was set. Libby had prepared Alex for his birthday surprise. She had wrapped his naked body in a black silk kimono and laid him spreadeagled, chest uppermost, on the bed. His limbs were restrained by leather wrist and ankle cuffs to the four bed posts. A purple studded collar was buckled round his neck, and the linked chain attached to the collar was tied to the far-left bedpost. His head was supported by two feather and down pillows, covered with red silk.

'Are you ready, Alex?'

He smirked. 'I have absolutely no idea what is about to happen, Libby, but bring it on!'

'First, let's drink a toast,' Libby said, opening a chilled bottle of Bollinger. She poured two glasses. 'Happy Birthday, Alex!' She glanced down at him, her eyes shining with excitement. She lifted the flute to her lips and took a small sip, and then padded over to the record player on the chest of drawers. She removed a record from its sleeve and placed it carefully on the turntable. All of a sudden, the trembling alto voice of Édith Piaf filled the room. 'Do you remember the cabaret at Chez Fleurie, my darling?' She never called him "darling" but, for some reason, it seemed appropriate. 'I want you to imagine you are in the club. Let your mind wander, Alex…'

He raised his eyebrows. She could see the lust in his eyes. 'I'm not sure I deserve this, Libby, but I'm not in a position to argue.' He looked at her and laughed, his heart pounding in his chest. His imagination was running wild.

The door opened and one slender stockinged leg appeared, caressing the side of the door with one heel of a red stiletto. Long red fingernails slithered round the entrance to caress the outstretched limb. The shape of a face appeared, the features difficult to discern; partially hidden behind a red diamanté-studded mask. She pouted her luscious lips, picked out in matching red matt lipstick. Her body twisted and turned erotically to "La Vie En Rose", her movement reminiscent of a middle eastern belly dancer. She paraded herself proudly, temptingly, in front of him. His eyes were glued to her, his senses alert, as she glided her body around the bed. Her dance was having the desired effect; his pupils were dark and dilated, a light film of sweat covered his forehead. She proffered him a sip of champagne, which he greedily devoured. As the music reached a crescendo, she slinked to one side of the room. This part of her dance was over.

His eyes refocused on the doorway. He watched as a black-gloved finger walked dramatically up and down the side of the door frame. She entered the room, her costume barely covering her womanly curves. She brushed one hand lightly against his naked instep, sliding the other up the inside of his thigh. She tantalised him, she paused, and then she withdrew, offering her hand instead, to the lady in red, the temptress. They danced together, gently intertwining their bodies, like snakes in a snake pit. He let out a deep sigh of pleasure; he was in ecstasy. The temptress offered him another sip of champagne and took a sip herself. The two women moved together to form a series of interwoven moving sculptures, driving Alex into even greater heights of excitement. They reminded him of the erotic stone carvings he had admired outside the Indian temples that he had visited the previous summer. As the music died down, they kissed one another passionately. Alex gasped; he couldn't believe how wonderful his treat was turning out to be.

And finally, a woman in cream appeared. Coy and yet elegant. She sauntered towards Alex and fed him another sip of bubbles from the crystal glass. He licked his lips hungrily. She ran her hand lightly from his shoulder, pausing to tickle the soft area of his inner arm, near his elbow; she knew he liked that. Alex shuddered with pleasure. She gently ruffled his chest hair with her nose, and continued downward over the stiffness of his manhood, until she finally reached his feet. She massaged each toe with tender care, using techniques that she had enjoyed in Paris when Roly had pleasured her. Their eyes locked together, and her lips brushed with his. She pulled away, and together, the three girls retreated from the bedroom. Just before Libby left, as an afterthought, she turned to place another record on the turntable. The quintessential sound of The Little Sparrow filled the room. "Non, Je Ne Regrette Rien". 'I will return to complete your birthday treat,' she said as she fed him yet more champagne. 'And I promise you, it will be an experience of a lifetime.' She saw a flicker of disappointment and frustration pass over Alex's face.

The three women crowded into Libby's bedroom and shut the door. They could no longer contain themselves; they dissolved into peals of laughter, their shoulders shaking with mirth.

'I can't believe we just did that! We were bloody brilliant!' Amelia remarked. 'And, by the way, Rachel, you're a pretty good kisser,' Amelia said, energetically slapping Rachel's bottom.

'Hey, what have I missed?' Libby asked. 'Thank you both, you were amazing, it worked. Alex was transported to heaven and back. And his treat hasn't finished yet.'

'Whoa, are you trying to make us envious, Libs?' Rachel laughed.

'Come on, you two, get your jeans back on and let's go for that Chardonnay I promised you.'

The glowing lights of The Rose and Crown shone as they walked down North Parade. They were in high spirits as they opened the door and found a small table near the window. Libby ordered a bottle of chilled Chardonnay and three glasses.

'Well, Libby, I don't know if Alex was excited, but it

certainly did the trick for me,' Amelia said in a seductive voice.

'Did I miss something?' Libby asked. 'Did you two go off script?'

'What happens in the bedroom stays in the bedroom!' Rachel said with a grin.

'We were fabulous,' Amelia said, laughing.

'It is a *very* ingenious idea, Libs. We could set up a business,' Rachel said, her eyes glittering with excitement. 'We would make a bloody fortune.'

'Could you imagine Alex, a lawyer, living off immoral earnings?' Libby said, stifling a laugh. 'But I took a risk,' she said, more seriously. 'Something happened to Alex back in the day when he was at university, and this might have brought back some horrible memories.'

Her two friends looked puzzled. 'What do you mean, Libs?'

She glanced from one to the other and shrugged her shoulders. 'Let's not talk about this now. But I think we have been a great success, so, here's to strong women everywhere,' she said, raising her bowser of wine. 'When I was at the French nightclub, I saw Alex in a different light. I'm used to his controlling ways, but, as you could see tonight, he adores being restrained and mildly humiliated. We really left him wanting more tonight! He is totally at my mercy,' said Libby jubilantly.

The time passed quickly.

'I could murder one of those toasted sandwiches, Libs, my treat.' Rachel went to order, leaving Libby and Amelia alone.

'Would Tom enjoy a treat like this, do you think?'

'God no, he's far too vanilla for anything like this.'

'What do you mean, vanilla?'

Amelia smiled. 'It's people who believe that sex is only for having babies, and always with the lights off.'

'Is that all you've got to look forward to, Amelia?'

'Thank goodness. I've just had a baby; I don't want another one for a long time.'

They talked, laughed and enjoyed their toasties and wine. Suddenly Libby looked at her watch. 'Oh my goodness, time has flown. I hope I left the heating on high enough for him. We've been gone for over an hour, I'd better dash. Thanks again, girls. I owe you.'

Thirty-Five

'Alex, I'm sorry I've been so long. The time passed in a flash. I'll just slip into something more comfortable, and I'll be with you in five…' Libby called as she leapt, two stairs at a time, to her bedroom. The effect of the wine was making her feel giddy, but she still had her wits about her. 'I'll be worth the wait,' she added, in a sultry voice. She would much prefer to call it a night, but she had promised him a treat. It had to be done. She slipped off her jeans and pulled her cream robe over her body, wriggling her hips lazily as she did so. She had enjoyed the role-play, and the drink with her friends in the pub, but this was just a step too far.

She paused outside the door to flick her hair back from her shoulders; she must remember that she was no longer a pawn, she was the queen. She walked confidently into the bedroom with her head held high. Her attention was immediately drawn to the sound of the record player as the needle scratched relentlessly on the vinyl, over and over again. She had forgotten to place the arm in the correct position for it to repeat. The clicking of the needle echoed round and round in her befuddled head. She turned her attention to Alex. He appeared to be asleep, his head bowed awkwardly, the purple collar taut round his neck. She padded to the side of his bed; perhaps she would be able to have an early night after all. Her brow creased in puzzlement when she noticed a thin trail of saliva and bile, running from the corner of his mouth, forming a pool on the floor beside him.

'Alex, I'm here,' she said seductively.

He stayed silent and still.

'Alex, wake up… I think you've had too much champagne,' she tutted. 'I'm back and I'm going to give you the treat of a lifetime.'

Libby stared down at him, rather annoyed; he appeared to be asleep. She placed her hand on one side of his arm. It was warm. 'Stop mucking around, I thought you would be excited to see me, not dead to the world…' She gave him a shake but there was no reaction at all. 'Alex, come on, you're frightening me now.'

A sudden chill coursed through her body. She put two fingers to the side of his neck to feel his pulse. Nothing. She froze with fear, her mind racing. 'Chest compressions… Oh God, Alex, don't leave me.' She bashed the middle of his chest with the side of her hand five times using the full weight of her body. She then put her ear to his mouth. Was he breathing? 'Oh God, what have I done?' She started the chest compressions again. A constant stream of bile dribbled from his mouth, but there was no sign of life. His chest was flat and still. Her hands shook uncontrollably as she unlocked the cuffs and the collar and heaved him onto his side. 'Come on, Alex, for God's sake, wake up.' He was unresponsive.

'He's dead.' Her hand flew to her mouth in horror. 'Make it go away. This can't be happening.' She shook him once again. 'Please, Alex,' she pleaded. She pulled one of his eyelids up, and then the other. His pupils were fixed and dilated. 'I can't believe it. I didn't mean to kill you, Alex. It was an accident,' she wailed. 'Think, Libby, think…' She fell back onto the chair, her heart beating fast. 'It's too late to call an ambulance; there's nothing anyone can do… He's gone.'

The true horror of what had happened was beginning to dawn on her. 'God, should I call the police?' She stared at his body and the unlocked bondage equipment laid out on the bed beside him. 'The police would assume that I had murdered him.' She stumbled to the bathroom and retched. Her body doubled over; she vomited until there was nothing left. She roughly pulled her matted hair away from her mouth and stared dismally into the darkness. 'Make a plan, make a plan,' she muttered under her breath.

'Why can't I think straight? Why did I drink so much wine? I was stupid. Stupid.' She had a vague memory of reading about something like this happening to a pop star. His wife had pretended that it was a sex game that had gone wrong, but the evidence didn't stack up. She ended up in prison, done for manslaughter. 'I can't do that; they would know that we tied him up and left him. I can't put my friends through this, we would all be put in prison.'

She went downstairs and switched on the coffee machine. She prepared herself a strong black coffee with two large teaspoons of sugar and racked her brain for an idea. Remembering a film she had seen, where something similar happened, she absentmindedly lifted the steaming cup to her lips. She was pretty sure that the wife and her lover had hidden the dead husband in a trunk and had put it into storage. And then they disappeared. The mystery had never been solved.

'Come on, Libby, think…' Alex had his school trunk stored in the attic and she knew that he could fit inside because he had once shown her how the boys, as a prank, used to hide in their trunks in the dormitory. As she drained the warm comforting liquid, a plan formed in her mind. She would hide his body in a bin bag inside the trunk and arrange for a "man with a van" to take it, with a few other items, to an archival storage facility. She thought there was one in Botley Road. And then she would simply disappear. Without a trace.

She stumbled back to the bedroom, willing him to move, to say something, anything, but all she could hear was the intermittent hum of traffic on the Banbury Road. She thought it strange that normal life continued in the outside world, and yet her own life had changed forever. She turned on the tap to run herself a hot bath and threw a scented bath bomb into the steaming water, listening to the gentle fizzing as it dissolved. She stepped out of her cream robe, throwing it carelessly onto the floor, and eased herself into the hot water. As she lowered her body, she could feel the tension ebbing away, replaced by deep and heavy exhaustion. It flashed through her mind that it would be simple to stretch out on her back, immerse her face and breathe the water deep into her lungs. A murder and a suicide; it would solve everything. She shook her head; this was not the answer. She knew she must not rest; she must act swiftly, before the body became stiff and cold.

Her mind switched from believing she was going to wake up from a deadly nightmare to thinking on her feet, working out the practical arrangements. She would use two strong garden bags, garden twine and packing tape to wrap the body. This would eliminate any suspicious odour; the body would start to smell after a few days. She would then pack him in the silver trunk downstairs. It would be too heavy to lift after it was fully packed. She would then arrange safe storage. Job done.

That was the straightforward part. But how could she disappear without a trace?

Dark thoughts crept into her head. Would the police think that she had killed Alex for the inheritance money? Of course, everyone would make that assumption. The police would search high and low to find her, to convict a killer – a murderer – on the loose. How wrong they would be. She suddenly remembered Roly and their conversation about how to disappear. She couldn't tell anyone, none of her friends, or the police, about what had happened. But she would contact Roly.

Reluctantly, she climbed out of the sanctuary of the bath and wrapped herself in Alex's navy-blue dressing gown. She inhaled the familiar scent of him, the tears streaming down her face. She placed the ladder against the hatch and climbed into the small attic space. The silver trunk was resting against the brickwork towards the back of the house. She clambered over years of unwanted clutter to unlatch the catch of the container. She sighed as she stared at the dusty university files that Alex had elected to keep. She thought idly, *why do we all keep the rubbish of our lives? We should chuck it away at the time, instead of leaving innocent family members to deal with the junk of our lives when we're gone.*

She piled the files and books carefully to one side until the trunk was empty. She struggled to lift the empty vessel over the mountains of rubbish bags, concerned about how she would lift the body and the trunk down the stairs. Mustering all her strength, she manoeuvred it through the hatch and dropped it onto the landing with an almighty crash. She turned and walked backwards down the steps to the safety of the landing. Lodging it against the top step, she slid the case downwards, holding the handle at one end. Her back ached as she struggled to control the momentum as it bounced noisily down each stair and ground to a halt at the bottom. Dragging it to the alcove underneath the front window, she drew the curtains against the black of the night.

Fortunately she had enough strong garden bags. Leaving them, the twine and the brown tape by the trunk, she returned to the bedroom. She would employ a similar technique for transporting his body downstairs. Except this time, she would have to drag his body down from the front. The sheer weight of his leaden body was extraordinary. She groaned with exhaustion but something in her, adrenaline, kept her mind and body focussed.

At last, she laid out his dead body on the polished wooden floor beside the trunk. Waving the first bag in the air to fully open it, she folded his legs together and stuffed them into the cavernous bag and tied it around his waist with garden twine. He was half gone. She stared at him, before returning upstairs to select a red fleece, his favourite, and she pulled it over his unruly curls. She thought how irrational she was, trying to keep him safe and warm, when in fact he was dead and getting colder by the minute.

Before placing the second bag over his head, their lips met. She let out a deep wail of agony. 'I'm so sorry, Alex.' She tied the second bag over the edge of the first, so the body was totally encased, and then she secured the seam with the wide brown tape. And then, he was gone. Summoning up the last vestiges of strength, she lifted the top half of the package and bent it into the space. The bottom half followed. It was a very tight fit, but she had been successful.

She inhaled deeply as she closed the lid of the trunk and locked it securely with the solid padlock. Selecting an Indian throw, she covered the trunk and placed a large vase of white lilies on the top.

No one would ever know the truth.

Thirty-Six

After a restless night's sleep, Libby opened her eyes. She instantly closed them again, willing the events of the night before to be nothing but a nightmare. She was shocked by how she could think with such clarity. How could she be this cold and calculating? Had she turned into a sociopath? She had just hidden her husband's dead body.

Her head churned with questions. *How did it happen? Was Alex strangled by the collar?* He had consumed a lot of alcohol, perhaps he choked on his own vomit. If only she hadn't stayed so long at the pub, she might have arrived back in time to save him. But whatever had happened, he was dead. There was no turning back.

She must work quickly. By concealing his body, she had bought herself some time to cover her tracks, consider her next steps and arrange a meeting with Roland.

The bed where Alex had lain was ruffled, the sheet stained with vomit and urine, damp and pale brown, edged with a thin line of darker brown. The silk pillows still held the impression of his head, the bondage equipment lay on top of the duvet just as she had left it. She glanced at the floor, a pool of bile, almost dry, seeped into the floorboards. She must hide the evidence, but not too thoroughly: too much disinfectant might raise suspicion. She worked tirelessly, using mild detergent, wearing protective rubber gloves; until the room looked ordinary, as if nothing had happened. She was satisfied with her work. Climbing into the attic, she put everything back in its place, and, scanning the dark space, she was content that everything looked normal. No one would ever know.

"Ordinary". "Normal". She thought how horribly ironic it was that, here she was trying to achieve ordinariness, normality, when everything was extraordinary; everything was far from normal.

She cleaned the whole house, obsessively moving every piece of the furniture, dusting every picture rail, until the house felt almost clinical. Dusty followed her into each room, studying her every movement. She felt unsettled by his presence, guilty, as his brown eyes stared unerringly at her. What would become of Dusty?

Her work was done. She poured herself another cup of coffee and lay down in the comforting folds of the settee. Her eyes were drawn to the elegant brown-and-gold Indian throw, and the extravagant display of lilies that enhanced the alcove to perfection. Although the overall shape did remind her of a coffin. She was tempted to leave the trunk there. It would be so overt and obvious that no-one would think to look there. The police would be more likely to search in the dark recesses of the house, rather than something like this, surely? Was she being rather naïve? She wished she had read more murder mysteries in her misspent youth.

She must be forensically aware. Astute.

She threw on her coat and cycled into town. She bought two simple "pay-as-you-go" phones from two different outlets and hurried back home to put them both on to charge and check that they were working. She entered Roland's number. 'Roly, is that you?'

'Hi, Libs. How are you doing?'

Hearing his soft comforting voice, all her strength and resolve left her in an instant. Deep sobs rose from the depths of her belly.

'Breathe, Libby. What on earth has happened?'

The tears streamed down her face, forming deep rivulets. 'Roly, please help me…'

There was silence. Neither person spoke. Eventually Roland sucked in a deep breath. 'What has he done to you, Libby?' he muttered.

Libby let out a strangled wail. 'I can't talk on the phone. I need to see you. It's urgent.'

'Okay, Libby. It sounds rather "cloak and dagger" to me, but where shall we meet?'

'The first bench on the left by the duck pond in the University Parks, in half an hour.' She glanced at her watch, 'Two o'clock?'

'I'll need to cancel my tutorial, but I'll be there.'

She rummaged in her wardrobe and selected a Hermès silk scarf and a large pair of sunglasses from her collection. She applied bright-red lipstick and glanced at her reflection in the mirror. She thought it strange that she looked like Jackie Kennedy – her husband had died tragically too. Finally she pulled out an old Burberry trench coat from the back of her wardrobe that she hadn't worn for years.

She went down to the hallway and selected a walking cane that Alex had made and paused to study herself in the long mirror by the front door. Her shoulders slumped. She looked like a cliché of a woman desperately trying not to be noticed; rather like a courier escaping the East German border during the Cold War. At least she was incognito; she would not be easily recognised. And it was the best she could do, given the short notice. She left the house by the kitchen door, turned left and limped her way towards the park, deciding to use the back gate because, as far as she knew, there was no CCTV at this entrance. The air was cold, but the sun shone brightly. She noticed that most women she passed were wearing some sort of scarf to keep warm, and some were also wearing sunglasses; perhaps, she was not quite as conspicuous as she felt.

As she approached the duck pond, she heard the call of the gulls as they swooped down towards the water to steal the tasty titbits that children had thrown into the murky water. She watched as the circular ripples spread on the surface of the water. It was like a reflection of her life; one tragic event radiates out and affects her whole life and everything she must do. 'Roly, thank you for agreeing to meet me.'

Roland reached forward to give her a gentle peck on her cheek, aware that her whole body was shaking. 'Libby, come and sit beside me, and tell me what is on your mind. And why are you limping?'

Libby's voice trembled with emotion as she recounted the events of the previous twenty-four hours. 'It was an accident…'

Roland's face turned puce, as he absorbed the reality of what had happened. 'Alex is dead. God, Libby, this is serious.' He balanced his glasses over his creased forehead and rubbed his eyes. 'What a bloody mess... Have you contacted the police?'

She shook her head in despair. 'They will think I murdered him, Roly. I will go to prison, and my friends will be dragged down with me. I can't...'

'It all seems so unfair. Alex was cruel to you, he treated you badly, he was blackmailing you. He was my friend, but I hated the way he treated you.' He paused. 'I don't think he deserved to die, but he did deserve to be punished. He was a damaged man, but he was too young to die.'

'Roly, I was trying to get our marriage back on the right track. It was a birthday treat that went horribly wrong...'

He pummelled his hands together nervously. 'I believe you, Libs, and I will help you. Tell me your plan.'

'I must disappear without a trace. I have no choice, Roly. I have to leave my life in Oxford behind and start a new life elsewhere.'

'Disappear?' He paused, stroking his chin in thought. 'I may be able to help you, Libs. I think I told you that I read a book recently on how to disappear, and, although it was fiction, it did give some good tips for how to vanish into thin air. You would need to use a new name, a new identity, a new look...'

'Tell me what to do and I will do it.'

'Libby, we'll need to make a list,' he said, pulling out a notebook and biro from his briefcase. 'Listen to me carefully. The first thing to remember is you cannot use your credit cards, bank cards, or any store cards. These will need to be destroyed. The police can easily trace you if you use any of these in an ATM. Be scrupulous about this. Have you got any cash in the house?'

'Yes, I'm pretty sure Alex has a bundle of cash in the safe. I don't know why, but it might have been something to do with cash payments for work. It all sounded a bit shady to me, but it will be useful to me now.'

Roly scribbled brief notes as he spoke. 'The next thing you must do is draw out cash from all your accounts, but not too much or you'll trigger an inquiry. Anything up to £5,000 is a safe bet, I think. Then gather all your jewellery together and put it all into a bag; you can flog it further down the line when you need more cash. I would also suggest that you go to several bullion dealers and buy sovereigns, using a bank transfer. They will post them out to you, special delivery, so you will receive them tomorrow. Sovereigns are small and valuable, easy to transport, and you can cash them in when you need to.' He paused, looking sympathetically at her. 'There is a lot to organise, Libs, but stay focussed. You can, and you will do this.'

She straightened her back and turned her head towards him, steely in her determination to do as Roly instructed.

'You will have to stop any activity on social media. Do you have a Facebook, Instagram, or a Twitter account?'

'I have a Facebook account, but I rarely post anything. I'm more of a Facebook stalker, I like to see what my friends are up to... I don't have Instagram or Twitter accounts. To be honest, I don't even know what they are!'

'Good. Close your Facebook account, and then dispose of your computer, but make a list first of the contacts you might need in the future from your database. And don't forget to dispose of Alex's laptop and mobile phone too.'

'There is so much I need to do,' she mumbled under her breath.

'Now for the practical arrangements: you must change your appearance. You could dye your hair black and dress like a goth, for example. It would help you to escape recognition by a chance encounter with a friend, you know how easy it is to bump into someone, quite by chance, when you're having an affair.' He chuckled. 'Also buy some glasses with clear lenses, they will help with your disguise.'

Libby blew into the air, trying to control the overwhelming feeling of panic.

'Now, we need to compose the story of your disappearance. The first thing you must do is dispose of the body. Contact a courier to take the trunk, plus a few other items to make it look more normal, to a local storage facility. Don't forget to use cash. Always use cash. And give a false name. Secondly, send a text to all your friends, saying that you and Alex have decided to go on an extended holiday to the continent. Keep the message short, friendly, but to the point. Within the next few days, it is imperative that you leave Oxford. I suggest you lay a false trail. You could catch a train to Liverpool, use one of your cards in a cash machine near the ferry, and then immediately buy another single ticket to go to your final destination. The police will think you have gone to Ireland. Does that sound like a plan?'

'Yes, it does,' Libby mused.

'When you go, Libby, I suggest you take as little stuff as you need. Stuff is not necessary and would be a cumbersome burden. You must leave your past life behind and move on. There is no room for sentimentality. We still have the thorny problem of your passport, but I think this is enough for now.'

Libby shuddered. 'But what about Dusty?'

'Good point. I really thought I'd covered everything. You must book him into kennels, telling them that you and your husband are touring the continent, and are likely to be away for at least a month, but say you'll confirm the return date asap.'

Libby pushed a second "pay-as-you-go" phone into Roland's hand. 'You have helped me so much already, Roly. I would understand if you wanted to cut all ties with me now, so you don't get implicated. But I thought if we both had a burner phone, we could remain in contact, should the need arise.'

'Libs, I won't desert you. You are an innocent victim; Alex emotionally abused you. You deserve another chance, and I will do my best to support you in whatever way I can. I do think it would be prudent, though, to keep our contact to a minimum.' Roland ripped out two pages of scribbled notes and handed them to Libby. 'Good luck, Libs. Draw a line in the sand. You can't change what has happened, but it is within your power to shape your future.'

Libby tied her scarf securely under her chin, repositioned her glasses and reached for her cane. 'Operation Thin Air starts now,' she said. 'I can't thank you enough.' They embraced warmly, and she turned and limped slowly towards the gate.

Thirty-Seven

She gazed out of the carriage window. The countryside sped past her eyes in a flash, just as the last few days had done. She had worked tirelessly through her list, crossing off each item as she did it. She ran through everything in her mind over and over again, checking and double-checking that she hadn't forgotten anything. The body had been safely dispatched. Tick. She had gathered cash from the safe, and from all her bank accounts, and she now kept it close to her in a belt under her coat. Tick. (She couldn't help but wonder what Alex had intended to do with literally thousands of pounds that he had stashed in the safe.) She had left her financial affairs as tidily as she could. Tick. She had disposed of all computers, mobile phones, and closed all activity on social media, including her friends WhatsApp group. Tick. She had sent text messages about their trip to the continent to all her friends and contacts. Tick. (She found it curious that the hardest thing of all was saying goodbye to Dusty; not her friends, but her dog.) She knew that she would never see him again. Her eyes welled with tears, but she could also cross this off her list. Tick.

She formed a tight fist and stretched out each finger in turn as she counted all the jobs that she had been instructed to complete. She was satisfied that "Operation Thin Air" had been successful. So far, so good.

As she looked around the half-empty carriage, she caught sight of her reflection in the window. She jumped. Her long hair was now jet black, held messily in place with long black braids. Her eyes, meticulously decorated with dramatic black eyeliner, forming the shape of two tear drops on her cheeks below. She had completed the look with a layer of deep-purple eyeshadow and matching lipstick. She wore a loose-fitting black cheesecloth dress – trussed in at the waist by a thick belt – dark tights and flat hobnail boots. She had teamed her outfit with an old army greatcoat, baggy enough to conceal the bulky items secured round her waist. She could barely recognise her own reflection. She smiled with satisfaction. Initially she had been tempted to try and merge into the background with an insignificant disguise, but this new look was far more powerful.

As the train pulled into Liverpool station, she felt the familiar bubble of anxiety as she stepped on to the platform and walked towards the exit. Hailing a taxi, she travelled to the ferry terminal. There, she found the nearest ATM and used her credit card for one last time to draw out more cash and to buy a coffee and a pastry at the cafe at the dockside. This would provide vital evidence for the police of her whereabouts, an inspirational red herring. She even treated herself to a packet of Marlboro Lights, something she'd been longing to do, but Alex had always forbidden it. As she cupped her black coffee, she considered her next steps. During the whirlwind of the last few days in Oxford, a small advert in one of the tabloids had caught her eye: a professional family of four living on the outskirts of Dartmouth urgently required a live-in nanny to look after their two children; a girl aged six and boy aged nine. She had contacted them on her burner phone, using a false name and identity details. They had offered her the position, including a three-month probationary period. She liked children, she had a wealth of teaching experience and Dartmouth was miles from Oxford. It was ideal.

As she strode back towards the station, she became aware of how many aggressive and belligerent looks she had attracted from complete strangers; she couldn't believe how quick they were to make instant and superficial judgements based simply on her appearance. She decided that, in future, it might be wise to ease back slightly on the makeup. The weight of the belt and the warmth of her coat made her feel hot and light-headed; beads of sweat formed on her forehead and her underarms felt moist. She bought a single ticket to Totnes, changing at Birmingham New Street. And then she would take a short bus ride to Dartmouth.

This time she was not as fortunate. The train to Birmingham was packed to the gills. She found a tiny space by the door and slumped down on her bulging rucksack on the grubby floor. She sighed as she studied the ankles of everyone crowding around her. The sharp clasp of one of her bracelets dug painfully into the skin on the side of her belly. This would be a long and uncomfortable journey.

She winced with pain as she opened her eyes, rubbing her cricked neck. The carriage had suddenly become a hive of activity. The train had arrived at Paddington Station. Passengers fought to retrieve their luggage from overhead lockers, and all were jostling for position by the automatic doors, thoughtlessly trampling over her in the process. She pushed her way up to standing, muttering with annoyance.

The connecting train to Totnes was, by contrast, quiet and half empty. She relaxed into her seat, feeling her pent-up emotion fade away. She watched as the hustle and bustle and flickering lights of Birmingham disappeared behind her, replaced by the tranquillity and darkness of the countryside. She felt like she was on a journey to the back of beyond.

But then she remembered. She was no longer the wife of a solicitor, living in the leafy suburbs of Oxford with her dog. Libby no longer existed. Her old life had been completely obliterated.

This was the beginning of her new life.

Her name is Charlie. She lives in Dartmouth and is employed to work as a nanny.

She has truly begun her new adventure.

Part 3

Thirty-Eight

Devon: Present day.

Her story is complete. The words of the last section of the book had flown onto the page, all her pent-up guilt released at last. It was easier to write the truth than to come up with a convincing fabrication. Although she knew that the story would incriminate her, she must own the blame, and she had to try to exonerate her friends who, some might argue, were accomplices.

She selected three publishers, careful to avoid the less scrupulous businesses who promised the earth for a huge fee. She meticulously prepared three submissions, which included the full manuscript, a covering letter, tailored to the requirements of individual publishers, and a synopsis.

The Humble Pawn.

Antonia Farouk.

Today was the day.

She checked and double-checked each submission. Her hand hovered over the keyboard, and then she pressed the button: once, twice, three times.

The truth was out. Her work was done.

***

Time was running out. She had submitted the true story and, if her manuscript was to be accepted, she knew it wouldn't take long for the police to piece everything together and track her down. But she wasn't ready. She had a lot to do, and she valued her freedom too much.

As she strolled down the cliff path and into the small town of Loss, a weight had been lifted from her shoulders. She breathed in the saltiness of the sea air and smiled. It had taken two years to write her story, and now she could do no more. It would probably be at least twelve weeks before she heard back from any publisher. She had no choice; she would just have to wait.

As she opened the door to the tiny cafe, the cheerful bell sounded to announce her arrival.

'Hello, my duck. What can I do you for? A latte? No children today then?'

'Hello, Bert, a latte would be wonderful, thank you. Bella and Dan are at school today, so I have a bit of time to myself.' Bert was one of the locals that had welcomed Charlie when she first arrived in Devon. The local community were inclined to be rather cliquey, and didn't always have time for the up-country folk, so Charlie felt honoured that she had been accepted into the fold so readily.

'I'll bring it over, Charlie. Go and sit yourself down.'

The metal chair was rather uncomfortable, but the cafe was warm and cosy, and she always enjoyed watching the hustle-bustle of the high street outside the window. Today, the narrow street was alive with people, young and old, going about their daily business. The fish shop opposite, usually thriving, was closed today. Charlie wondered why, and then remembered it was Monday, a day off for the local fishermen. Next to the fish shop was a typical seaside shop, selling all the things you never knew you needed: expensive glass ornaments, single coffee-cup froth whisks, funky fat bins, and white-framed art of the sea, the sky and hundreds of gulls. The shopkeepers of these kinds of shops all looked weirdly the same: middle-aged, messy hair tied in a bun, donning floral pinafore dresses, and flat, pink leather shoes fastened with a sensible buckle.

The bell sounded, heralding another customer. A tall gentleman of oriental origin strode into the cafe, holding a briefcase in one hand and a folded newspaper in the other. Charlie gasped. How could this be possible? She covered one side of her face with an outstretched hand, trying to look inconspicuous. What were the chances of Alex's son walking into a small cafe in an insignificant town in Devon? She bit her lip, a tight ball of sickness rising from her belly. Would he recognise her?

'Here you are, my love,' Bert said, handing Charlie a steaming latte. 'This should warm the cockles of your heart.' Libby muttered her thanks, but Bert seemed intent on having a conversation. 'Are you coming to the knees-up on Saturday at the pub? Sandrine is the guest musician; she's a mate of yours isn't she, Charlie? It should be a cracking night!'

'Yes, I'll probably be there,' she whispered. She willed Bert to go away and leave her alone, he was drawing unwanted attention to her. As she self-consciously sipped her coffee, she became aware of his bemused stare. Should she escape? Or was it too late?

'Excuse me, I hope you'll forgive me, but you look familiar. Do I know you?' The young man stooped over her, his brow creased in puzzlement. Charlie raised her head and their eyes locked. Although her hair was still dyed black, she had become careless with her disguised appearance, using considerably less makeup than she had done, and not wearing glasses.

'No, you don't know me.' She pursed her lips. 'Is this some kind of chat-up line? I'm old enough to be your mother.'

Suddenly his expression changed. 'I know it's you, Libby, despite your rather feeble disguise. You've got a rather poor crown on your upper-central incisor that doesn't match with the others. I remember it well.'

'Okay, Tai. We need to talk, but probably not here.' The palms of her hands were bathed in sweat.

'Where is my father? Is he living with you down here? I've got so many questions. Why did you run away from Oxford?'

Bert strode up to them. 'What's going on, Charlie? Is this bloke bothering you? I can't be doing with this kind of thing in my cafe,' he said, looking accusingly at Tai.

Charlie was quick to diffuse the situation. 'He's an old acquaintance of mine, Bert. What are the chances of that, huh?'

Bert smiled benevolently. 'I think you'd better buy a lottery ticket, having this kind of luck, Missy.' Satisfied, he walked back behind the counter.

'Have you got your car here, Tai? I don't want everyone overhearing what I've got to say.'

He nodded, quickly draining his coffee. 'It's parked just along the road. It's a dark green Bentley. I'll see you there in five minutes.' He stood, gathered his coat, newspaper and briefcase, and politely nodded his thanks to Bert.

They sat side by side on the sumptuous leather seats.

'I can't believe I've found you. I hope you know that you and my father are officially on the Missing Persons list?' he said curtly. 'Where is he? Where is my father?'

'I'd better start at the beginning.' She recounted the cruelty and control that Alex had shown towards her from the beginning of their marriage. She had suffered for years. He had been unfaithful to her, he had manipulated his mother's will, he had lied and cheated. But despite everything, she wanted to make it all better. 'Because I loved him.' She described their trip to Paris. 'I was willing to do anything he asked for, anything at all, even going into a sex club in Paris, because that is what he wanted.' She described how she arranged a birthday treat for him, 'Something I knew that he would like.' She recounted the careful planning, the cooperation of her friends, the event itself. 'But, Tai, it all went wrong.' Her shoulders shuddered with grief as she described the horror of what had happened. 'So you see, the only thing I could think to do was to hide his body and for me to disappear without a trace.'

The air in the car was hot and stuffy. She could feel her heart beating in her chest

'Did you lose your mind, Libby? The police would have understood.'

'I don't know, Tai. I've been over it time and time again. Maybe in hindsight, I might have done it all differently. It was a huge shock to find Alex the way he was. I will have to live with that for the rest of my life.'

Tai stared into space. 'I'm trying to understand, Libby. There must have been a lot going on in your mind that evening. But surely, can't you go to the police now and explain. It might be better in the long run. You can't run away forever.'

'I can't do it, Tai. Imagine the agony of being dragged through the courts, having to disclose intimate details, implicating my friends… It would be all over the tabloids.'

'I could arrange for you to have the best lawyer money can buy. I do understand how difficult my father must have been. He was damaged by my mother and her friend, he was sexually assaulted, and this is something I will have to live for the rest of my life.'

'I'm so sorry, it must be hard for you.' Libby reached across and clamped his hands in hers. 'I need you to understand, Tai. Please don't go to the police.' She looked quizzically at him. 'What are you doing here anyway?'

'I inherited a house in Tiverton from my mother. I intend to spend the next three months down here, because I have a placement in Derriford Hospital in Plymouth. It's a very convenient location, and I like to come to Loss for some sea air and grab some respite from my relentless study.' He paused. 'A competent lawyer could fight your corner for you.' He sighed heavily with the weight of his sorrow. 'I have to confess that I am disappointed and very sad that I will never have the chance to get to know my father. But I have to ask you, where is he? Where is his body?'

'You will find out in the fullness of time, but, for now, you'll just have to be patient. I don't want to implicate you in all this, Tai. You have your whole life to live. And I have things I must do before I can start to think about clearing my name.'

Tai rubbed his face roughly with his hands. 'But I have to be completely scrupulous, or I'll lose my career. I have no choice. I don't know where you live, so all I can do is tell the police that I spotted you in a cafe and that you looked like one of the missing people that they are searching for. I'm sure they get dozens of calls like this. Keep your head down, and it might all blow over. I'm so sorry, Libby, but I can't be a party to this.'

Thirty-Nine

Charlie opened the lid of her computer. Three pings sounded in quick succession. She clicked open first email:

Dear Antonia Farouk,

Thank you for sending through your manuscript and supporting documents. We are delighted to offer you a publishing contract for *The Humble Pawn*. We are impressed by the honesty and validity of your story. Please consider the attached contract. The advance is to be negotiated, should you decide to accept our terms and conditions.

We look forward to hearing from you.

Yours sincerely,
Simon Alchester,

On behalf of Stork Publishing,
Cavendish House,
356 Fleet Street,
London
E45 8CB

Her hand flew to her mouth. She hadn't expected such a quick response, but she wasn't entirely surprised. She scrolled through the contract; there didn't seem to be any catches in the small print. Not only that, but the publishing company was also offering her a substantial advance for the honour of publishing her book. It seemed a novel idea to actually be given a fee for all the work and time she had devoted to her writing. A reward for all the agony and pain.

She opened the second email. Another offer with no obvious catches. She threw her hands in the air jubilantly.

But it was the third email that caught her eye. It was from Brendon and Moseley Books: a small bespoke publishing company based in the Scottish Highlands. She read and reread the contract. This was a scrupulous, honest contract, not asking for any money upfront, and contained a modest itemisation of expenses likely to be incurred during the editing, printing and marketing process. The publisher would receive reimbursement from the profits of the sales.

Charlie flicked on to the website and read the author reviews which were enthusiastic and insightful. She did briefly worry about providing an author photo for the website, but this was a concern for further down the line.

She breathed in a deep sigh of satisfaction, but then worries crept into the dark recesses of her mind. She couldn't accept any sum of money because she didn't have a bank account, or any formal means of identification. This was the first obvious barrier. She felt, on balance, that the big publishing companies were thriving enterprises, they probably didn't need her custom, or yet another "would be" ever-hopeful first-time author. This wasn't a barrier, but more of a personal conundrum.

She returned to the contract offered by Brendon and Moseley Books. Of course she wouldn't have the thorny problem of how to accept an advance, but this, for her, was irrelevant. Everything felt right about this company. The website shone with enthusiasm and optimism about releasing the work of authors they respected and valued, out into the big wide world. The editors were authors in their own right, and they were prepared to take a risk, to believe in the authors and their stories. She appreciated the honesty and integrity of this company.

Her mind was made up.

***

Since her meeting with Tai, Charlie had realised that time was short. She had warmed to Tai from the very first moment that she met him. And when they had sat together in the car two days before, and she had told her story, she felt that Tai had understood, and empathised with, the misery that she suffered during her marriage to his father. But he also expressed his sadness about being denied the opportunity to get to know him. Charlie felt deep sorrow on his behalf. The manner in which Tai was conceived had a big part to play in why Alex had behaved in the way he had; the control and coercive behaviour. But Alex's mother had told Libby when she visited the rest home, that he had a tendency to seek control from an early age. The sexual assault that Alex was subjected to was undoubtedly a significant factor, but it was also in Alex's genetic makeup. She wondered how Tai might have turned out if Alex had been able to take an active role in his life. Perhaps he would have suffered more. No one will ever know the answer, and it is impossible to change the course of history. She understood why Tai had to inform the police: he was a medical student, and any kind of criminal activity would have robbed him of his career. But Charlie couldn't help but feel disappointed, saddened, that she was going to be shopped by Alex's son.

She cast her mind back to the sailing trip to Salcombe back in the summer with the family. How, one stormy evening, she and the children's father, James, had gone ashore to buy provisions from the local store. How a middle-aged couple standing behind them in the queue thought they recognised her face from a photo in the newspaper: one of two missing persons living in Oxford. From that day, she had waited for the police to contact her, but so far she had heard nothing. Perhaps she would have the same fortune after Tai's contact with the police, but she feared not. Now that her story, *The Humble Pawn*, was to be published, and the truth of events will be public; she will eventually be traced. The sharks were circling. The net was closing in.

Charlie was looking forward to the music evening at The Ferry Boat Inn. Sandy always provided high-quality entertainment, the beer was good and the company even better. Tonight the pub was bubbling with locals, all enjoying a pint and a chat. Charlie pushed her way to the bar and bought two pints of beer, one for herself and one for Sandy, and then found a table in front of the small stage area designated for the musicians. Two large speakers partially concealed her view, but it was good enough. She settled into her chair and glanced around. She didn't know many of the punters, but she recognised most of them by sight; they were always kind and courteous towards her. She was particularly fond of old Jimmy, a wonderful local character, who has gone fishing almost every day for most of his life on his boat, *Maverick*. She enjoyed his company, and he always shared a few wise titbits, learnt from his experiences on his journey through life.

Tonight, Charlie felt an inexplicable sense of sadness. Loss had become somewhere she could call home. Although her host family weren't perfect, she had grown fond of the children, and she loved her self-contained flat in the north wing of High Cliff. Sandy had become a very close friend, and she felt sad that she had been unable to share much of her previous life with her. She had a strange feeling that her time here was rapidly coming to an end. And she wasn't ready.

The murmurings of anticipation rose, as Sandrine bounced her way onto the stage area. Tonight she wore a short flouncy gypsy skirt, edged with a wide frill. Her white linen shirt enhanced her olive skin, falling loosely, enticingly, over the curves of her body. Her sleeves were rolled up, as if she was ready to get stuck into the washing up, but she wore it easily and with class. Her elegant ankle boots drew the eye to her slim shapely legs and finished off her outfit stylishly. Charlie gazed at her with pride and admiration. She looked beautiful. But the most eye-catching part of Sandrine was the embellishment of a tattoo of the fern on her right hand, which encircled her missing finger. Sandrine celebrated how she overcame her disability, and now shone like the shiniest star in the sky.

As she started to sing, the crowd gathered round her and listened intently, their faces etched with pleasure, admiration and lust. Sandy had the talent to draw in her audience; she always had them eating out of her hands.

Tonight, it was as if Sandy was putting on a concert just for her. She sang with energy and emotion, and Charlie listened, breathing in the sentiments of her words, appreciating every single note, every strum of her guitar. Sandy seemed to know that their time together would soon be drawing to an end.

All too soon, Sandy announced her last song: "It's Over" by Roy Orbison. Two young women climbed onto the stage behind her – her backing singers. Sandy smiled at them. 'Are you ready?' She then fixed her gaze on Charlie, and she sang with heartfelt emotion; the words seemed to spill from deep within her soul, like a gentle stream meandering down the mountainside.

Charlie's eyes brimmed with tears and her bottom lip quivered. They both knew.

At the end of the night, Sandy took Charlie by the hand. 'Come back to my flat, Charlie. I've got a bottle of bubbly in the fridge. Please say you'll come.'

Charlie smiled and nodded her head. She thought about a wise saying that she had heard, about when an opportunity comes along, you should grab hold of it with both hands or you'll surely find that it's passed you by. 'You're amazing, Sandy – such a star. And you have been such a special friend to me.' Tears ran freely down her face as she gently stroked Sandy's hair. 'I need you tonight.'

'Why do you say it like it's all over?' Sandy asked quietly. 'Come on,' she urged, not waiting for an answer. 'Let's talk later. I'll leave the sound equipment here tonight and clear up tomorrow,' she said, zipping up the cover of her guitar. 'Come on. Let's go.'

Charlie took a last lingering look round the pub that she had come to love. As they were just leaving, old Jimmy struggled out of his chair, his twinkling eyes almost totally buried in the deep ruddy fold of his cheeks. 'Mind how you go,' he said, 'and don't do anything I wouldn't do…' He threw back his head, opened his mouth and chuckled with mirth. 'I'm just a silly old duffer, go and have some fun. You deserve it,' he said, gazing at each of them in turn. He turned his attention to Charlie, cupping her hands in his. 'And whatever has happened in your life to make you sad, and fearful, remember that you are very special, a precious gem. Everything will work out in the end for you, my lovely.'

As they walked towards Sandy's flat they were both lost in their own thoughts. Sandy was puzzled as to why this all felt like this was the grand finale of a beautiful film. She reflected on old Jimmy, how he had sensed that Charlie was hiding something. She knew he was the wise old man of the sea. She must believe the words that he spoke.

Charlie looked around in wonderment. Sandy's flat was illuminated by a multitude of fairy lights and a collection of candles, all flickering in the semi-darkness. The wood burner in the centre of the room cast a warm, comfortable glow, and a deep sheepskin rug lay in front of the fire. The walls were decorated with monochrome prints of musicians from the sixties and seventies: The Beatles, The Rolling Stones, The Kinks and many more. A random selection of guitars filled one corner of the room, enticing Sandy to play.

'What's troubling you, Charlie? I have a woman's sixth sense, so spill the beans. I want to know. You can tell me anything, I will be discreet.'

Charlie screwed her eyes in despair. 'I've led a double life and I'm in turmoil. But I've discovered a place, Loss, and more importantly, special people, so please don't worry about me.'

'What do you mean, a double life?'

'I was married to a very difficult man.'

'Married? You've never told me this.'

'He bullied me, he controlled me. I tried to make it work, Sandy. I tried everything, I really did.' Her body twisted with the pain of her words. 'I left him behind, and ran away…'

'That was brave. I don't blame you; I think I'd have done the same.' She glanced at Charlie's face, etched with agony. 'Let's have a drink, we'll talk more tomorrow.'

'Sandy, can I ask you to do something for me, if I have to leave?'

'Of course, Charlie, anything…'

'I'm worried about Dan; will you keep an eye on him? You mentioned that your friend, who is a dance teacher, could give him some lessons. I know he would absolutely love this, and I've a feeling it could be the making of him. He is going through a really tough time; he's being bullied at school, and his parents are not very understanding. I would worry less if I knew that you were there for him. Would you do this for me, Sandy?'

'Of course I will, but please don't go…' She pulled Charlie into her arms and they clung together, each wanting the precious moment to last forever.

'Just relax, my friend. I'll massage the tension out of your body.' Sandy gently undressed her friend and covered her lovingly with a soft throw. She started to work on her densely knotted shoulders until nothing mattered anymore.

'That was fantastic, Sandy, come and join me under the throw and I will do the same for you.' They lay together on the rug, their bodies intertwined, and they freely enjoyed the pleasure only a like-minded woman could provide. Later when the fire had died down, they climbed into bed, held each other tightly and drifted into a dreamless sleep.

Forty

It was early evening when the doorbell rang. She peered out of the window to see a police car on the drive. Two police officers and a middle-aged couple stood by the front door. Her heart missed a beat. They were the people from Salcombe, who thought they had recognised her. Charlie's eyes darted to the rucksack in the corner, which she kept ready and packed for emergencies, in case she had to act quickly. Throwing on her money belt and waterproof jacket, she pulled open the door which led to the spiral fire escape. The wind stung her cheeks as she clambered down the greasy steps. She unlocked the car door, her hands shaking, and decided to head for the narrow streets of Dartmouth, where she might be able to lose her pursuer. She didn't have any real plan.

After about a mile, she noticed the flashing blue lights lighting up her rear-view mirror. 'They're onto me already,' she wailed through gritted teeth. She drove the battered old banger as fast as she could down the lane and skidded out onto the main road, just managing to keep the car under control. The rain lashed the windscreen. The wind tore at the wipers. She blinked against the blurred flash of headlights from the oncoming traffic. The distant wail of the police sirens rang through her head, like an angry demon. She would soon be on the main hill leading into Dartmouth. She quickly made a plan to drive into the maze of back roads in Dartmouth; she thought she might be able to lose them there. But she realised with horror, that the brakes were fading. No wonder this road had escape routes, it was steeper than she thought. 'Come on, Libby, you can do this.' She changed down a gear, the engine screaming. Suddenly she slammed her foot down on the brakes, narrowly missing three drunks who had been foolish enough to lurch across the road. They waved their cider cans high into the air and gesticulated rudely. The end of the hill was fast approaching. Charlie gripped the steering wheel, her knuckles white, praying that nothing was coming the other way. She couldn't see lights or hear the sirens anymore.

Suddenly she was there. She threw the car into a sharp right to stay on the road, but the tail skidded across and clipped the kerb. Now the car was going slower, but still too fast, and not really under control. A car loomed up in front of her, showing only side lights. Swerving hard left to miss it, she squeezed between a parked lorry and a huge plant pot. She bumped over the kerb and careered straight into the murky waters of the River Dart. She felt a sharp pain as she was thrown against the seat belt. Fortunately, it was high water, so the car didn't have far to fall. Time stood still. She stared in front of her, her body frozen with fear. The murky water gushed around her feet. She pushed against the door, but the pressure of the water held it tightly closed. She tried the passenger door, but she couldn't open it either. The car was tilting, nose down, so she clambered to the back and pushed against one of the rear doors with all her might. This time it swung open. She grabbed her rucksack containing all her worldly possessions, and, linking her arm through one of the shoulder straps, she plunged into the freezing water. She kicked away from the car, gasping for air, as she ingested the muddy water. Turning her head, she could just see a tiny blue light disappearing into the far distance. The car was sinking quickly now, amidst a sea of bubbles.

She decided not to go back on shore, but to swim to a yacht moored up nearby on the Trots. This could be her chance. The weight of her clothes dragged her down, her breath shallow and laboured. She approached the yacht shrouded in darkness. Fortunately, the stern ladder had been left out. She threw her rucksack onto the boat, grabbed the backstay and slid unceremoniously into the cockpit, like a large slippery cod being landed. She looked nervously towards the land and saw the blue light travelling towards the town. Her whole body shivered uncontrollably as she threw her head over the side of the boat and emptied the contents of her stomach. She tried the hatch, but it was secured by a stout-looking padlock. She remembered that, during the sailing weekend back in the summer, James had told her that most yachtsmen kept a spare set of keys somewhere. She searched high and low, before reaching under the gas bottle, and sure enough, attached to a floating key ring, was a bunch of keys. It didn't take her long to unlock the hatch and climb down the steps into the relative warmth of the cabin.

She rummaged in a side locker and pulled out a couple of towels. She stripped off and roughly rubbed herself down. Not daring to put a light on, she grabbed her miniature light pen from her bag instead, and hunted around for something to wear. She threw on some old clothes that she found in one of the lockers. She also discovered a tin of cocoa and some long-life milk. If she could get the stove working, she could have a warming drink.

Before long the kettle was beginning to sing, and she was able to think more clearly about what to do next. The adrenalin pumped through her body, denying her any prospect of sleep. She would ride out the storm and hopefully, by dawn, she could slip out of Dartmouth and head east. She would navigate using her burner phone. Her eyes narrowed as she studied the charts, the small beam of light trembling in the darkness. The charts meant nothing to her.

Everything would look different in the morning. Pouring herself a small tot of whisky, she lay on one of the bunks and buried herself deep in a sleeping bag. At last, she drifted into a fitful sleep, lulled by the gentle waves of calmer water.

She woke at dawn and climbed out into the cockpit. The navy sky was painted with a deep red-and-purple strip of colour. A weak ball of light rose in the east, the river flat and calm; these were good conditions for motor sailing. But she must leave now, under the cover of darkness.

She switched on the batteries and remembered to turn on the seacocks for the engine-cooling water. She twisted open the fuel cap and checked the level; thankfully the tank was nearly full. As an afterthought, she positioned a towel over the painted name of the boat to avoid recognition. She had learnt a little about sailing when she had joined the family on a weekend's boating trip, not much, just enough.

The engine burst into life, leaving a thin trail of smoke behind. She untied the stern line, and then the bowline, and gently eased the boat out of her mooring. She sighed with relief, as the elements nudged the bow in the right direction. As the yacht gathered momentum, the gentle breeze caressed her face, and she inhaled the heady taste of freedom.

As Dartmouth diminished and the boat headed out towards the open sea, she pulled out a small section of jib, to take full advantage of the prevailing wind. Her phone navigation system was simple to understand and operate, and she began to relax, the tension draining away with every breath. Glancing back she could just see the outline of Dartmouth castle. 'I will return one day.'

Life had dealt her some bitter blows, but she had made some good friends along the way. Sandy had become a special part of her life. Glancing to starboard, she could just see the thin yellow line of sand where she had discovered the freedom of naturism; the joy of swimming naked in the sea and walking along the sand, hand in hand, to dry in the sun. Sandy was her friend and her lover. She had helped her to understand more about herself. Charlie had discovered that she was able to love a man or a woman; it is the deep love of another human being that matters, whether they are masculine or feminine is unimportant. She felt sad that she had been unable to share much of her life story with Sandy, but the time would come, they would meet again.

Setting up the auto helm, she reached for her phone and idly flicked through her news feed. Two news items caught her eye. The first article reported the escape of a fugitive – a missing person from Oxford – who had escaped a police chase in Dartmouth and had then disappeared into thin air. She scanned the rest of the article, not ready to face the reality of an intense search that was about to be launched. She felt quietly content that it hadn't been Tai who had informed the police of her whereabouts.

Her eyes widened as she scrolled through the second article. It described a new facility – a refuge for men – that had been recently set up in Totnes. The refuge aimed to provide a safe house for men who are experiencing domestic abuse, sexual abuse and violence. For men who might feel isolated, scared or confused. Or might feel ashamed or afraid to tell anyone about their situation. The article emphasised that no person should live in fear of abuse. The name of the innovator of this new and invaluable project leapt out at her from the page: Mr Tai Wilkinson. Her heart swelled with pride. This young man, who she had only recently had the privilege of meeting, had achieved something immense, something positive, from all the disappointment and sadness in his life.

Alex had been a victim of sexual abuse, and he had been unable to talk about it for years. If there had been a men's refuge nearby to help and support him, his life might have taken a different direction.

She reflected on all the twists and turns in her own life. Her struggles with mental health, the deep cracks in her own marriage, being controlled and suffering emotional abuse from the man she loved. Words can heal wounds and convey love, but thoughtless words have the power to do untold damage. But she didn't want Alex to die. She had wanted to make their relationship better; to make their marriage work. Her heart ached with sadness that she would never see him again. The guilt would never leave her.

There were so many questions left unanswered. Money was far from her mind, but she wondered what would happen to Alex's inheritance. Would his brothers contest the will? She hoped they would. But the most pressing question of all: how long would it take before the police, or some other unfortunate individual, discovered Alex's body? She knew it was only a matter of time. Condemned to a life undercover, she would always look over her shoulder. She would find the answers in the fullness of time, but, for now, she must leave it all behind. She smiled. She had left the humble pawn behind and had become queen in the shadows; ruler of her own destiny.

She turned to look one last time as the outline of the land merged into the sea. She would return to the shores of Blighty one day, but, for now, she must focus on her future.

A new name. A new identity. A new life in France.

Acknowledgements

My grateful thanks to:

The amazing team at The Book Guild, Rosie Lowe, Holly Porter and all those who work tirelessly behind the scenes. Thank you for your professionalism, support, guidance and expertise.

Wendy Spray and Jo Daley for your emotional and editorial support, wise words, encouragement and precious friendship.

Nathalie, my beautiful French friend for your advice on language and culture.

My wonderful and endlessly patient partner and my incredible family for encouraging and supporting my creativity, and for enriching my life in so many ways.

In the end, I take full responsibility for any errors found in this book. The faults are all mine.

Mental Health Contact Information

If you have been affected by issues raised in this book and need support:

Getting help for domestic violence and abuse – NHS

https://www.nhs.uk › live-well › getting-help-for-domestic-violence
https://refuge.org.uk/i-need-help-now/other-support-services/support-for-men/

Emergency housing – ManKind Initiative

https://mankind.org.uk/help-for-victims/emergency-housing/

Male victims of domestic abuse – Please call: 01823 334244
https://www.mankind.org.uk

Children and young people affected by mental health issues can find support, information and details about their local NHS mental health services at www.youngminds.org.uk/find-help or call Childline on 0800 1111.

For adults, whether you're concerned about yourself or a loved one, you can find local NHS urgent mental health helplines and a list of mental health charities, organisations and support groups offering expert advice on the NHS website at www.nhs.uk/conditions/stress-anxiety-depression/mental-health-helplines/ or call the Samaritans; 116 123

Queen in the Shadows

Liz van Santen

Looks can't hide your true identity. It's the eyes that give you away... the soul behind them. The intent. The shadows.

Vicki Peterson

Prologue

She blinked her eyes against the horror of darkness. She could not rid herself of her terrifying nightmare. The sins of the past. She saw his body, bound to the bed, lifeless; his skin, pale, almost translucent; bile leaking from the corner of his mouth. She hadn't meant to kill him, it was an accident. Nothing more than a tragic accident. It sounds trivial, doesn't it? Insignificant? But it was not. Her face twisted with pain. Rather like the domino effect, one event – a fatal accident – initiated a succession of events. A cumulative effect, like ripples on the surface of the water. Actions have consequences.

The
Book
Guild

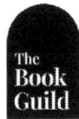

For writing and publishing news, or
recommendations of new titles to read,
sign up to the Book Guild newsletter:

SCAN ME